The Riverdale Vampire Collection

Classic and Modern Vampire Stories

Riverdale Electronic Books, Inc.
Cumming, Georgia

The Riverdale Vampire Collection

Classic and Modern Vampire Stories

J.T. McDaniel,
Editor

The Riverdale Vampire Collection

Introduction and Notes © 2009, J.T. McDaniel. All rights reserved.

Published by:
Riverdale Electronic Books, Inc.
4420 Bonneville Drive
Cumming, Georgia 30041

ISBN: 978-1-932606-27-0
Also available in Amazon Kindle and ePub formats:
eISBN: 978-1-932606-28-7
Kindle ASIN: B002RL9OYS

Published in the United States of America

Contents

Introduction
J.T. McDaniel

I have loved vampires—fictional ones, at least—ever since I was a kid sitting up after the news on Friday nights watching Ghoulardi (the late Ernie Anderson[1]) mercilessly razz the collection of el-cheapo horror movies that he ran in that time slot. Once in a while there would be a good movie, which always seemed to confuse the host, who frequently expressed astonishment that such a thing had managed to get on his show, but mostly they were pretty bad. These were by no means all vampire movies—for a good idea, just take a good look at American-International's early 1960s catalogue—but sometimes you got vampires, sometime werewolves—including Michael Landon as a teenaged one[2]—and kilted ghosts stalking the quaking cardboard stone halls of a haunted Scottish castle. Another time it was Jack Nicholson practically orgasmic in the dentist's chair in the original *Little Shop of Horrors*[3], which didn't have any vampires, but was argu-

---

1 Ernie Anderson (1923–1997) created the Ghoulardi character on WJW-TV in Cleveland in 1963, hosting the late Friday *Shock Theater* (mostly horror and science fiction movies) through 1966. His usual costume included a fake beard, sunglasses missing one lens, and a fright wig. I was somewhat addicted to the show as a teenager, and at other times found it mildly disorienting when Anderson would appear during the day introducing "regular" movies in a jacket and tie and looking disconcertingly like somebody's father (which, of course, he was). After leaving Cleveland he moved to Los Angeles, where he gained semi-anonymous national prominence as the main promo announcer for ABC, was a popular voice-over artist, and in the years prior to his death worked as the original announcer on *America's Funniest Home Videos*. His son, director Paul Thomas Anderson, dedicated his film *Boogie Nights*, released shortly after his fathers death, in Anderson's memory.
2 *I was a Teenage Werewolf*, 1957, American International Pictures, starred Michael Landon and Whit Bissell. B&W, 76 minutes.
3 *Little Shop of Horrors*, 1960, American International Pictures, starred Jonathan Haze, Jackie Joseph, and Mel Welles. Jack Nicholson was billed well down in the credits originally, but recent DVD releases now generally put him on the cover as he is by far the best-known actor in the film to today's audiences. B&W, 72 minutes.

1

ably funnier than the later musical.

For the good vampire movies, or good horror movies in general, there were theatres, mostly downtown. Many a time I made the bus trip to Cleveland to catch Christopher Lee at the Allen, or Loewe's State, or the old Hippodrome[4]. One of these old downtown theatres was probably where I first saw Hammer's *Dracula* (which we got here as *The Horror of Dracula*). In many ways, Count Dooku might be considered an extension of Dracula, cape, ominous voice, and all. Lee was generally under-utilized through much of his career, in good part because at 6' 5" he was usually quite a bit taller than the actors he would have to work with.

Now back in those days (the mid-'60s, mainly) kids not only *could* read, but generally did. Vampire literature naturally came in for review. Everything was fair game, from the latest issue of *Famous Monsters of Filmland* magazine, to Bram Stoker's *Dracula*, which was a bit of a challenge for a twelve-year-old. What the hell *is* a calèche, anyway? Well, as it turns out, it certainly was *not* the ominous closed coach of the movies, but more like the carriages used to haul tourists around Central Park in New York. Discovering this fact made the wolves circling as Harker waited in the Transylvanian woods for his driver to return significantly more ominous, now that it was obvious he was sitting in an open carriage and not tucked away behind closed doors and windows.

I even attempted to read Montague Summers' *The Vampire: His Kith and Kin.* I say "attempted" because many of the quotations are untranslated Latin and Greek, which remain just as opaque today as they were 40-odd

---

4   The Cleveland Hippodrome Theater (colloquially referred to as the "Hipp") was located at 720 Euclid Avenue, with a second entrance on Prospect Avenue. Built in 1907, the theatre originally seated 3,548, but a remodeling in 1931 increased capacity to a bit over 4,000. The remodeling also included a conversion to an exclusively motion-picture theater, with a part of the stage removed (though what remained behind the movie screen was still larger than the stage at the Hannah, once Cleveland's only commercial legitimate theater (and somewhat notorious for having acoustics so bad that it was jokingly referred to as "the only theater in the world where Ethel Merman needs a microphone," though a 2008 remodeling is said to have fixed those problems). The Hippodrome was considered one of the most acoustically perfect theaters in the world, and in earlier years had been a favorite concert venue for a number of noted performers, including Enrico Caruso. While a number of other old vaudeville and movie-palace era theaters in Cleveland were later converted to legitimate houses farther up Euclid Avenue in the Playhouse Square area (except for the Stillman, which was converted into an indoor parking garage), the Hippodrome (which would have made an ideal venue for opera and ballet), was torn down in 1981 and replaced by a parking lot. The Editor notes a sense of personal loss not only for the theater, and the big rehearsal halls located above the auditorium in the office building that fronted Euclid Avenue, where he learned more than a few musical roles, but for the small apartment building located behind the theater on Prospect Avenue, where he used to live. The apartment building shared the fate of the theater.

years ago. I still have my copy, and sometimes even refer to it, but I still can't read Greek, nor pick out enough Latin to be useful. It makes for definite gaps in the narrative.

The first time, perhaps obviously with a little kid involved, a lot of things I read just went over my head. When I first read *Carmilla* I think I was more impressed by the general absence of blood than by the obvious lesbian overtones. A twelve-year-old doesn't know from lesbians, at least not back in 1961. The first time I saw the best of the filmed versions, The Vampire Lovers[5], I think I was more impressed by Ingrid Pitt's body (not to mention Madeline Smith's breasts) than anything else, but I was out of the Army by then, so it was okay to notice such things.

A vampire's bite has long been a literary and cinematic metaphor for sexual intercourse. Some authors make this rather more explicit than others, but the rule nearly always applies. In *The Vampire Lovers*, the bite marks would appear on the victim's breast, which not only made them normally less conspicuous than the usual position on the throat, but also provided the director with a good excuse to show the victims topless. I don't think many of the male moviegoers complained (the breasts in question were all lovely), though what their wives and girlfriends had to say may have been a bit less favorable.

The only thing that perplexed me about this film was the title, which I can only attribute to a belief on the part of the studio that their audience might not be all that conversant with 19th century literature and thus went for the suggestive instead.

The lesbian theme in *Carmilla* is obvious. Author Jacob Thomson, who wrote the modern stories in this book, has suggested that this isn't limited to the obvious lesbianism implied in *Carmilla*, but may also be found, in a less obvious form, in works such as *Dracula*. "British girls' boarding schools were a favorite theme in Victorian pornography—and haven't, for that matter, declined very much in that regard today," he related, adding "and there are hints in *Dracula* that Lucy and Mina may have been somewhat closer than mere friends in their school days."

In the cinema, Dracula seems to have been everywhere. A good part of this may come from the fact that the American publisher failed to follow proper procedures, and the novel has never been subject to copyright in this country.[6] This freed the studios and other adapters from the problems encountered by Murnau, whose *Nosferatu*, even with changes in locale, character names, and much of the plot, was ruled to have been plagiarized

5   *The Vampire Lovers*, 1970, Hammer Films, starred Ingrid Pitt, Madeline Smith, Peter Cushing, and Kate O'Mara. Color, 91 minutes.

6   The copyright on *Dracula* in the UK, and much of the rest of the world, did not expire until 1962.

from *Dracula* and ordered destroyed.[7]

In America as well, the story was frequently adapted, twisted, mangled, and otherwise made to fit some screen writer's notion of just how Stoker could have improved his story. Characters were dropped, or combined—particular in the case of Lucy and Mina—or had their roles switched. Copolla's version[8] was fairly close to the novel, even including Quincy Morris and Arthur Holmwood, who were almost always left out of earlier versions. Other adaptations were far looser.

Nor, despite having his name in the title, did Dracula himself always appear in the films. In Hammer's Brides of Dracula[9] the vampire is an entirely different character, Baron Meinster, and Dracula is merely an off-screen presence explaining the baron's condition. Van Helsing, in the person of Peter Cushing, does appear.

If the studio or distributor had a vampire movie, they liked to at least put Dracula into the title, and sometimes renamed one of the characters to represent the Count. The practice was a bit like the way a large number of Italian Machiste, Samson, or Goliath movies were imported into the United States with the main character renamed Hercules. At least with the vampire movies, the majority were made in English, avoiding the often unintentionally humorous dubbing of the Hercules movies.[10]

Most cultures have held beliefs in vampires, or something very like them. In southern Africa the Zulus once believed that it was unsafe for a lone person to enter a hut containing a corpse, but that safety required that never less than three should enter together. Nor is this an unusual notion. In primitive societies[11] everywhere the belief was common that the spirits of the dead were often overtly hostile to the living.

---

7 The destruction order was carried out, and for many years the film was believed to have been lost. However, as release copies had already been distributed, enough segments survived that it was later possible to restore the film. A number of DVD versions are available in the United States, most of them rather poor, but an excellent restoration, which includes the reconstructed orchestral score written in 1922, is available from Kino International.

8 *Bram Stoker's Dracula*, 1992, American Zoetrope. Directed by Francis Ford Coppola and starring Anthony Hopkins, Gary Oldman, Keanu Reeves, and Winona Ryder.

9 *The Brides of Dracula*, 1960, Hammer/Universal, starring Peter Cushing, Yvonne Monlaur, David Peel, and Martita Hunt. Color, 85 minutes.

10 Perhaps the strangest dubbing of any Hercules movie was that employed in the 1970 *Hercules in New York*, which was filmed in English featuring mostly American actors. The lead, however, was played by Arnold Schwarzenegger (billed as Arnold Strong in his first film role), and for the original release his voice was dubbed, making him sound entirely too much like one of the characters on a Saturday morning kids' adventure cartoon. The effect is even more jarring now, when viewers are used to Schwarzenegger's accent, and the rather silly film does seem to improve slightly in the un-dubbed version, which is an option on the DVD.

11 Primitive in the sense of being scientifically unsophisticated, though not necessarily in any cultural sense.

There might even be some logical basis for this. If someone died of a contagious disease anyone who came into close contact with the body might well contract the same disease and die in turn. Tuberculosis was known to linger in a particular house, sometimes taking out entire families, or even more than one family as the house was resold or rented.[12] The real causes of TB then being unknown, it was not unusual for the wasting condition of its victims to be blamed on vampiric predation.

In Turkish and Greek vampire mythology, the first victims were usually those closest to the newly-minted vampire. It was only later, when the immediate family had been destroyed, that the vampire would widen his depredations into the broader community.

In a time when even physicians were woefully ignorant of the actual causes of disease, the influence of vampires was often suspected, particularly in the Balkans. If people in a Carpathian village began to waste away and die, it just seemed somehow more logical to blame a vampire—which the people firmly believed to be real—rather than a germ that they could not only *not* see, but whose very existence had yet to be discovered. A vampire, they reasoned, could be seen, caught, and destroyed.

Nor was it that difficult to find the vampire. Legend suggested that mounting a virgin boy on a virgin stallion and leading the horse through a cemetery would do the trick, as the horse would balk as it was led across the vampire's grave. In practice, the villagers were just as likely to simply open the most recent graves to see if the bodies exhibited obvious signs of vampirism. These included things such as blood on the mouth, lengthening of the teeth, and the body bloated with the victims' blood. As a corpse's gums naturally shrink (making the teeth look longer), blood naturally seeps from the mouth and nose, and decomposition causes the body to appear bloated, the signs were often found.

The transition of the vampire from legend and myth to literature and film followed naturally. The simple reality is that people *enjoy* being scared, as long as the sensation does not involve any real danger. Just look at the popularity of roller coasters.

The stories selected for this collection range from classic to new. The oldest, John Polidori's *The Vampyre*, is generally considered one of, if not *the*, oldest of vampire stories. Published in the April 1819 issue of *New Monthly Magazine*, and at that time incorrectly attributed to Lord Byron, it was, in fact, written by his personal physician, inspired by the fragmentary tale Byron concocted as a diversion on the same night that Mary Shelley conceived the idea that would grow into *Frankenstein*. It was shortly there-

---

12   For a fictionalized account of this type of incident, see Upton Sinclair's novel *The Jungle*.

after published as a book, though today we would hardly consider it to be a book-length work.

Byron himself commented on the story after hearing of the death of Polidori, generally believed to be a suicide, though ruled natural by the coroner, in 1821, as quoted in *Conversations of Lord Byron: Noted During a Residence With His Lordship at Pisa in the Years 1821 and 1822,* by Thomas Medwin, Esq.

> I was convinced something very unpleasant hung over me last night: I expected to hear that somebody I knew was dead:—so it turns out! Poor Polidori is gone! When he was my physician, he was always talking of Prussic Acid [Hydrogen Cyanide. ED.], oil of amber, blowing into veins, suffocating by charcoal, and compounding poisons; but for a different purpose to what the Pontic Monarch did, for he has prescribed a dose whose effect, Murray says, was so instantaneous that he went off without a spasm or struggle. It seems that disappointment was the cause of this rash act. He had entertained too sanguine hopes of his "Vampyre," which in consequence of its being attributed to me, was got up as a melo-drame at Paris. The foundation of the story *was* mine; but I was forced to disown the publication, lest the world should suppose that I had vanity enough, or was egotist enough, to write in that ridiculous manner about myself. [He alluded to the Preface and Postscript, containing accounts of his residence at Geneva and in the Isle of Mitylene. (Note in original. ED.)] Notwithstanding which, the French editions still persevere in including it with my works. My real "Vampyre" I gave at the end of "Mazeppa,"; something in the same way that I told it one night at Diodati, when Monk Lewis, and Shelley and his wife were present.

This book includes three works by modern author and editor Jacob Thomson. One of these, *Castle Grosshelm,* has previously been published only on the author's website. The title, according to Thomson, is "a very bad *Star Wars* gag by way of *Space Balls.*" "*Grosshelm*" literally translates as "big helmet." The story itself hasn't the slightest connection with *Star Wars,* but is set in post World War II Romania.

Not all vampires are created equal, either in literature or in "real" life. At the bottom of the scale is the simple revenant. This vampire is little more than a corpse, re-animated by a malevolent spirit, and usually having no remaining personality. Like a shark, it simply moves around and eats indiscriminately. In some ways the revenant is similar to the cinematic zombie, except that it wants blood instead of brains.

You don't find this sort of creature very often in literature. One suspects that this is mostly because they're not very interesting. Always hungry, attacking everyone encountered, and motivated only by an insatiable hunger for blood, the revenant vampire is useful for a brief cameo for shock effect, as in Anne Rice's *Interview With The Vampire*, where one pops up in the Balkans, much to the horror of the more sophisticated protagonists. They don't make very good lead characters.

We are, perhaps, most familiar with a more elegant vampire, as often as not a nobleman, exemplified by Polidori's Lord Ruthven, or Stoker's Count Dracula. One might note a certain parallel between these two, as Ruthven, by the end of the tale, has inherited his father's loftier title of Earl of Marsden (earl being the British equivalent of the continental count). Ruthven does seem to be rather the more social of the two, and by far the younger given that most of the events in *The Vampyre* apparently occur prior to the death of his father. Count Dracula, by way of contrast, is presented as being several hundred years old, and intimated to be the actual Vlad Dracula (1431–1476), who was bloodthirsty enough in his own right, though the real Dracula seemed to prefer spilling it to drinking it.

In his novel *The Alukam,* Jacob Thomson presented yet another type of vampire, drawing on Jewish mystical traditions to create a protagonist who could utterly ignore the usual collection of crosses, holy water, garlic, and such, and was forced to spend most of the week awake, resting only on the Jewish sabbath. A secondary character from that novel appears in Thomson's short story *The Predator*, which appears in this volume. The novel itself is also excerpted here, in a semi-blatant attempt to get a few more people to buy the book.

Also hearkening back to Jewish mysticism, by way of Babylonian folklore, is the story of Lilith, supposedly Adam's first wife, who left him after he insisted that he would always have to be on top during sex, and that she should be subservient to him. It was only after this that God created Eve. Lilith's story, found in the *Midrash*, has become something of a feminist staple, being seen as a tale of sexual equality quashed by unjust male domination. In the Jewish mystical tradition, after abandoning Adam, Lilith exiled herself to the wilderness and became the mother of a race of demons who would persecute Adam's descendants. In particular, she was the mother of the succubi, and is sometimes portrayed as having herself transformed into a succubus.

While a succubus is not strictly a vampire, given that she drains her victim by sexual means, rather than by drinking his blood, I believe the creature is close enough to a vampire to merit inclusion in this collection. The tale contained herein, Honoré de Balzac's *The Succubus*, is from his

Droll Tales (*Contes Drolatiques*), and is a thoroughly Catholic story with an inquisitorial theme. From a modern viewpoint, the seeming religious fervor of the protagonists sounds suspiciously like sexual obsession fueled by repression. That which we desire, but cannot have because of "divine" law, is most simply dealt with by killing it.

Then again, vampires also destroy that which they love.

The Vampyre
John Polidori
1819

Extract of a Letter from Geneva

"I breathe freely in the neighbourhood of this lake; the ground upon which I tread has been subdued from the earliest ages; the principal objects which immediately strike my eye, bring to my recollection scenes, in which man acted the hero and was the chief object of interest. Not to look back to earlier times of battles and sieges, here is the bust of Rousseau—here is a house with an inscription denoting that the Genevan philosopher first drew breath under its roof. A little out of the town is Ferney, the residence of Voltaire; where that wonderful, though certainly in many respects contemptible, character, received, like the hermits of old, the visits of pilgrims, not only from his own nation, but from the farthest boundaries of Europe. Here too is Bonnet's abode, and, a few steps beyond, the house of that astonishing woman Madame de Stael: perhaps the first of her sex, who has really proved its often claimed equality with, the nobler man. We have before had women who have written interesting novels and poems, in which their tact at observing drawing-room characters has availed them; but never since the days of Heloise have those faculties which are peculiar to man, been developed as the possible inheritance of woman. Though even here, as in the case of Heloise, our sex have not been backward in alledging the existence of an Abeilard in the person of M. Schlegel as the inspirer of her works. But to proceed: upon the same side of the lake, Gibbon, Bonnivard, Bradshaw, and others mark, as it were, the stages for our progress; whilst upon the other side there is one house, built by Diodati, the friend of Milton, which has contained within its walls, for several months, that poet whom we have so often read together, and who—if human passions remain the same, and human feelings, like chords, on being swept by nature's impulses shall vibrate as before—will be placed by posterity in the first rank of our English Poets. You must have heard, or the Third Canto of *Childe Harold* will have informed you, that Lord Byron resided many months in this neighbourhood. I went with some friends a few days ago, after having seen Ferney, to view this mansion. I trod the floors with the same feelings of awe and respect as we did, together, those of Shakespeare's dwelling at Stratford. I sat down in a chair of the saloon, and satisfied myself that I was resting on what he had made his constant seat. I found a servant there who had lived with him; she, however, gave me but little information. She pointed out his bed-chamber upon the same level as the saloon and dining-room, and informed me that he retired to rest at three, got up at two, and employed himself a long time over his toilette; that he never went to sleep without a pair of pistols and a dagger by his side, and that he never eat animal food. He apparently spent some part of every day upon the lake in an English boat. There is a balcony from the saloon which looks upon the lake and the mountain Jura; and I imagine, that it must have been hence, he contemplated the storm *so* magnificently described in the Third Canto; for you have from here a most extensive view of all the points he has therein depicted. I can fancy him like the scathed pine, whilst all around was sunk to repose, still waking to observe, what gave but a weak image of the storms which had desolated his own breast.

> The sky is changed!—and such a change; Oh, night!
> And storm and darkness, ye are wond'rous strong,
> Yet lovely in your strength, as is the light
> Of a dark eye in woman! Far along
> From peak to peak, the rattling crags among,
> Leaps the lire thunder! Not from one lone cloud,
> But every mountain now hath found a tongue,
> And Jura answers thro' her misty shroud,
> Back to the joyous Alps who call to her aloud!
>
> And this is in the night:—Most glorious night!
> Thou wer't not sent for slumber! let me be
> A sharer in thy far and fierce delight,—
> A portion of the tempest and of me!
> How the lit lake shines a phosphoric sea,
> And the big rain comet dancing to the earth!
> And now again 'tis black,—and now the glee
> Of the loud hills shakes with its mountain mirth,
> As if they did rejoice o'er a young; earthquake's birth,

Now where the swift Rhine cleaves his way between
Heights which appear, as lovers who have parted
In haste, whose mining depths so intervene,
That they can meet no more, tho' broken hearted;
Tho' in their souls which thus each other thwarted,
Love was the very root of the fond rage
Which blighted their life's bloom, and then departed—
Itself expired, but leaving; them an age
Of years all winter—war within themselves to wage.

"I went down to the little port, if I may use the expression, wherein his vessel used to lay, and conversed with the cottager, who had the care of it. You may smile, but I have my pleasure in thus helping my personification of the individual I admire, by attaining to the knowledge of those circumstances which were daily around him. I have made numerous enquiries in the town concerning him, but can learn nothing. He only went into society there once, when M. Pictet took him to the house of a lady to spend the evening. They say he is a very singular man, and seem to think him very uncivil. Amongst other things they relate, that having invited M. Pictet and Bonstetten to dinner, he went on the lake to Chillon, leaving a gentleman who travelled with him to receive them and make his apologies. Another evening, being invited to the house of Lady D—— H——, he promised to attend, but upon approaching the windows of her ladyship's villa, and perceiving the room to be full of company, he set down his friend, desiring him to plead his excuse, and immediately returned home. This will serve as a contradiction to the report which you tell me is current in England, of his having been avoided by his countrymen on the continent. The case happens to be directly the reverse, as he has been generally sought by them, though on most occasions, apparently without success. It is said, indeed, that upon paying his first visit at Coppet, following the servant who had announced his name, he was surprised to meet a lady carried out fainting; but before he had been seated many minutes, the same lady, who had been so affected at the sound of his name, returned and conversed with him a considerable time—such is female curiosity and affectation! He visited Coppet frequently, and of course associated there with several of his countrymen, who evinced no reluctance to moot him whom his enemies alone would represent as an outcast.

"Though I have been so unsuccessful in this town, I have been more fortunate in my enquiries elsewhere. There is a society three or four miles from Geneva, the centre of which is the Countess of Breuss, a Russian lady, well acquainted with the agrémens de la Société, and who has collected them round herself at her mansion. It was chiefly here, I find, that the gentleman who travelled with Lord Byron, as physician, sought for society. He used almost every day to cross the lake by himself, in one of their flat-bottomed boats, and return after passing the evening with his friends, about eleven or twelve at night, often whilst the storms were raging in the circling summits of the mountains around. As he became intimate, from long acquaintance, with several of the families in this neighbourhood, I have gathered from their accounts some excellent traits of his lordship's character, which I will relate to you at some future opportunity. I must, however, free him from one imputation attached to him—of having in his house two sisters as the partakers of his revels. This is, like many other charges which have been brought against his lordship, entirely destitute of truth. His only companion was the physician I have already mentioned. The report originated from the following circumstance: Mr. Percy Bysshe Shelly, a gentleman well known for extravagance of doctrine, and for his daring, in their profession, even to sign himself with the title of Atheos in the Album at Chamouny, having taken a house below, in which he resided with Miss M.W. Godwin and Miss Clermont, (the daughters of the celebrated Mr. Godwin) they were frequently visitors at Diodati, and were often seen upon the lake with his Lordship, which gave rise to the report, the truth of which is here positively denied.

"Among other things which the lady, from whom I procured these anecdotes, related to me, she mentioned the outline of a ghost story by Lord Byron. It appears that one evening Lord B., Mr. P. B. Shelly, the two ladies and the gentleman before alluded to, after having perused a German work, which was entitled *Phantasmagoriana*[13], began relating ghost stories; when his lordship having recited the beginning of *Christabel*, then unpublished, the whole took so strong a hold of Mr. Shelly's mind, that he suddenly started up and ran out of the room. The physician and Lord Byron followed, and discovered him leaning against a mantle-piece, with cold drops of perspiration trickling down his face. After having given him something to refresh him, upon enquiring into the cause of his alarm, they found that his wild imagination having pictured to him the bosom of one of the ladies with eyes (which was reported of a lady in the neighbourhood where he lived) he was obliged to leave the room in order to destroy the impression. It was afterwards proposed, in the course of conversation, that each of the company present should write a tale depending upon some supernatural agency, which was undertaken by Lord B., the physician, and Miss M. W.

---

13   There was, in fact, no German work of this title. Further research indicates that the party actually read a French translation, *Fantasmagoriana, ou Recueil d'Histoires d'Apparitions de Spectres, Revenans, Fantômes, etc.; traduit de l'allemand, par un Amateur,* of the German *Das Gespensterbuch* (The Ghost Book).

Godwin.[14] My friend, the lady above referred to, had in her possession the outline of each of these stories; I obtained them as a great favour, and herewith Forward them to you, as I was assured you would feel as much curiosity as myself, to peruse the *ébauches* of so great a genius, and those immediately under his influence."

---

14 Since published under the title of *Frankenstein: or the Modern Prometheus.* (Note in original. M.W. Godwin was, of course, Mary Wolstoncraft Shelley. The physician mentioned in this section was Polidori himself. Ed.)

The Vampyre
Introduction

The superstition upon which this tale is founded is very general in the East. Among the Arabians it appears to be common: it did not, however, extend itself to the Greeks until after the establishment of Christianity; and it has only assumed its present form since the division of the Latin and Greek churches; at which time, the idea becoming prevalent, that a Latin body could not corrupt if buried in their territory, it gradually increased, and formed the subject of many wonderful stories, still extant, of the dead rising from their graves, and feeding upon the blood of the young and beautiful. In the West it spread, with some slight variation, all over Hungary, Poland, Austria, and Lorraine, where the belief existed, that vampyres nightly imbibed a certain portion of the blood of their victims, who became emaciated, lost their strength, and speedily died of consumptions; whilst these human blood-suckers fattened—and their veins became distended to such a state of repletion, as to cause the blood to flow from all the passages of their bodies, and even from the very pores of their skins.

In the London Journal, of March, 1732, is a curious, and, of course, credible account of a particular case of vampyrism, which is stated to have occurred at Madreyga, in Hungary. It appears, that upon an examination of the commander-in-chief and magistrates of the place, they positively and unanimously affirmed, that, about five years before, a certain Heyduke[15], named Arnold Paul, had been heard to say, that, at Cassovia, on the frontiers of the Turkish Servia, he had been tormented by a vampyre, but had found a way to rid himself of the evil, by eating some of the earth out of the vampyre's grave, and rubbing himself with his blood. This precaution, however, did not prevent him from becoming a vampyre himself;[16] for, about

---

15 Mercenary.
16 The universal belief is, that a person sucked by a vampyre becomes a vampyre himself, and sucks in his turn. (Note in original. ED.)

14

twenty or thirty days after his death and burial, many persons complained of having been tormented by him, and a deposition was made, that four persons had been deprived of life by his attacks. To prevent further mischief, the inhabitants having consulted their *Hadagni*,[17] took up the body, and found it (as is supposed to be usual in cases of vampyrism) fresh, and entirely free from corruption, and emitting at the mouth, nose, and ears, pure and florid blood. Proof having been thus obtained, they resorted to the accustomed remedy. A stake was driven entirely through the heart and body of Arnold Paul, at which he is reported to have cried out as dreadfully as if he had been alive. This done, they cut off his head, burned his body, and threw the ashes into his grave. The same measures were adopted with the corses of those persons who had previously died from vampyrism, lest they should, in their turn, become agents upon others who survived them.

This monstrous rodomontade is here related, because it seems better adapted to illustrate the subject of the present observations than any other instance which could be adduced. In many parts of Greece it is considered as a sort of punishment after death, for some heinous crime committed whilst in existence, that the deceased is not only doomed to vampyrise, but compelled to confine his infernal visitations solely to those beings he loved most while upon earth, those to whom he was bound by ties of kindred and affection. A supposition alluded to in the *Giaour.*

> But first on earth, as Vampyre sent,
> Thy corse shall from its tomb be rent;
> Then ghastly haunt the native place,
> And suck the blood of all thy race;
> There from thy daughter, sister, wife,
> At midnight drain the stream of life;
> Yet loathe the banquet which perforce
> Must feed thy livid living corse,
> Thy victims, ere they yet expire,
> Shall know the demon for their sire;
> As cursing thee, thou cursing them,
> Thy flowers are withered on the stem.
> But one that for thy crime must fall,
> The youngest, best beloved of all,
> Shall bless thee with a father's name—
> That word shall wrap thy heart in flame!
> Yet thou must end thy task and mark
> Her cheek's last tinge—her eye's last spark,

---

17   Chief Bailiff (Note in original. Ed.)

And the last glassy glance must view
Which freezes o'er its lifeless blue;
Then with unhallowed hand shall tear
The tresses of her yellow hair,
Of which, in life a lock when shorn
Affection's fondest pledge was worn—
But now is borne away by thee
Memorial of thine agony!
Yet with thine own best blood shall drip;
Thy gnashing tooth, and haggard lip;
Then stalking to thy sullen grave,
Go—and with Gouls and Afrits rave,
Till these in horror shrink away
From spectre more accursed than they.

Mr. Southey[18] has also introduced in his wild but beautiful poem of *Thalaba*, the vampyre corse of the Arabian maid Oneiza, who is represented as having returned from the grave for the purpose of tormenting him she best loved whilst in existence. But this cannot be supposed to have resulted from the sinfulness of her life, she being portrayed throughout the whole of the tale as a complete type of purity and innocence. The veracious Tournefort[19] gives a long account in his travels of several astonishing cases of vampyrism, to which he pretends to have been an eyewitness; and Calmet[20], in his great work upon this subject, besides a variety of anecdotes, and traditionary narratives illustrative of its effects, has put forth some learned dissertations, tending to prove it to be a classical, as well as barbarian error.

Many curious and interesting notices on this singularly horrible superstition might be added; though the present may suffice for the limits of a note, necessarily devoted to explanation, and which may now be concluded by merely remarking, that though the term Vampyre is the one in most general acceptation, there are several others synonimous with it, made use of in various parts of the world: as *Vroucolocha, Vardoulacha, Goul, Broucoloka,* &c.

---

18 Robert Southey, Poet Laureate of England from 1813–1843. In addition to his poetry, Southey produced several biographies, was a popular translator of Spanish and Portuguese works, and wrote several novels. One of these, *The Doctor*, is best remembered as the original source of the children's story of the three bears.

19 Joseph Pitton de Tournefort (1656–1708), French botanist. This is probably a reference to stories contained in his *Relation d'un voyage du Levant*, published posthumously in 1708.

20 Dom Antoine Augustin Calmet (1672–1757), French Benedictine monk. He published extensively on Biblical texts, but is best known among vampire scholars for his 1746 treatise which at least *seemed* to indicate that such creatures might be real.

The Vampyre

It happened that in the midst of the dissipations attendant upon a London winter, there appeared at the various parties of the leaders of the *ton*[21] a nobleman, more remarkable for his singularities, than his rank. He gazed upon the mirth around him, as if he could not participate therein. Apparently, the light laughter of the fair only attracted his attention, that he might by a look quell it, and throw fear into those breasts where thoughtlessness reigned. Those who felt this sensation of awe, could not explain whence it arose: some attributed it to the dead grey eye, which, fixing upon the object's face, did not seem to penetrate, and at one glance to pierce through to the inward workings of the heart; but fell upon the cheek with a leaden ray that weighed upon the skin it could not pass. His peculiarities caused him to be invited to every house; all wished to see him, and those who had been accustomed to violent excitement, and now felt the weight of *ennui*, were pleased at having something in their presence capable of engaging their attention. In spite of the deadly hue of his face, which never gained a warmer tint, either from the blush of modesty, or from the strong emotion of passion, though its form and outline were beautiful, many of the female hunters after notoriety attempted to win his attentions, and gain, at least, some marks of what they might term affection: Lady Mercer, who had been the mockery of every monster shewn in drawing-rooms since her marriage, threw herself in his way, and did all but put on the dress of a mountebank, to attract his notice: — though in vain: — when she stood before him, though his eyes were apparently fixed upon her's, still it seemed as if they were unperceived; — even her unappalled impudence was baffled, and she left the field. But though the common adulteress could not influence even the guidance of his eyes, it was not that the female sex was indifferent to him: yet such was the apparent caution with which he spoke to the virtuous

---

21 Pronounced "tone," the British upper classes, and particularly the fashionable members of that class, during the Georgian period.

wife and innocent daughter, that few knew he ever addressed himself to females. He had, however, the reputation of a winning tongue; and whether it was that it even overcame the dread of his singular character, or that they were moved by his apparent hatred of vice, he was as often among those females who form the boast of their sex from their domestic virtues, as among those who sully it by their vices.

About the same time, there came to London a young gentleman of the name of Aubrey: he was an orphan left with an only sister in the possession of great wealth, by parents who died while he was yet in childhood. Left also to himself by guardians, who thought it their duty merely to take care of his fortune, while they relinquished the more important charge of his mind to the care of mercenary subalterns, he cultivated more his imagination than his judgment. He had, hence, that high romantic feeling of honour and candour, which daily ruins so many milliners' apprentices. He believed all to sympathise with virtue, and thought that vice was thrown in by Providence merely for the picturesque effect of the scene, as we see in romances: he thought that the misery of a cottage merely consisted in the vesting of clothes, which were as warm, but which were better adapted to the painter's eye by their irregular folds and various coloured patches. He thought, in fine, that the dreams of poets were the realities of life. He was handsome, frank, and rich: for these reasons, upon his entering into the gay circles, many mothers surrounded him, striving which should describe with least truth their languishing or romping favourites: the daughters at the same time, by their brightening countenances when he approached, and by their sparkling eyes, when he opened his lips, soon led him into false notions of his talents and his merit. Attached as he was to the romance of his solitary hours, he was startled at finding, that, except in the tallow and wax candles that flickered, not from the presence of a ghost, but from want of snuffing, there was no foundation in real life for any of that congeries of pleasing pictures and descriptions contained in those volumes, from which he had formed his study. Finding, however, some compensation in his gratified vanity, he was about to relinquish his dreams, when the extraordinary being we have above described, crossed him in his career.

He watched him; and the very impossibility of forming an idea of the character of a man entirely absorbed in himself, who gave few other signs of his observation of external objects, than the tacit assent to their existence, implied by the avoidance of their contact: allowing his imagination to picture every thing that flattered its propensity to extravagant ideas, he soon formed this object into the hero of a romance, and determined to observe the offspring of his fancy, rather than the person before him. He became acquainted with him, paid him attentions, and so far advanced upon his notice, that his presence was always recognised. He gradually learnt that

Lord Ruthven's affairs were embarrassed, and soon found, from the notes of preparation in —— Street, that he was about to travel. Desirous of gaining some information respecting this singular character, who, till now, had only whetted his curiosity, he hinted to his guardians, that it was time for him to perform the tour, which for many generations has been thought necessary to enable the young to take some rapid steps in the career of vice towards putting themselves upon an equality with the aged, and not allowing them to appear as if fallen from the skies, whenever scandalous intrigues are mentioned as the subjects of pleasantry or of praise, according to the degree of skill shewn in carrying them on. They consented: and Aubrey immediately mentioning his intentions to Lord Ruthven, was surprised to receive from him a proposal to join him. Flattered by such a mark of esteem from him, who, apparently, had nothing in common with other men, he gladly accepted it, and in a few days they had passed the circling waters.

Hitherto, Aubrey had had no opportunity of studying Lord Ruthven's character, and now he found, that, though many more of his actions were exposed to his view, the results offered different conclusions from the apparent motives to his conduct. His companion was profuse in his liberality;—the idle, the vagabond, and the beggar, received from his hand more than enough to relieve their immediate wants. But Aubrey could not avoid remarking, that it was not upon the virtuous, reduced to indigence by the misfortunes attendant even upon virtue, that he bestowed his alms;—these were sent from the door with hardly suppressed sneers; but when the profligate came to ask something, not to relieve his wants, but to allow him to wallow in his lust, or to sink him still deeper in his iniquity, he was sent away with rich charity. This was, however, attributed by him to the greater importunity of the vicious, which generally prevails over the retiring bashfulness of the virtuous indigent. There was one circumstance about the charity of his Lordship, which was still more impressed upon his mind: all those upon whom it was bestowed, inevitably found that there was a curse upon it, for they were all either led to the scaffold, or sunk to the lowest and the most abject misery. At Brussels and other towns through which they passed, Aubrey was surprised at the apparent eagerness with which his companion sought for the centres of all fashionable vice; there he entered into all the spirit of the faro table: he betted, and always gambled with success, except where the known sharper was his antagonist, and then he lost even more than he gained; but it was always with the same unchanging face, with which he generally watched the society around: it was not, however, so when he encountered the rash youthful novice, or the luckless father of a numerous family; then his very wish seemed fortune's law—this apparent abstractedness of mind was laid aside, and his eyes sparkled with more fire than that of the cat whilst dallying with the half-dead mouse. In every town, he left the formerly affluent youth, torn from the circle he adorned, cursing, in the solitude of a dungeon, the fate that had drawn him within the reach of this fiend; whilst many a father sat frantic, amidst the speaking looks of mute hungry children, without a single farthing of his late immense wealth, wherewith to buy even sufficient to satisfy their present craving.

Yet he took no money from the gambling table; but immediately lost, to the ruiner of many, the last gilder he had just snatched from the convulsive grasp of the innocent: this might but be the result of a certain degree of knowledge, which was not, however, capable of combating the cunning of the more experienced. Aubrey often wished to represent this to his friend, and beg him to resign that charity and pleasure which proved the ruin of all, and did not tend to his own profit;—but he delayed it—for each day he hoped his friend would give him some opportunity of speaking frankly and openly to him; however, this never occurred. Lord Ruthven in his carriage, and amidst the various wild and rich scenes of nature, was always the same: his eye spoke less than his lip; and though Aubrey was near the object of his curiosity, he obtained no greater gratification from it than the constant excitement of vainly wishing to break that mystery, which to his exalted imagination began to assume the appearance of something supernatural.

They soon arrived at Rome, and Aubrey for a time lost sight of his companion; he left him in daily attendance upon the morning circle of an Italian countess, whilst he went in search of the memorials of another almost deserted city. Whilst he was thus engaged, letters arrived from England, which he opened with eager impatience; the first was from his sister, breathing nothing but affection; the others were from his guardians, the latter astonished him; if it had before entered into his imagination that there was an evil power resident in his companion, these seemed to give him sufficient reason for the belief. His guardians insisted upon his immediately leaving his friend, and urged, that his character was dreadfully vicious, for that the possession of irresistible powers of seduction, rendered his licentious habits more dangerous to society. It had been discovered, that his contempt for the adulteress had not originated in hatred of her character; but that he had required, to enhance his gratification, that his victim, the partner of his guilt, should be hurled from the pinnacle of unsullied virtue, down to the lowest abyss of infamy and degradation: in fine, that all those females whom he had sought, apparently on account of their virtue, had, since his departure, thrown even the mask aside, and had not scrupled to expose the whole deformity of their vices to the public gaze.

Aubrey determined upon leaving one, whose character had not yet shown a single bright point on which to rest the eye. He resolved to invent some plausible pretext for abandoning him altogether, purposing, in the mean while, to watch him more closely, and to let no slight circumstances pass by unnoticed. He entered into the same circle, and soon perceived, that his Lordship was endeavouring to work upon the inexperience of the daughter of the lady whose house he chiefly frequented. In Italy, it is seldom that an unmarried female is met with in society; he was therefore obliged to carry on his plans in secret; but Aubrey's eye followed him in all his windings, and soon discovered that an assignation had been appointed, which would most likely end in the ruin of an innocent, though thoughtless girl. Losing no time, he entered the apartment of Lord Ruthven, and abruptly asked him his intentions with respect to the lady, informing him at the same time that he was aware of his being about to meet her that very night. Lord Ruthven answered, that his intentions were such as he supposed all would have upon such an occasion; and upon being pressed whether he intended to marry her, merely laughed. Aubrey retired; and, immediately writing a note, to say, that from that moment he must decline accompanying his Lordship in the remainder of their proposed tour, he ordered his servant to seek other apartments, and calling upon the mother of the lady, informed her of all he knew, not only with regard to her daughter, but also concerning the character of his Lordship. The assignation was prevented. Lord Ruthven next day merely sent his servant to notify his complete assent to a separation; but did not hint any suspicion of his plans having been foiled by Aubrey's interposition.

Having left Rome, Aubrey directed his steps towards Greece, and crossing the Peninsula, soon found himself at Athens. He then fixed his residence in the house of a Greek; and soon occupied himself in tracing the faded records of ancient glory upon monuments that apparently, ashamed of chronicling the deeds of freemen only before slaves, had hidden themselves beneath the sheltering soil or many coloured lichen. Under the same roof as himself, existed a being, so beautiful and delicate, that she might have formed the model for a painter, wishing; to portray on canvass the promised hope of the faithful in Mahomet's paradise, save that her eyes spoke too much mind for any one to think she could belong to those who had no souls. As she danced upon the plain, or tripped along the mountain's side, one would have thought the gazelle a poor type of her beauties; for who would have exchanged her eye, apparently the eye of animated nature, for that sleepy luxurious look of the animal suited but to the taste of an epicure. The light step of Ianthe often accompanied Aubrey in his search after antiquities, and often would the unconscious girl, engaged in the pursuit of a Kashmere butterfly, show the whole beauty of her form, floating as it were upon the wind, to the eager gaze of him, who forgot the

letters he had just decyphered upon an almost effaced tablet, in the contemplation of her sylph-like figure. Often would her tresses falling, as she
flitted around, exhibit in the sun's ray such delicately brilliant and swiftly
fading hues, as might well excuse the forgetfulness of the antiquary, who let
escape from his mind the very object he had before thought of vital importance to the proper interpretation of a passage in Pausanias[22]. But why attempt to describe charms which all feel, but none can appreciate? — It was
innocence, youth, and beauty, unaffected by crowded drawing-rooms and
stifling balls. Whilst he drew those remains of which he wished to preserve
a memorial for his future hours, she would stand by, and watch the magic
effects of his pencil, in tracing the scenes of her native place; she would
then describe to him the circling dance upon the open plain, would paint,
to him in all the glowing colours of youthful memory, the marriage pomp
she remembered viewing in her infancy; and then, turning to subjects that
had evidently made a greater impression upon her mind, would tell him
all the supernatural tales of her nurse. Her earnestness and apparent belief
of what she narrated, excited the interest even of Aubrey; and often as she
told him the tale of the living vampyre, who had passed years amidst his
friends, and dearest ties, forced every year, by feeding upon the life of a
lovely female to prolong his existence for the ensuing months, his blood
would run cold, whilst he attempted to laugh her out of such idle and horrible fantasies; but Ianthe cited to him the names of old men, who had at
last detected one living among themselves, after several of their near rela-
tives and children had been found marked with the stamp of the fiend's
appetite, and when she found him so incredulous, she begged of him to
believe her, for it had been remarked, that those who had dared to question their existence, always had some proof given, which obliged them,
with grief and heartbreaking, to confess it was true. She detailed to him the
traditional appearance of these monsters, and his horror was increased,
by hearing a pretty accurate description of Lord Ruthven; he, however,
still persisted in persuading her, that there could be no truth in her fears,
though at the same time he wondered at the many coincidences which had
all tended to excite a belief in the supernatural power of Lord Ruthven.

Aubrey began to attach himself more and more to Ianthe; her innocence, so contrasted with all the affected virtues of the women among
whom he had sought for his vision of romance, won his heart; and while he
ridiculed the idea of a young man of English habits, marrying an uneducat-
ed Greek girl, still he found himself more and more attached to the almost
fairy form before him. He would tear himself at times from her, and, forming a plan for some antiquarian research, he would depart, determined not

---

22   A Greek traveler and writer of the 2nd Century CE, most noted for his *Description of
      Greece.*

to return until his object was attained; but he always found it impossible to fix his attention upon the ruins around him, whilst in his mind he retained an image that seemed alone the rightful possessor of his thoughts. Ianthe was unconscious of his love, and was ever the same frank infantile being he had found: known. She always seemed to part from him with reluctance; but it was because she had no longer any one with whom she could visit her favourite haunts, whilst her guardian was occupied in sketching or uncovering some fragment which had yet escaped the destructive hand of time. She had appealed to her parents on the subject of Vampyres, and they both, with several present, affirmed their existence, pale with horror at the very name. Soon after, Aubrey determined to proceed upon one of his excursions, which was to detain him for a few hours; when they heard the name of the place, they all at once begged of him not to return at night, as he must necessarily pass through a wood, where no Greek would ever remain, after the day had closed, upon any consideration. They described it as the resort of the vampyres in their nocturnal orgies, and denounced the most heavy evils as impending upon him who dared to cross their path. Aubrey made light of their representations, and tried to laugh them out of the idea; but when he saw them shudder at his daring thus to mock a superior, infernal power, the very name of which apparently made their blood freeze, he was silent.

Next morning Aubrey set off upon his excursion unattended; he was surprised to observe the melancholy face of his host, and was concerned to find that his words, mocking the belief of those horrible fiends, had inspired them with such terror. When he was about to depart, Ianthe came to the side of his horse, and earnestly begged of him to return, ere night allowed the power of these beings to be put in action;—he promised. He was, however, so occupied in his research, that he did not perceive that day-light would soon end, and that in the horizon there was one of those specks which, in the warmer climates, so rapidly gather into a tremendous mass, and pour all their rage upon the devoted country. "He at last, however, mounted his horse, determined to make up by speed for his delay: but it was too late. Twilight, in these southern climates, is almost unknown; immediately the sun sets, night begins: and ere he had advanced far, the power of the storm was above—its echoing thunders had scarcely an interval of rest—its thick heavy rain forced its way through the canopying foliage, whilst the blue forked lightning seemed to fall and radiate at his very feet. Suddenly his horse took fright, and he was carried with dreadful rapidity through the entangled forest. The animal at last, through fatigue, stopped, and he found, by the glare of lightning, that he was in the neighbourhood of a hovel that hardly lifted itself up from the masses of dead leaves and brushwood which surrounded it. Dismounting, he approached, hoping to find some one to guide him to the town, or at least trusting to obtain shelter from the pelting of the storm. As he approached, the thunders, for a moment silent, allowed him to hear the dreadful shrieks of a woman mingling with the stifled, exultant mockery of a laugh, continued in one almost unbroken sound;—he was startled: but, roused by the thunder which again rolled over his head, he, with a sudden effort, forced open the door of the hut. He found himself in utter darkness: the sound, however, guided him. He was apparently unperceived; for, though he called, still the sounds continued, and no notice was taken of him.

He found himself in contact with some one, whom he immediately seized; when a voice cried, "Again baffled!" to which a loud laugh succeeded; and he felt himself grappled by one whose strength seemed superhuman: determined to sell his life as dearly as he could, he struggled; but it was in vain: he was lifted from his feet and hurled with enormous force against the ground:—his enemy threw himself upon him, and kneeling upon his breast, had placed his hands upon his throat—when the glare of many torches penetrating through the hole that gave light in the day, disturbed him;—he instantly rose, and, leaving his prey, rushed through the door, and in a moment the crashing of the branches, as he broke through the wood, was no longer heard. The storm was now still; and Aubrey, incapable of moving, was soon heard by those without. They entered; the light of their torches fell upon the mud walls, and the thatch loaded on every individual straw with heavy flakes of soot. At the desire of Aubrey they searched for her who had attracted him by her cries; he was again left in darkness; but what was his horror, when the light of the torches once more burst upon him, to perceive the airy form of his fair conductress brought in a lifeless corse. He shut his eyes, hoping that it was but a vision arising from his disturbed imagination; but he again saw the same form, when he unclosed them, stretched by his side. There was no colour upon her cheek, not even upon her lip; yet there was a stillness about her face that seemed almost as attaching as the life that once dwelt there:—upon her neck and breast was blood, and upon her throat were the marks of teeth having opened the vein:—to this the men pointed, crying, simultaneously struck with horror, "A Vampyre! a Vampyre!" A litter was quickly formed, and Aubrey was laid by the side of her who had lately been to him the object of so many bright and fairy visions, now fallen with the flower of life that had died within her. He knew not what his thoughts were—his mind was benumbed and seemed to shun reflection, and take refuge in vacancy—he held almost unconsciously in his hand a naked dagger of a particular construction, which had been found in the hut. They were soon met by different parties who had been engaged in the search of her whom a mother had missed. Their lamentable cries, as they approached the city, forewarned the parents of some dreadful catastrophe.—To describe their grief would be impossible; but when they ascertained the cause of their child's death, they looked at Aubrey, and pointed to the corse. They were inconsolable; both died broken-hearted.

Aubrey being put to bed was seized with a most violent fever, and was often delirious; in these intervals he would call upon Lord Ruthven and upon Ianthe—by some unaccountable combination he seemed to beg of his former companion to spare the being he loved. At other times he would imprecate maledictions upon his head, and curse him as her destroyer. Lord Ruthven, chanced at this time to arrive at Athens, and, from whatever motive, upon hearing of the state of Aubrey, immediately placed himself in the same house, and became his constant attendant. When the latter recovered from his delirium, he was horrified and startled at the sight of him whose image he had now combined with that of a Vampyre; but Lord Ruthven, by his kind words, implying almost repentance for the fault that had caused their separation, and still more by the attention, anxiety, and care which he showed, soon reconciled him to his presence. His lordship seemed quite changed; he no longer appeared that apathetic being who had so astonished Aubrey; but as soon as his convalescence began to be rapid, he again gradually retired into the same state of mind, and Aubrey perceived no difference from the former man, except that at times he was surprised to meet his gaze fixed intently upon him, with a smile of malicious exultation playing upon his lips: he knew not why, but this smile haunted him. During the last stage of the invalid's recovery, Lord Ruthven was apparently engaged in watching the tideless waves raised by the cooling breeze, or in marking the progress of those orbs, circling, like our world, the moveless sun;—indeed, he appeared to wish to avoid the eyes of all.

Aubrey's mind, by this shock, was much weakened, and that elasticity of spirit which had once so distinguished him now seemed to have fled for ever. He was now as much a lover of solitude and silence as Lord Ruthven; but much as he wished for solitude, his mind could not find it in the neighbourhood of Athens; if he sought it amidst the ruins he had formerly frequented, Ianthe's form stood by his side—if he sought it in the woods, her light step would appear wandering amidst the underwood, in quest of the modest violet; then suddenly turning round, would show, to his wild imagination, her pale face and wounded throat, with a meek smile upon her lips. He determined to fly scenes, every feature of which created such bitter associations in his mind. He proposed to Lord Ruthven, to whom he held himself bound by the tender care he had taken of him during his illness, that they should visit those parts of Greece neither had yet seen. They travelled in every direction, and sought every spot to which a recollection could be attached: but though they thus hastened from place to place, yet they seemed not to heed what they gazed upon. They heard much of robbers, but they gradually began to slight these reports, which they imagined were only the invention of individuals, whose interest it was to excite the generosity of those whom they defended from pretended dangers. In consequence of thus neglecting the advice of the inhabitants, on one occasion they travelled with only a few guards, more to serve as guides than as a defence. Upon entering, however, a narrow defile, at the bottom of which was the bed of a torrent, with large masses of rock brought down from the neighbouring precipices, they had reason to repent their negligence; for scarcely were the whole of the party engaged in the narrow pass, when they were startled by the whistling of bullets close to their heads, and by the echoed report of several guns. In an instant their guards had left them, and, placing themselves behind rocks, had begun to fire in the direction whence the report came. Lord Ruthven and Aubrey, imitating their example, retired for a moment behind the sheltering turn of the defile: but ashamed of being thus detained by a foe, who with insulting shouts bade them advance, and being exposed to unresisting slaughter, if any of the robbers should climb above and take them in the rear, they determined at once to rush forward in search of the enemy. Hardly had they lost the shelter of the rock, when Lord Ruthven received a shot in the shoulder, which brought him to the ground. Aubrey hastened to his assistance; and, no longer heeding the contest or his own peril, was soon surprised by seeing the robbers' faces around him—his guards having, upon Lord Ruthven's being wounded, immediately thrown up their arms and surrendered.

By promises of great reward, Aubrey soon induced them to convey his wounded friend to a neighbouring cabin; and having agreed upon a ransom, he was no more disturbed by their presence—they being content merely to guard the entrance till their comrade should return with the promised sum, for which he had an order. Lord Ruthven's strength rapidly decreased; in two days mortification ensued, and death seemed advancing with hasty steps. His conduct and appearance had not changed; he seemed as unconscious of pain as he had been of the objects about him: but towards the close of the last evening, his mind became apparently uneasy, and his eye often fixed upon Aubrey, who was induced to offer his assistance with more than usual earnestness—"Assist me! you may save me—you may do more than that—I mean not my life, I heed the death of my existence as little as that of the passing day; but you may save my honour, your friend's honour."—"How? tell me how? I would do any thing," replied Aubrey.—"I need but little—my life ebbs apace—I cannot explain the whole—but if you would conceal all you know of me, my honour were free from stain in the world's mouth—and if my death were unknown for some time in England— I— I— but life."—"It shall not be known."— "Swear!" cried the dying man, raising himself with exultant violence, "Swear by all your soul reveres, by all your nature fears, swear that, for a year and a day you will not impart your knowledge of my crimes or death to any living being in any way, whatever may happen, or whatever you may see."— His eyes seemed bursting from their sockets: "I swear!" said Aubrey; he sunk laughing upon his pillow, and breathed no more.

Aubrey retired to rest, but did not sleep; the many circumstances attending his acquaintance with this man rose upon his mind, and he knew not why; when he remembered his oath a cold shivering came over him, as if from the presentiment of something horrible awaiting him. Rising early in the morning, he was about to enter the hovel in which he had left the corpse, when a robber met him, and informed him that it was no longer there, having been conveyed by himself and comrades, upon his retiring, to the pinnacle of a neighbouring mount, according to a promise they had given his lordship, that it should be exposed to the first cold ray of the moon that rose after his death. Aubrey astonished, and taking several of the men, determined to go and bury it upon the spot where it lay. But, when he had mounted to the summit he found no trace of either the corpse or the clothes, though the robbers swore they pointed out the identical rock on which they had laid the body. For a time his mind was bewildered in conjectures, but he at last returned, convinced that they had buried the corpse for the sake of the clothes.

Weary of a country in which he had met with such terrible misfortunes, and in which all apparently conspired to heighten that superstitious melancholy that had seized upon his mind, he resolved to leave it, and soon arrived at Smyrna. While waiting for a vessel to convey him to Otranto, or to Naples, he occupied himself in arranging those effects he had with him belonging to Lord Ruthven. Amongst other things there was a case containing several weapons of offence, more or less adapted to ensure the death of the victim. There were several daggers and ataghans. Whilst turning them over, and examining their curious forms, what was his surprise at finding a sheath apparently ornamented in the same style as the dagger discovered in the fatal hut—he shuddered—hastening to gain further proof, he found the weapon, and his horror may be imagined when he discovered that it fitted, though peculiarly shaped, the sheath he held in his hand. His eyes seemed to need no further certainty—they seemed gazing to be bound to the dagger; yet still he wished to disbelieve; but the particular form, the same varying tints upon the haft and sheath were alike in splendour on both, and left no room for doubt; there were also drops of blood on each.

He left Smyrna, and on his way home, at Rome, his first inquiries were concerning the lady he had attempted to snatch from Lord Ruthven's seductive arts. Her parents were in distress, their fortune ruined, and she had not been heard of since the departure of his lordship. Aubrey's mind became almost broken under so many repeated horrors; he was afraid that this lady had fallen a victim to the destroyer of Ianthe. He became morose and silent; and his only occupation consisted in urging the speed of the postilions, as if he were going to save the life of some one he held dear. He arrived at Calais; a breeze, which seemed obedient to his will, soon wafted him to the English shores; and he hastened to the mansion of his fathers, and there, for a moment, appeared to lose, in the embraces and caresses of his sister, all memory of the past. If she before, by her infantine caresses, had gained his affection, now that the woman began to appear, she was still more attaching as a companion.

Miss Aubrey had not that winning grace which gains the gaze and applause of the drawing-room assemblies. There was none of that light brilliancy which only exists in the heated atmosphere of a crowded apartment. Her blue eye was never lit up by the levity of the mind beneath. There was a melancholy charm about it which did not seem to arise from misfortune, but from some feeling within, that appeared to indicate a soul conscious of a brighter realm. Her step was not that light footing, which strays where'er a butterfly or a colour may attract—it was sedate and pensive. When alone, her face was never brightened by the smile of joy; but when her brother breathed to her his affection, and would in her presence forget those griefs she knew destroyed his rest, who would have exchanged her smile for that of the voluptuary? It seemed as if those eyes,—that face were then playing in the light of their own native sphere. She was yet only eighteen, and had not been presented to the world, it having been thought by her guardians more fit that her presentation should be delayed until her brother's return from the continent, when he might be her protector. It was now, therefore, resolved that the next drawing-room, which was fast approaching, should be the epoch of her entry into the "busy scene." Aubrey would rather have remained in the mansion of his fathers, and fed upon the melancholy which overpowered him. He could not feel interest about the frivolities of fashionable strangers, when his mind had been so torn by the events he had witnessed; but he determined to sacrifice his own comfort to the protection of his sister. They soon arrived in town, and prepared for the next day, which had been announced as a drawing-room.

The crowd was excessive—a drawing-room had not been held for a long time, and all who were anxious to bask in the smile of royalty, hastened thither. Aubrey was there with his sister. While he was standing in a corner by himself, heedless of all around him, engaged in the remembrance that the first time he had seen Lord Ruthven was in that very place—he felt himself suddenly seized by the arm, and a voice he recognized too well, sounded in his ear—"Remember your oath." He had hardly courage to turn, fearful of seeing a spectre that would blast him, when he perceived, at a little distance, the same figure which had attracted his notice on this spot upon his first entry into society. He gazed till his limbs almost refusing to bear their weight, he was obliged to take the arm of a friend, and forcing a passage through the crowd, he threw himself into his carriage, and was driven home. He paced the room with hurried steps, and fixed his hands upon his head, as if he were afraid his thoughts were bursting from his brain. Lord Ruthven again before him—circumstances started up in dreadful array—the dagger—his oath.— He roused himself, he could not believe it possible—the dead rise again!— He thought his imagination had conjured up the image his mind was resting upon. It was impossible that it could be real—he determined, therefore, to go again into society; for though he attempted to ask concerning Lord Ruthven, the name hung upon his lips, and he could not succeed in gaining information. He went a few nights after with his sister to the assembly of a near relation. Leaving her under the protection of a matron, he retired into a recess, and there gave himself up to his own devouring thoughts. Perceiving, at last, that many were leaving, he roused himself, and entering another room, found his sister surrounded by several, apparently in earnest conversation; he attempted to pass and get near her, when one, whom he requested to move, turned round, and revealed to him those features he most abhorred. He sprang forward, seized his sister's arm, and, with hurried step, forced her towards the street: at the door he found himself impeded by the crowd of servants who were waiting for their lords; and while he was engaged in passing them, he again heard that voice whisper close to him—"Remember your oath!"—He did not dare to turn, but, hurrying his sister, soon reached home.

Aubrey became almost distracted. If before his mind had been absorbed by one subject, how much more completely was it engrossed, now that the certainty of the monster's living again pressed upon his thoughts. His sister's attentions were now unheeded, and it was in vain that she intreated him to explain to her what had caused his abrupt conduct. He only uttered a few words, and those terrified her. The more he thought, the more he was bewildered. His oath startled him;—was he then to allow this monster to roam, bearing ruin upon his breath, amidst all he held dear, and not avert its progress? His very sister might have been touched by him. But even if he were to break his oath, and disclose his suspicions, who would believe him? He thought of employing his own hand to free the world from such a wretch; but death, he remembered, had been already mocked. For days he remained in this state; shut up in his room, he saw no one, and eat only when his sister came, who, with eyes streaming with tears, besought him, for her sake, to support nature. At last, no longer capable of bearing stillness and solitude, he left his house, roamed from street to street, anxious to fly that image which haunted him. His dress became neglected, and he wandered, as often exposed to the noon-day sun as to the midnight damps. He was no longer to be recognized; at first he returned with the evening to the house; but at last he laid him down to rest wherever fatigue overtook him. His sister, anxious for his safety, employed people to follow him; but they were soon distanced by him who fled from a pursuer swifter than any—from thought. His conduct, however, suddenly changed. Struck with the idea that he left by his absence the whole of his friends, with a fiend amongst them, of whose presence they were unconscious, he determined to enter again into society, and watch him closely, anxious to forewarn, in spite of his oath, all whom Lord Ruthven approached with intimacy. But when he entered into a room, his haggard and suspicious looks were so striking, his inward shudderings so visible, that his sister was at last obliged to beg of him to abstain from seeking, for her sake, a society which affected him so strongly. When, however, remonstrance proved unavailing, the guardians thought proper to interpose, and, fearing that his mind was becoming alienated, they thought it high time to resume again that trust which had been before imposed upon them by Aubrey's parents.

Desirous of saving him from the injuries and sufferings he had daily encountered in his wanderings, and of preventing him from exposing to the general eye those marks of what they considered folly, they engaged a physician to reside in the house, and take constant care of him. He hardly appeared to notice it, so completely was his mind absorbed by one terrible subject. His incoherence became at last so great, that he was confined to his chamber. There he would often lie for days, incapable of being roused. He had become emaciated, his eyes had attained a glassy lustre;—the only sign of affection and recollection remaining displayed itself upon the entry of his sister; then he would sometimes start, and, seizing her hands, with looks that severely afflicted her, he would desire her not to touch him. "Oh, do not touch him—if your love for me is aught, do not go near him!" When, however, she inquired to whom he referred, his only answer was, "True! true!" and again he sank into a state, whence not even she could rouse him. This lasted many months: gradually, however, as the year was passing, his incoherences became less frequent, and his mind threw off a portion of its gloom, whilst his guardians observed, that several times in the day he would count upon his fingers a definite number, and then smile.

The time had nearly elapsed, when, upon the last day of the year, one of his guardians entering his room, began to converse with his physician upon the melancholy circumstance of Aubrey's being in so awful a situation, when his sister was going next day to be married. Instantly Aubrey's attention was attracted; he asked anxiously to whom. Glad of this mark of returning intellect, of which they feared he had been deprived, they mentioned the name of the Earl of Marsden. Thinking this was a young Earl whom he had met with in society, Aubrey seemed pleased, and astonished them still more by his expressing his intention to be present at the nuptials, and desiring to see his sister. They answered not, but in a few minutes his sister was with him. He was apparently again capable of being affected by the influence of her lovely smile; for he pressed her to his breast, and kissed her cheek, wet with tears, flowing at the thought of her brother's being once more alive to the feelings of affection. He began to speak with all his wonted warmth, and to congratulate her upon her marriage with a person so distinguished for rank and every accomplishment; when he suddenly perceived a locket upon her breast; opening it, what was his surprise at beholding the features of the monster who had so long influenced his life. He seized the portrait in a paroxysm of rage, and trampled it under foot. Upon her asking him why he thus destroyed the resemblance of her future husband, he looked as if he did not understand her—then seizing her hands, and gazing on her with a frantic expression of countenance, he bade her swear that she would never wed this monster, for he—But he could not advance—it seemed as if that voice again bade him remember his oath—he turned suddenly round, thinking Lord Ruthven was near him but saw no one. In the meantime the guardians and physician, who had heard the whole, and thought this was but a return of his disorder, entered, and forcing him from Miss Aubrey, desired her to leave him. He fell upon his knees to them, he implored, he begged of them to delay but for one day. They, attributing this to the insanity they imagined had taken possession of his mind, endeavoured to pacify him, and retired.

Lord Ruthven had called the morning after the drawing-room, and had been refused with every one else. When he heard of Aubrey's ill health, he readily understood himself to be the cause of it; but when he learned that he was deemed insane, his exultation and pleasure could hardly be concealed from those among whom he had gained this information. He hastened to the house of his former companion, and, by constant attendance, and the pretence of great affection for the brother and interest in his fate, he gradually won the ear of Miss Aubrey. Who could resist his power? His tongue had dangers and toils to recount—could speak of himself as of an individual having no sympathy with any being on the crowded earth, save with her to whom he addressed himself;—could tell how, since he knew her, his existence, had begun to seem worthy of preservation, if it were merely that he might listen to her soothing accents;—in fine, he knew so well how to use the serpent's art, or such was the will of fate, that he gained her affections. The title of the elder branch[23] falling at length to him, he obtained an important embassy, which served as an excuse for hastening the marriage, (in spite of her brother's deranged state,) which was to take place the very day before his departure for the continent.

Aubrey, when he was left by the physician and his guardians, attempted to bribe the servants, but in vain. He asked for pen and paper; it was given him; be wrote a letter to his sister, conjuring her, as she valued her own happiness, her own honour, and the honour of those now in the grave, who once held her in their arms as their hope and the hope of their house, to delay but for a few hours that marriage, on which he denounced the most heavy curses. The servants promised they would deliver it; but giving it to the physician, he thought it better not to harass any more the mind of Miss Aubrey by, what he considered, the ravings of a maniac. Night passed on without rest to the busy inmates of the house; and Aubrey heard, with a horror that may more easily be conceived than described, the notes of busy preparation. Morning came, and the sound of carriages broke upon his ear. Aubrey grew almost frantic. The curiosity of the servants at last overcame their vigilance, they gradually stole away, leaving him in the custody of an helpless old woman. He seized the opportunity, with one bound was out of the room, and in a moment found himself in the apartment where all were nearly assembled. Lord Ruthven was the first to perceive him: he immediately approached, and, taking his arm by force, hurried him from the room, speechless with rage. When on the staircase, Lord Ruthven whispered in his ear— "Remember your oath, and know, if not my bride to day, your sister is dishonoured. Women are frail!" So saying, he pushed him towards his attendants, who, roused by the old woman, had come in search of him. Aubrey could no longer support himself; his rage not finding vent, had broken a blood-vessel, and he was conveyed to bed. This was not mentioned to his sister, who was not present when he entered, as the physician was afraid of agitating her. The marriage was solemnized, and the bride and bridegroom left London.

Aubrey's weakness increased; the effusion of blood produced symptoms of the near approach of death. He desired his sister's guardians might be called, and when the midnight hour had struck, he related composedly what the reader has perused—he died immediately after.

The guardians hastened to protect Miss Aubrey; but when they arrived, it was too late. Lord Ruthven had disappeared, and Aubrey's sister had glutted the thirst of a VAMPYRE!

---

23 In the British nobility, a long established custom was for a nobleman who possessed more than one title to bestow the lower ranking title on his eldest son. A noble referred to as Lord So-and-so would usually be a baron, as higher ranks were usually referred to by their title. In this story, Ruthven was probably the family name, while Marsden would be the family estate to which the earldom attached.

Extract of a Letter
Containing an Account
of
Lord Byron's Residence
in the
Island of Mitylene

"The world was all before him, where to choose his place of rest, and Providence his guide."

In sailing through the Grecian Archipelago, on board one of his Majesty's vessels, in the year 1812, we put into the harbour of Mitylene, in the island of that name. The beauty of this place, and the certain supply of cattle and vegetables always to be had there, induce many British vessels to visit it—both men of war and merchantmen; and though it lies rather out of the track for ships bound to Smyrna, its bounties amply repay for the deviation of a voyage. We landed, as usual, at the bottom of the bay, and whilst the men were employed in watering, and the purser bargaining for cattle with the natives, the clergyman and myself took a ramble to the cave called Homer's School, and other places, where we had been before. On the brow of Mount Ida (a small monticule so named) we met with and engaged a young Greek as our guide, who told us he had come from Scio with an English lord, who left the island four days previous to our arrival in his felucca. "He engaged me as a pilot," said the Greek, "and would have taken me with him; but I did not choose to quit Mitylene, where I am likely to get married. He was an odd, but a very good man. The cottage over the hill, facing the river, belongs to him, and he has left an old man in charge of it: he gave Dominick, the wine-trader, six hundred zechines for it, (about £250 English currency,) and has resided there about fourteen months, though not constantly; for he sails in his felucca very often to the different islands."

This account excited our curiosity very much, and we lost no time in

33

hastening to the house where our countryman had resided. We were kindly received by an old man, who conducted us over the mansion. It consisted of four apartments on the ground-floor—an entrance hall, a drawing-room, a sitting parlour, and a bed-room, with a spacious closet annexed. They were all simply decorated: plain green-stained walls, marble tables on either side, a large myrtle in the centre, and a small fountain beneath, which could be made to play through the branches by moving a spring fixed in the side of a small bronze Venus in a leaning posture; a large couch or sofa completed the furniture. In the hall stood half a dozen English cane chairs, and an empty book-case: there were no mirrors, nor a single painting. The bedchamber had merely a large mattress spread on the floor, with two stuffed cotton quilts and a pillow—the common bed throughout Greece. In the sitting-room we observed a marble recess, formerly, the old man told us, filled with books and papers, which were then in a large seaman's chest in the closet: it was open, but we did not think ourselves justified in examining the contents. On the tablet of the recess lay Voltaire's, Shakspeare's, Boileau's, and Rousseau's works complete; Volney's *Ruins of Empires*; Zimmerman, in the German language; Klopstock;s *Messiah*; Kotzebue's novels; Schiller's play of *The Robbers*; Milton's *Paradise Lost*, an Italian edition, printed at Parma in 1810; several small pamphlets from the Greek press at Constantinople, much torn, but no English book of any description. Most of these books were filled with marginal notes, written with a pencil, in Italian and Latin. The *Messiah* was literally scribbled all over, and marked with slips of paper, on which also were remarks.

The old man said: "The lord had been reading these books the evening before he sailed, and forgot to place them with the others; but," said he, "there they must lie until his return; for he is so particular, that were I to move one thing without orders, he would frown upon me for a week together; he is otherways very good. I once did him a service; and I have the produce of this farm for the trouble of taking care of it, except twenty zechines which I pay to an aged Armenian who resides in a small cottage in the wood, and whom the lord brought here from Adrianople; I don't know for what reason."

The appearance of the house externally was pleasing. The portico in front was fifty paces long and fourteen broad, and the fluted marble pillars with black plinths and fret-work cornices, (as it is now customary in Grecian architecture,) were considerably higher than the roof. The roof, surrounded by a light stone balustrade, was covered by a fine Turkey carpet, beneath an awning of strong coarse linen. Most of the house-tops are thus furnished, as upon them the Greeks pass their evenings in smoking, drinking light wines, such as "lachryma christi," eating fruit, and enjoying the evening breeze.

On the left hand as we entered the house, a small streamlet glided away, grapes, oranges and limes were clustering together on its borders, and under the shade of two large myrtle bushes, a marble seat with an ornamental wooden back was placed, on which we were told, the lord passed many of his evenings and nights till twelve o'clock, reading, writing, and talking to himself. "I suppose," said the old man, "*praying*, for he was very devout, and always attended our church twice a week, besides Sundays."

The view from this seat was what may be termed "a bird's-eye view." A line of rich vineyards led the eye to Mount Calcla, covered with olive and myrtle trees in bloom, and on the summit of which an ancient Greek temple appeared in majestic decay. A small stream issuing from the ruins descended in broken cascades, until it was lost in the woods near the mountain's base. The sea smooth as glass, and an horizon unshadowed by a single cloud, terminates the view in front; and a little on the left, through a vista of lofty chestnut and palm-trees, several small islands were distinctly observed, studding the light blue wave with spots of emerald green. I seldom enjoyed a view more than I did this; but our enquiries were fruitless as to the name of the person who had resided in this romantic solitude: none knew his name but Dominick, his banker, who had gone to Candia. "The Armenian," said our conductor, "could tell, but I am sure he will not,"— "And cannot you tell, old friend?" said I— "If I can," said he, "I dare not." We had not time to visit the Armenian, but on our return to the town we learnt several particulars of the isolated lord. He had portioned eight young girls when he was last upon the island, and even danced with them at the nuptial feast. He gave a cow to one man, horses to others, and cotton and silk to the girls who live by weaving these articles. He also bought a new boat for a fisherman who had lost his own in a gale, and he often gave Greek Testaments to the poor children. In short, he appeared to us, from all we collected, to have been a very eccentric and benevolent character. One circumstance we learnt, which our old friend at the cottage thought proper not to disclose. He had a most beautiful daughter, with whom the lord was often seen walking on the sea-shore, and he had bought her a piano-forte, and taught her himself the use of it.

Such was the information with which we departed from the peaceful isle of Mitylene; our imaginations all on the rack, guessing who this rambler in Greece could be. He had money it was evident: he had philanthropy of disposition, and all those eccentricities which mark peculiar genius. Arrived at Palermo, all our doubts were dispelled. Falling in company with Mr. Foster, the architect, a pupil of Wyatt's, who had been travelling in Egypt and Greece, "The individual," said he, "about whom you are so anxious, is Lord Byron; I met him in my travels on the island of Tenedos, and I also visited him at Mitylene." We had never then heard of his lordship's fame, as we had been some years from home; but "Childe Harolde" being put into our hands we recognized the recluse of Calcla in every page. Deeply did we regret not having been more curious in our researches at the cottage, but we consoled ourselves with the idea of returning to Mitylene on some future day; but to me that day will never return. I make this statement, believing it not quite uninteresting, and in justice to his lordship's good name, which has been grossly slandered. He has been described as of an unfeeling disposition, averse to associating with human nature, or contributing in any way to sooth its sorrows, or add to its pleasures. The fact is directly the reverse, as may be plainly gathered from these little anecdotes. All the finer feelings of the heart, so elegantly depicted in his lordship's poems, seem to have their seat in his bosom. Tenderness, sympathy, and charity appear to guide all his actions: and his courting the repose of solitude is an additional reason for marking him as a being on whose heart Religion hath set her seal, and over whose head Benevolence hath thrown her mantle. No man can read the preceding pleasing "traits" without feeling proud of him as a countryman. With respect to his loves or pleasures, I do not assume a right to give an opinion. Reports are ever to be received with caution, particularly when directed against man's moral integrity; and he who dares justify himself before that awful tribunal where all must appear, alone may censure the errors of a fellow-mortal. Lord Byron's character is worthy of his genius. To do good in secret, and shun the world's applause, is the surest testimony of a virtuous heart and self-approving conscience.

Carmilla
J. Sheridan LeFanu
1872

Prologue

U pon a paper attached to the Narrative which follows, Doctor Hesselius has written a rather elaborate note, which he accompanies with a reference to his Essay on the strange subject which the MS. illuminates.

This mysterious subject he treats, in that Essay, with his usual learning and acumen, and with remarkable directness and condensation. It will form but one volume of the series of that extraordinary man's collected papers.

As I publish the case, in this volume, simply to interest the "laity," I shall forestall the intelligent lady, who relates it, in nothing; and after due consideration, I have determined, therefore, to abstain from presenting any précis of the learned Doctors reasoning, or extract from his statement on a subject which he describes as "involving, not improbably, some of the profoundest arcana of our dual existence, and its intermediates."

I was anxious on discovering this paper, to reopen the correspondence commenced by Doctor Hesselius, so many years before, with a person so clever and careful as his informant seems to have been. Much to my regret, however, I found that she had died in the interval.

She, probably, could have added little to the Narrative, which she communicates in the following pages with, so far as I can pronounce, such conscientious particularity.

I
An Early Fright

In Styria,[24] we, though by no means magnificent people, inhabit a castle, or *schloss*. A small income, in that part of the world, goes a great way. Eight or nine hundred a year does wonders. Scantily enough ours would have answered among wealthy people at home. My father is English, and I bear an English name, although I never saw England. But here, in this lonely and primitive place, where everything is so marvelously cheap, I really don't see how ever so much more money would at all materially add to our comforts, or even luxuries.

My father was in the Austrian service, and retired upon a pension and his patrimony, and purchased this feudal residence, and the small estate on which it stands, a bargain.

Nothing can be more picturesque or solitary. It stands on a slight eminence in a forest. The road, very old and narrow, passes in front of its drawbridge, never raised in my time, and its moat, stocked with perch, and sailed over by many swans, and floating on its surface white fleets of water lilies.

Over all this the *schloss* shows its many-windowed front; its towers, and its Gothic chapel.

The forest opens in an irregular and very picturesque glade before its gate, and at the right a steep Gothic bridge carries the road over a stream that winds in deep shadow through the wood. I have said that this is a very lonely place. Judge whether I say truth. Looking from the hall door towards the road, the forest in which our castle stands extends fifteen miles to the right, and twelve to the left. The nearest inhabited village is about seven of your English miles to the left. The nearest inhabited *schloss* of any historic associations, is that of old General Spielsdorf, nearly twenty miles away to the right.

---

24   Styria, or Steiermark, is a south-eastern Austrian state. The capitol is Graz, perhaps best known today outside Austria as the birthplace of Arnold Schwarzenegger.

I have said "the nearest *inhabited* village," because there is, only three miles westward, that is to say in the direction of General Spielsdorf's *schloss*, a ruined village, with its quaint little church, now roofless, in the aisle of which are the moldering tombs of the proud family of Karnstein, now extinct, who once owned the equally desolate chateau which, in the thick of the forest, overlooks the silent ruins of the town.

Respecting the cause of the desertion of this striking and melancholy spot, there is a legend which I shall relate to you another time.

I must tell you now, how very small is the party who constitute the inhabitants of our castle. I don't include servants, or those dependents who occupy rooms in the buildings attached to the *schloss*. Listen, and wonder! My father, who is the kindest man on earth, but growing old; and I, at the date of my story, only nineteen. Eight years have passed since then.

I and my father constituted the family at the *schloss*. My mother, a Styrian lady, died in my infancy, but I had a good-natured governess, who had been with me from, I might almost say, my infancy. I could not remember the time when her fat, benignant face was not a familiar picture in my memory.

This was Madame Perrodon, a native of Berne, whose care and good nature now in part supplied to me the loss of my mother, whom I do not even remember, so early I lost her. She made a third at our little dinner party. There was a fourth, Mademoiselle De Lafontaine, a lady such as you term, I believe, a "finishing governess." She spoke French and German, Madame Perrodon French and broken English, to which my father and I added English, which, partly to prevent its becoming a lost language among us, and partly from patriotic motives, we spoke every day. The consequence was a Babel, at which strangers used to laugh, and which I shall make no attempt to reproduce in this narrative. And there were two or three young lady friends besides, pretty nearly of my own age, who were occasional visitors, for longer or shorter terms; and these visits I sometimes returned.

These were our regular social resources; but of course there were chance visits from "neighbours" of only five or six leagues distance. My life was, notwithstanding, rather a solitary one, I can assure you.

My *gouvernantes* had just so much control over me as you might conjecture such sage persons would have in the case of a rather spoiled girl, whose only parent allowed her pretty nearly her own way in everything.

The first occurrence in my existence, which produced a terrible impression upon my mind, which, in fact, never has been effaced, was one of the very earliest incidents of my life which I can recollect. Some people will think it so trifling that it should not be recorded here. You will see, however, by-and-by, why I mention it. The nursery, as it was called, though I had it all to myself, was a large room in the upper story of the castle, with a steep oak roof. I can't have been more than six years old, when one night I awoke, and looking round the room from my bed, failed to see the nursery maid. Neither was my nurse there; and I thought myself alone. I was not frightened, for I was one of those happy children who are studiously kept in ignorance of ghost stories, of fairy tales, and of all such lore as makes us cover up our heads when the door cracks suddenly, or the flicker of an expiring candle makes the shadow of a bedpost dance upon the wall, nearer to our faces. I was vexed and insulted at finding myself, as I conceived, neglected, and I began to whimper, preparatory to a hearty bout of roaring; when to my surprise, I saw a solemn, but very pretty face looking at me from the side of the bed. It was that of a young lady who was kneeling, with her hands under the coverlet. I looked at her with a kind of pleased wonder, and ceased whimpering. She caressed me with her hands, and lay down beside me on the bed, and drew me towards her, smiling; I felt immediately delightfully soothed, and fell asleep again. I was wakened by a sensation as if two needles ran into my breast very deep at the same moment, and I cried loudly. The lady started back, with her eyes fixed on me, and then slipped down upon the floor, and, as I thought, hid herself under the bed.

I was now for the first time frightened, and I yelled with all my might and main. Nurse, nursery maid, housekeeper, all came running in, and hearing my story, they made light of it, soothing me all they could meanwhile. But, child as I was, I could perceive that their faces were pale with an unwonted look of anxiety, and I saw them look under the bed, and about the room, and peep under tables and pluck open cupboards; and the housekeeper whispered to the nurse: "Lay your hand along that hollow in the bed; someone *did* lie there, so sure as you did not; the place is still warm."

I remember the nursery maid petting me, and all three examining my chest, where I told them I felt the puncture, and pronouncing that there was no sign visible that any such thing had happened to me.

The housekeeper and the two other servants who were in charge of the nursery, remained sitting up all night; and from that time a servant always sat up in the nursery until I was about fourteen.

I was very nervous for a long time after this. A doctor was called in, he was pallid and elderly. How well I remember his long saturnine face, slightly pitted with smallpox, and his chestnut wig. For a good while, every second day, he came and gave me medicine, which of course I hated.

The morning after I saw this apparition I was in a state of terror, and could not bear to be left alone, daylight though it was, for a moment.

I remember my father coming up and standing at the bedside, and talking cheerfully, and asking the nurse a number of questions, and laughing very heartily at one of the answers; and patting me on the shoulder, and kissing me, and telling me not to be frightened, that it was nothing but a dream and could not hurt me.

But I was not comforted, for I knew the visit of the strange woman was *not* a dream; and I was *awfully* frightened.

I was a little consoled by the nursery maid's assuring me that it was she who had come and looked at me, and lain down beside me in the bed, and that I must have been half-dreaming not to have known her face. But this, though supported by the nurse, did not quite satisfy me.

I remembered, in the course of that day, a venerable old man, in a black cassock, coming into the room with the nurse and housekeeper, and talking a little to them, and very kindly to me; his face was very sweet and gentle, and he told me they were going to pray, and joined my hands together, and desired me to say, softly, while they were praying, "Lord, hear all good prayers for us, for Jesus' sake." I think these were the very words, for I often repeated them to myself, and my nurse used for years to make me say them in my prayers.

I remembered so well the thoughtful sweet face of that white-haired old man, in his black cassock, as he stood in that rude, lofty, brown room, with the clumsy furniture of a fashion three hundred years old about him, and the scanty light entering its shadowy atmosphere through the small lattice. He kneeled, and the three women with him, and he prayed aloud with an earnest quavering voice for, what appeared to me, a long time. I forget all my life preceding that event, and for some time after it is all obscure also, but the scenes I have just described stand out vivid as the isolated pictures of the phantasmagoria surrounded by darkness.

II
A Guest

I am now going to tell you something so strange that it will require all your faith in my veracity to believe my story. It is not only true, nevertheless, but truth of which I have been an eyewitness.

It was a sweet summer evening, and my father asked me, as he sometimes did, to take a little ramble with him along that beautiful forest vista which I have mentioned as lying in front of the *schloss*.

"General Spielsdorf cannot come to us so soon as I had hoped," said my father, as we pursued our walk.

He was to have paid us a visit of some weeks, and we had expected his arrival next day. He was to have brought with him a young lady, his niece and ward, Mademoiselle Rheinfeldt, whom I had never seen, but whom I had heard described as a very charming girl, and in whose society I had promised myself many happy days. I was more disappointed than a young lady living in a town, or a bustling neighborhood can possibly imagine. This visit, and the new acquaintance it promised, had furnished my day dream for many weeks.

"And how soon does he come?" I asked.

"Not till autumn. Not for two months, I dare say," he answered. "And I am very glad now, dear, that you never knew Mademoiselle Rheinfeldt."

"And why?" I asked, both mortified and curious.

"Because the poor young lady is dead," he replied. "I quite forgot I had not told you, but you were not in the room when I received the General's letter this evening."

I was very much shocked. General Spielsdorf had mentioned in his first letter, six or seven weeks before, that she was not so well as he would wish her, but there was nothing to suggest the remotest suspicion of danger.

"Here is the General's letter," he said, handing it to me. "I am afraid he is in great affliction; the letter appears to me to have been written very nearly in distraction."

We sat down on a rude bench, under a group of magnificent lime trees. The sun was setting with all its melancholy splendour behind the sylvan horizon, and the stream that flows beside our home, and passes under the steep old bridge I have mentioned, wound through many a group of noble trees, almost at our feet, reflecting in its current the fading crimson of the sky. General Spielsdorf's letter was so extraordinary, so vehement, and in some places so self-contradictory, that I read it twice over—the second time aloud to my father—and was still unable to account for it, except by supposing that grief had unsettled his mind.

It said, "I have lost my darling daughter, for as such I loved her. During the last days of dear Bertha's illness I was not able to write to you.

"Before then I had no idea of her danger. I have lost her, and now learn *all*, too late. She died in the peace of innocence, and in the glorious hope of a blessed futurity. The fiend who betrayed our infatuated hospitality has done it all. I thought I was receiving into my house innocence, gaiety, a charming companion for my lost Bertha. Heavens! what a fool have I been!

"I thank God my child died without a suspicion of the cause of her sufferings. She is gone without so much as conjecturing the nature of her illness, and the accursed passion of the agent of all this misery. I devote my remaining days to tracking and extinguishing a monster. I am told I may hope to accomplish my righteous and merciful purpose. At present there is scarcely a gleam of light to guide me. I curse my conceited incredulity, my despicable affectation of superiority, my blindness, my obstinacy—all—too late. I cannot write or talk collectedly now. I am distracted. So soon as I shall have a little recovered, I mean to devote myself for a time to enquiry, which may possibly lead me as far as Vienna. Some time in the autumn, two months hence, or earlier if I live, I will see you—that is, if you permit me; I will then tell you all that I scarce dare put upon paper now. Farewell. Pray for me, dear friend."

In these terms ended this strange letter. Though I had never seen Bertha Rheinfeldt my eyes filled with tears at the sudden intelligence; I was startled, as well as profoundly disappointed.

The sun had now set, and it was twilight by the time I had returned the General's letter to my father.

It was a soft clear evening, and we loitered, speculating upon the possible meanings of the violent and incoherent sentences which I had just been reading. We had nearly a mile to walk before reaching the road that passes the *schloss* in front, and by that time the moon was shining brilliantly. At the drawbridge we met Madame Perrodon and Mademoiselle De Lafontaine, who had come out, without their bonnets, to enjoy the exquisite moonlight.

We heard their voices gabbling in animated dialogue as we approached. We joined them at the drawbridge, and turned about to admire with them the beautiful scene.

The glade through which we had just walked lay before us. At our left the narrow road wound away under clumps of lordly trees, and was lost to sight amid the thickening forest. At the right the same road crosses the steep and picturesque bridge, near which stands a ruined tower which once guarded that pass; and beyond the bridge an abrupt eminence rises, covered with trees, and showing in the shadows some grey ivy-clustered rocks.

Over the sward and low grounds a thin film of mist was stealing like smoke, marking the distances with a transparent veil; and here and there we could see the river faintly flashing in the moonlight.

No softer, sweeter scene could be imagined. The news I had just heard made it melancholy; but nothing could disturb its character of profound serenity, and the enchanted glory and vagueness of the prospect.

My father, who enjoyed the picturesque, and I, stood looking in silence over the expanse beneath us. The two good governesses, standing a little way behind us, discoursed upon the scene, and were eloquent upon the moon.

Madame Perrodon was fat, middle-aged, and romantic, and talked and sighed poetically. Mademoiselle De Lafontaine—in right of her father who was a German, assumed to be psychological, metaphysical, and something of a mystic—now declared that when the moon shone with a light so intense it was well known that it indicated a special spiritual activity. The effect of the full moon in such a state of brilliancy was manifold. It acted on dreams, it acted on lunacy, it acted on nervous people, it had marvelous physical influences connected with life. Mademoiselle related that her cousin, who was mate of a merchant ship, having taken a nap on deck on such a night, lying on his back, with his face full in the light on the moon, had wakened, after a dream of an old woman clawing him by the cheek, with his features horribly drawn to one side; and his countenance had never quite recovered its equilibrium.

"The moon, this night," she said, "is full of idyllic and magnetic influence—and see, when you look behind you at the front of the *schloss* how all its windows flash and twinkle with that silvery splendour, as if unseen hands had lighted up the rooms to receive fairy guests."

There are indolent styles of the spirits in which, indisposed to talk ourselves, the talk of others is pleasant to our listless ears; and I gazed on, pleased with the tinkle of the ladies' conversation.

"I have got into one of my moping moods tonight," said my father, after a silence, and quoting Shakespeare, whom, by way of keeping up our English, he used to read aloud, he said:

"'In truth I know not why I am so sad.
It wearies me: you say it wearies you;
But how I got it—came by it.'

"I forget the rest. But I feel as if some great misfortune were hanging over us. I suppose the poor General's afflicted letter has had something to do with it."

At this moment the unwonted sound of carriage wheels and many hoofs upon the road, arrested our attention.

They seemed to be approaching from the high ground overlooking the bridge, and very soon the equipage emerged from that point. Two horsemen first crossed the bridge, then came a carriage drawn by four horses, and two men rode behind.

It seemed to be the traveling carriage of a person of rank; and we were all immediately absorbed in watching that very unusual spectacle. It became, in a few moments, greatly more interesting, for just as the carriage had passed the summit of the steep bridge, one of the leaders, taking fright, communicated his panic to the rest, and after a plunge or two, the whole team broke into a wild gallop together, and dashing between the horsemen who rode in front, came thundering along the road towards us with the speed of a hurricane.

The excitement of the scene was made more painful by the clear, long-drawn screams of a female voice from the carriage window.

We all advanced in curiosity and horror; me rather in silence, the rest with various ejaculations of terror.

Our suspense did not last long. Just before you reach the castle drawbridge, on the route they were coming, there stands by the roadside a magnificent lime tree, on the other stands an ancient stone cross, at sight of which the horses, now going at a pace that was perfectly frightful, swerved so as to bring the wheel over the projecting roots of the tree.

I knew what was coming. I covered my eyes, unable to see it out, and turned my head away; at the same moment I heard a cry from my lady friends, who had gone on a little.

Curiosity opened my eyes, and I saw a scene of utter confusion. Two of the horses were on the ground, the carriage lay upon its side with two wheels in the air; the men were busy removing the traces, and a lady, with a commanding air and figure had got out, and stood with clasped hands, raising the handkerchief that was in them every now and then to her eyes.

Through the carriage door was now lifted a young lady, who appeared to be lifeless. My dear old father was already beside the elder lady, with his hat in his hand, evidently tendering his aid and the resources of his *schloss*. The lady did not appear to hear him, or to have eyes for anything but the slender girl who was being placed against the slope of the bank.

I approached; the young lady was apparently stunned, but she was certainly not dead. My father, who piqued himself on being something of a physician, had just had his fingers on her wrist and assured the lady, who declared herself her mother, that her pulse, though faint and irregular, was undoubtedly still distinguishable. The lady clasped her hands and looked upward, as if in a momentary transport of gratitude; but immediately she broke out again in that theatrical way which is, I believe, natural to some people.

She was what is called a fine looking woman for her time of life, and must have been handsome; she was tall, but not thin, and dressed in black velvet, and looked rather pale, but with a proud and commanding countenance, though now agitated strangely.

"Who was ever being so born to calamity?" I heard her say, with clasped hands, as I came up. "Here am I, on a journey of life and death, in prosecuting which to lose an hour is possibly to lose all. My child will not have recovered sufficiently to resume her route for who can say how long. I must leave her: I cannot, dare not, delay. How far on, sir, can you tell, is the nearest village? I must leave her there; and shall not see my darling, or even hear of her till my return, three months hence."

I plucked my father by the coat, and whispered earnestly in his ear: "Oh! papa, pray ask her to let her stay with us—it would be so delightful. Do, pray."

"If Madame will entrust her child to the care of my daughter, and of her good *gouvernante*, Madame Perrodon, and permit her to remain as our guest, under my charge, until her return, it will confer a distinction and an obligation upon us, and we shall treat her with all the care and devotion which so sacred a trust deserves."

"I cannot do that, sir, it would be to task your kindness and chivalry too cruelly," said the lady, distractedly.

"It would, on the contrary, be to confer on us a very great kindness at the moment when we most need it. My daughter has just been disappointed by a cruel misfortune, in a visit from which she had long anticipated a great deal of happiness. If you confide this young lady to our care it will be her best consolation. The nearest village on your route is distant, and affords no such inn as you could think of placing your daughter at; you cannot allow her to continue her journey for any considerable distance without danger. If, as you say, you cannot suspend your journey, you must part with her tonight, and nowhere could you do so with more honest assurances of care and tenderness than here."

There was something in this lady's air and appearance so distinguished and even imposing, and in her manner so engaging, as to impress one, quite apart from the dignity of her equipage, with a conviction that she was a person of consequence.

By this time the carriage was replaced in its upright position, and the horses, quite tractable, in the traces again.

The lady threw on her daughter a glance which I fancied was not quite so affectionate as one might have anticipated from the beginning of the scene; then she beckoned slightly to my father, and withdrew two or three steps with him out of hearing; and talked to him with a fixed and stern countenance, not at all like that with which she had hitherto spoken.

I was filled with wonder that my father did not seem to perceive the change, and also unspeakably curious to learn what it could be that she was speaking, almost in his ear, with so much earnestness and rapidity.

Two or three minutes at most I think she remained thus employed, then she turned, and a few steps brought her to where her daughter lay, supported by Madame Perrodon. She kneeled beside her for a moment and whispered, as Madame supposed, a little benediction in her ear; then hastily kissing her she stepped into her carriage, the door was closed, the footmen in stately liveries jumped up behind, the outriders spurred on, the postilions cracked their whips, the horses plunged and broke suddenly into a furious canter that threatened soon again to become a gallop, and the carriage whirled away, followed at the same rapid pace by the two horsemen in the rear.

III
We Compare Notes

We followed the *cortege* with our eyes until it was swiftly lost to sight in the misty wood; and the very sound of the hoofs and the wheels died away in the silent night air.

Nothing remained to assure us that the adventure had not been an illusion of a moment but the young lady, who just at that moment opened her eyes. I could not see, for her face was turned from me, but she raised her head, evidently looking about her, and I heard a very sweet voice ask complainingly, "Where is mamma?"

Our good Madame Perrodon answered tenderly, and added some comfortable assurances.

I then heard her ask:

"Where am I? What is this place?" and after that she said, "I don't see the carriage; and Matska, where is she?"

Madame answered all her questions in so far as she understood them; and gradually the young lady remembered how the misadventure came about, and was glad to hear that no one in, or in attendance on, the carriage was hurt; and on learning that her mamma had left her here, till her return in about three months, she wept.

I was going to add my consolations to those of Madame Perrodon when Mademoiselle De Lafontaine placed her hand upon my arm, saying:

"Don't approach, one at a time is as much as she can at present converse with; a very little excitement would possibly overpower her now."

As soon as she is comfortably in bed, I thought, I will run up to her room and see her.

My father in the meantime had sent a servant on horseback for the physician, who lived about two leagues[25] away; and a bedroom was being prepared for the young lady's reception.

---

25   Roughly six miles.

The stranger now rose, and leaning on Madame's arm, walked slowly over the drawbridge and into the castle gate.

In the hall, servants waited to receive her, and she was conducted forthwith to her room. The room we usually sat in as our drawing room is long, having four windows, that looked over the moat and drawbridge, upon the forest scene I have just described.

It is furnished in old carved oak, with large carved cabinets, and the chairs are cushioned with crimson Utrecht velvet. The walls are covered with tapestry, and surrounded with great gold frames, the figures being as large as life, in ancient and very curious costume, and the subjects represented are hunting, hawking, and generally festive. It is not too stately to be extremely comfortable; and here we had our tea, for with his usual patriotic leanings he insisted that the national beverage should make its appearance regularly with our coffee and chocolate.

We sat here this night, and with candles lighted, were talking over the adventure of the evening.

Madame Perrodon and Mademoiselle De Lafontaine were both of our party. The young stranger had hardly lain down in her bed when she sank into a deep sleep; and those ladies had left her in the care of a servant.

"How do you like our guest?" I asked, as soon as Madame entered. "Tell me all about her?"

"I like her extremely," answered Madame, "she is, I almost think, the prettiest creature I ever saw; about your age, and so gentle and nice."

"She is absolutely beautiful," threw in Mademoiselle, who had peeped for a moment into the stranger's room.

"And such a sweet voice!" added Madame Perrodon.

"Did you remark a woman in the carriage, after it was set up again, who did not get out," inquired Mademoiselle, "but only looked from the window?"

"No, we had not seen her."

Then she described a hideous black woman, with a sort of coloured turban on her head, and who was gazing all the time from the carriage window, nodding and grinning derisively towards the ladies, with gleaming eyes and large white eyeballs, and her teeth set as if in fury.

"Did you remark what an ill-looking pack of men the servants were?" asked Madame.

"Yes," said my father, who had just come in, "ugly, hang-dog looking fellows as ever I beheld in my life. I hope they mayn't rob the poor lady in the forest. They are clever rogues, however; they got everything to rights in a minute."

"I dare say they are worn out with too long traveling," said Madame.

"Besides looking wicked, their faces were so strangely lean, and dark, and sullen. I am very curious, I own; but I dare say the young lady will tell you all about it tomorrow, if she is sufficiently recovered."

"I don't think she will," said my father, with a mysterious smile, and a little nod of his head, as if he knew more about it than he cared to tell us.

This made us all the more inquisitive as to what had passed between him and the lady in the black velvet, in the brief but earnest interview that had immediately preceded her departure.

We were scarcely alone, when I entreated him to tell me. He did not need much pressing.

"There is no particular reason why I should not tell you. She expressed a reluctance to trouble us with the care of her daughter, saying she was in delicate health, and nervous, but not subject to any kind of seizure—she volunteered that—nor to any illusion; being, in fact, perfectly sane."

"How very odd to say all that!" I interpolated. "It was so unnecessary."

"At all events it *was* said," he laughed, "and as you wish to know all that passed, which was indeed very little, I tell you. She then said, "I am making a long journey of *vital* importance—she emphasized the word—rapid and secret; I shall return for my child in three months; in the meantime, she will be silent as to who we are, whence we come, and whither we are traveling." That is all she said. She spoke very pure French. When she said the word "secret," she paused for a few seconds, looking sternly, her eyes fixed on mine. I fancy she makes a great point of that. You saw how quickly she was gone. I hope I have not done a very foolish thing, in taking charge of the young lady."

For my part, I was delighted. I was longing to see and talk to her; and only waiting till the doctor should give me leave. You, who live in towns, can have no idea how great an event the introduction of a new friend is, in such a solitude as surrounded us.

The doctor did not arrive till nearly one o'clock; but I could no more have gone to my bed and slept, than I could have overtaken, on foot, the carriage in which the princess in black velvet had driven away.

When the physician came down to the drawing room, it was to report very favourably upon his patient. She was now sitting up, her pulse quite regular, apparently perfectly well. She had sustained no injury, and the little shock to her nerves had passed away quite harmlessly. There could be no harm certainly in my seeing her, if we both wished it; and, with this permission I sent, forthwith, to know whether she would allow me to visit her for a few minutes in her room.

The servant returned immediately to say that she desired nothing more.

You may be sure I was not long in availing myself of this permission.

Our visitor lay in one of the handsomest rooms in the *schloss*. It was, perhaps, a little stately. There was a somber piece of tapestry opposite the foot of the bed, representing Cleopatra with the asps to her bosom; and other solemn classic scenes were displayed, a little faded, upon the other walls. But there was gold carving, and rich and varied colour enough in the other decorations of the room, to more than redeem the gloom of the old tapestry.

There were candles at the bedside. She was sitting up; her slender pretty figure enveloped in the soft silk dressing gown, embroidered with flowers, and lined with thick quilted silk, which her mother had thrown over her feet as she lay upon the ground.

What was it that, as I reached the bedside and had just begun my little greeting, struck me dumb in a moment, and made me recoil a step or two from before her? I will tell you.

I saw the very face which had visited me in my childhood at night, which remained so fixed in my memory, and on which I had for so many years so often ruminated with horror, when no one suspected of what I was thinking.

It was pretty, even beautiful; and when I first beheld it, wore the same melancholy expression.

But this almost instantly lighted into a strange fixed smile of recognition.

There was a silence of fully a minute, and then at length she spoke; I could not.

"How wonderful!" she exclaimed. "Twelve years ago, I saw your face in a dream, and it has haunted me ever since."

"Wonderful indeed!" I repeated, overcoming with an effort the horror that had for a time suspended my utterances. "Twelve years ago, in vision or reality, I certainly saw you. I could not forget your face. It has remained before my eyes ever since."

Her smile had softened. Whatever I had fancied strange in it was gone, and it and her dimpling cheeks were now delightfully pretty and intelligent.

I felt reassured, and continued more in the vein which hospitality indicated, to bid her welcome, and to tell her how much pleasure her accidental arrival had given us all, and especially what a happiness it was to me.

I took her hand as I spoke. I was a little shy, as lonely people are, but the situation made me eloquent, and even bold. She pressed my hand, she laid hers upon it, and her eyes glowed, as, looking hastily into mine, she smiled again, and blushed.

She answered my welcome very prettily. I sat down beside her, still wondering; and she said:

"I must tell you my vision about you; it is so very strange that you and I should have had, each of the other so vivid a dream, that each should have seen, I you and you me, looking as we do now, when of course we both were mere children. I was a child, about six years old, and I awoke from a confused and troubled dream, and found myself in a room, unlike my nursery, wainscoted clumsily in some dark wood, and with cupboards and bedsteads, and chairs, and benches placed about it. The beds were, I thought, all empty, and the room itself without anyone but myself in it; and I, after looking about me for some time, and admiring especially an iron candlestick with two branches, which I should certainly know again, crept under one of the beds to reach the window; but as I got from under the bed, I heard someone crying; and looking up, while I was still upon my knees, I saw you—most assuredly you—as I see you now; a beautiful young lady, with golden hair and large blue eyes, and lips—your lips—you as you are here.

"Your looks won me; I climbed on the bed and put my arms about you, and I think we both fell asleep. I was aroused by a scream; you were sitting up screaming. I was frightened, and slipped down upon the ground, and, it seemed to me, lost consciousness for a moment; and when I came to myself, I was again in my nursery at home. Your face I have never forgotten since. I could not be misled by mere resemblance. "You are the lady whom I saw then."

It was now my turn to relate my corresponding vision, which I did, to the undisguised wonder of my new acquaintance.

"I don't know which should be most afraid of the other," she said, again smiling— "If you were less pretty I think I should be very much afraid of you, but being as you are, and you and I both so young, I feel only that I have made your acquaintance twelve years ago, and have already a right to your intimacy; at all events it does seem as if we were destined, from our earliest childhood, to be friends. I wonder whether you feel as strangely drawn towards me as I do to you; I have never had a friend—shall I find one now?" She sighed, and her fine dark eyes gazed passionately on me.

Now the truth is, I felt rather unaccountably towards the beautiful stranger. I did feel, as she said, "drawn towards her," but there was also something of repulsion. In this ambiguous feeling, however, the sense of attraction immensely prevailed. She interested and won me; she was so beautiful and so indescribably engaging.

I perceived now something of languor and exhaustion stealing over her, and hastened to bid her good night.

"The doctor thinks," I added, "that you ought to have a maid to sit up with you tonight; one of ours is waiting, and you will find her a very useful and quiet creature."

"How kind of you, but I could not sleep, I never could with an attendant in the room. I shan't require any assistance—and, shall I confess my weakness, I am haunted with a terror of robbers. Our house was robbed once, and two servants murdered, so I always lock my door. It has become a habit—and you look so kind I know you will forgive me. I see there is a key in the lock."

She held me close in her pretty arms for a moment and whispered in my ear, "Good night, darling, it is very hard to part with you, but good night; tomorrow, but not early, I shall see you again."

She sank back on the pillow with a sigh, and her fine eyes followed me with a fond and melancholy gaze, and she murmured again, "Good night, dear friend."

Young people like, and even love, on impulse. I was flattered by the evident, though as yet undeserved, fondness she showed me. I liked the confidence with which she at once received me. She was determined that we should be very near friends.

Next day came and we met again. I was delighted with my companion; that is to say, in many respects.

Her looks lost nothing in daylight[26]—she was certainly the most beautiful creature I had ever seen, and the unpleasant remembrance of the face presented in my early dream, had lost the effect of the first unexpected recognition.

She confessed that she had experienced a similar shock on seeing me, and precisely the same faint antipathy that had mingled with my admiration of her. We now laughed together over our momentary horrors.

---

26 As the reader may have also noted in *The Vampyre*, and may likewise discover from reading Dracula, it was not unknown for vampires to venture out in the daylight in the 19th Century (after 137 years, I don't think I'm giving away any plot points here). It has been suggested that the idea that sunlight will destroy a vampire was first firmly implanted in the public mind by Murnau in *Nosferatu*, where this method is used to destroy Count Orlock at the conclusion of the film. Thereafter, it is suggested, others carried on in the same vein until the idea became firmly established. Some recent television shows, such as Moonlight, have reverted to the older idea, that sunlight may not be particularly pleasant for a vampire, but neither is it instantly fatal.

IV
Her Habits—A Saunter

Itold you that I was charmed with her in most particulars.

There were some that did not please me so well.

She was above the middle height of women. I shall begin by describing her.

She was slender, and wonderfully graceful. Except that her movements were languid—very languid—indeed, there was nothing in her appearance to indicate an invalid. Her complexion was rich and brilliant; her features were small and beautifully formed; her eyes large, dark, and lustrous; her hair was quite wonderful, I never saw hair so magnificently thick and long when it was down about her shoulders; I have often placed my hands under it, and laughed with wonder at its weight. It was exquisitely fine and soft, and in colour a rich very dark brown, with something of gold. I loved to let it down, tumbling with its own weight, as, in her room, she lay back in her chair talking in her sweet low voice, I used to fold and braid it, and spread it out and play with it. Heavens! If I had but known all!

I said there were particulars which did not please me. I have told you that her confidence won me the first night I saw her; but I found that she exercised with respect to herself, her mother, her history, everything in fact connected with her life, plans, and people, an ever wakeful reserve. I dare say I was unreasonable, perhaps I was wrong; I dare say I ought to have respected the solemn injunction laid upon my father by the stately lady in black velvet. But curiosity is a restless and unscrupulous passion, and no one girl can endure, with patience, that hers should be baffled by another. What harm could it do anyone to tell me what I so ardently desired to know? Had she no trust in my good sense or honour? Why would she not believe me when I assured her, so solemnly, that I would not divulge one syllable of what she told me to any mortal breathing.

There was a coldness, it seemed to me, beyond her years, in her smiling melancholy persistent refusal to afford me the least ray of light.

I cannot say we quarreled upon this point, for she would not quarrel upon any. It was, of course, very unfair of me to press her, very ill-bred, but I really could not help it; and I might just as well have let it alone.

What she did tell me amounted, in my unconscionable estimation—to nothing.

It was all summed up in three very vague disclosures:

First—Her name was Carmilla.

Second—Her family was very ancient and noble.

Third—Her home lay in the direction of the west.

She would not tell me the name of her family, nor their armourial bearings, nor the name of their estate, nor even that of the country they lived in.

You are not to suppose that I worried her incessantly on these subjects. I watched opportunity, and rather insinuated than urged my inquiries. Once or twice, indeed, I did attack her more directly. But no matter what my tactics, utter failure was invariably the result. Reproaches and caresses were all lost upon her. But I must add this, that her evasion was conducted with so pretty a melancholy and deprecation, with so many, and even passionate declarations of her liking for me, and trust in my honour, and with so many promises that I should at last know all, that I could not find it in my heart long to be offended with her.

She used to place her pretty arms about my neck, draw me to her, and laying her cheek to mine, murmur with her lips near my ear, "Dearest, your little heart is wounded; think me not cruel because I obey the irresistible law of my strength and weakness; if your dear heart is wounded, my wild heart bleeds with yours. In the rapture of my enormous humiliation I live in your warm life, and you shall die—die, sweetly—into mine. I cannot help it; as I draw near to you, you, in your turn, will draw near to others, and learn the rapture of that cruelty, which yet is love; so, for a while, seek to know no more of me and mine, but trust me with all your loving spirit."

And when she had spoken such a rhapsody, she would press me more closely in her trembling embrace, and her lips in soft kisses gently glow upon my cheek.

Her agitations and her language were unintelligible to me.

From these foolish embraces, which were not of very frequent occurrence, I must allow, I used to wish to extricate myself; but my energies seemed to fail me. Her murmured words sounded like a lullaby in my ear, and soothed my resistance into a trance, from which I only seemed to recover myself when she withdrew her arms.

In these mysterious moods I did not like her. I experienced a strange tumultuous excitement that was pleasurable, ever and anon, mingled with a vague sense of fear and disgust. I had no distinct thoughts about her while such scenes lasted, but I was conscious of a love growing into adoration, and also of abhorrence. This I know is paradox, but I can make no other attempt to explain the feeling.

I now write, after an interval of more than ten years, with a trembling hand, with a confused and horrible recollection of certain occurrences and situations, in the ordeal through which I was unconsciously passing; though with a vivid and very sharp remembrance of the main current of my story.

But, I suspect, in all lives there are certain emotional scenes, those in which our passions have been most wildly and terribly roused, that are of all others the most vaguely and dimly remembered.

Sometimes after an hour of apathy, my strange and beautiful companion would take my hand and hold it with a fond pressure, renewed again and again; blushing softly, gazing in my face with languid and burning eyes, and breathing so fast that her dress rose and fell with the tumultuous respiration. It was like the ardour of a lover; it embarrassed me; it was hateful and yet over-powering; and with gloating eyes she drew me to her, and her hot lips traveled along my cheek in kisses; and she would whisper, almost in sobs, "You are mine, you *shall* be mine, you and I are one for ever." Then she has thrown herself back in her chair, with her small hands over her eyes, leaving me trembling.

"Are we related," I used to ask; "what can you mean by all this? I remind you perhaps of someone whom you love; but you must not, I hate it; I don't know you—I don't know myself when you look so and talk so."

She used to sigh at my vehemence, then turn away and drop my hand.

Respecting these very extraordinary manifestations I strove in vain to form any satisfactory theory—I could not refer them to affectation or trick. It was unmistakably the momentary breaking out of suppressed instinct and emotion. Was she, notwithstanding her mother's volunteered denial, subject to brief visitations of insanity; or was there here a disguise and a romance? I had read in old storybooks of such things. What if a boyish lover had found his way into the house, and sought to prosecute his suit in masquerade, with the assistance of a clever old adventuress. But there were many things against this hypothesis, highly interesting as it was to my vanity.

I could boast of no little attentions such as masculine gallantry delights to offer. Between these passionate moments there were long intervals of commonplace, of gaiety, of brooding melancholy, during which, except that I detected her eyes so full of melancholy fire, following me, at times I might have been as nothing to her. Except in these brief periods of mysterious excitement her ways were girlish; and there was always a languor about her, quite incompatible with a masculine system in a state of health. In some respects her habits were odd. Perhaps not so singular in the opinion of a town lady like you, as they appeared to us rustic people. She used to come down very late, generally not till one o'clock, she would then take a cup of chocolate, but eat nothing; we then went out for a walk, which was a mere saunter, and she seemed, almost immediately, exhausted, and either returned to the *schloss* or sat on one of the benches that were placed, here and there, among the trees. This was a bodily languor in which her mind did not sympathize. She was always an animated talker, and very intelligent.

She sometimes alluded for a moment to her own home, or mentioned an adventure or situation, or an early recollection, which indicated a people of strange manners, and described customs of which we knew nothing. I gathered from these chance hints that her native country was much more remote than I had at first fancied.

As we sat thus one afternoon under the trees a funeral passed us by. It was that of a pretty young girl, whom I had often seen, the daughter of one of the rangers of the forest. The poor man was walking behind the coffin of his darling; she was his only child, and he looked quite heartbroken. Peasants walking two-and-two came behind, they were singing a funeral hymn.

I rose to mark my respect as they passed, and joined in the hymn they were very sweetly singing.

My companion shook me a little roughly, and I turned surprised.

She said brusquely, "Don't you perceive how discordant that is?"

"I think it very sweet, on the contrary," I answered, vexed at the interruption, and very uncomfortable, lest the people who composed the little procession should observe and resent what was passing.

I resumed, therefore, instantly, and was again interrupted. "You pierce my ears," said Carmilla, almost angrily, and stopping her ears with her tiny fingers. "Besides, how can you tell that your religion and mine are the same; your forms wound me, and I hate funerals. What a fuss! Why you must die — *everyone* must die; and all are happier when they do. Come home."

"My father has gone on with the clergyman to the churchyard. I thought you knew she was to be buried today."

"She? I don't trouble my head about peasants. I don't know who she is," answered Carmilla, with a flash from her fine eyes.

"She is the poor girl who fancied she saw a ghost a fortnight ago, and has been dying ever since, till yesterday, when she expired."

"Tell me nothing about ghosts. I shan't sleep tonight if you do."

"I hope there is no plague or fever coming; all this looks very like it," I continued. "The swineherd's young wife died only a week ago, and she thought something seized her by the throat as she lay in her bed, and nearly strangled her. Papa says such horrible fancies do accompany some forms of fever. She was quite well the day before. She sank afterwards, and died before a week."

"Well, *her* funeral is over, I hope, and *her* hymn sung; and our ears shan't be tortured with that discord and jargon. It has made me nervous. Sit down here, beside me; sit close; hold my hand; press it hard-hard-harder."

We had moved a little back, and had come to another seat.

She sat down. Her face underwent a change that alarmed and even terrified me for a moment. It darkened, and became horribly livid; her teeth and hands were clenched, and she frowned and compressed her lips, while she stared down upon the ground at her feet, and trembled all over with a continued shudder as irrepressible as ague. All her energies seemed strained to suppress a fit, with which she was then breathlessly tugging; and at length a low convulsive cry of suffering broke from her, and gradually the hysteria subsided. "There! That comes of strangling people with hymns!" she said at last. "Hold me, hold me still. It is passing away."

And so gradually it did; and perhaps to dissipate the somber impression which the spectacle had left upon me, she became unusually animated and chatty; and so we got home.

This was the first time I had seen her exhibit any definable symptoms of that delicacy of health which her mother had spoken of. It was the first time, also, I had seen her exhibit anything like temper.

Both passed away like a summer cloud; and never but once afterwards did I witness on her part a momentary sign of anger. I will tell you how it happened.

She and I were looking out of one of the long drawing room windows, when there entered the courtyard, over the drawbridge, a figure of a wanderer whom I knew very well. He used to visit the *schloss* generally twice a year.

It was the figure of a hunchback, with the sharp lean features that generally accompany deformity. He wore a pointed black beard, and he was smiling from ear to ear, showing his white fangs. He was dressed in buff, black, and scarlet, and crossed with more straps and belts than I could count, from which hung all manner of things. Behind, he carried a magic lantern, and two boxes, which I well knew, in one of which was a salamander, and in the other a mandrake.[27] These monsters used to make my fa-

---

27   In legend, the salamander was a lizard-like creature that could be spontaneously generated from fire. It has been suggested that this notion developed after people saw the actual creature, unknowingly carried in with the firewood, quite understandably rushing out of the fireplace once the log was ignited. Mandrake roots are said to resemble a human body, and legend says that a mandrake will scream when pulled from the ground, inevitably killing the foolish chap who pulled it. They

ther laugh. They were compounded of parts of monkeys, parrots squirrels, fish, and hedgehogs, dried and stitched together with great neatness and startling effect. He had a fiddle, a box of conjuring apparatus, a pair of foils and masks attached to his belt, several other mysterious cases dangling about him, and a black staff with copper ferrules in his hand. His companion was a rough spare dog, that followed at his heels, but stopped short, suspiciously at the drawbridge, and in a little while began to howl dismally.

In the meantime, the mountebank, standing in the midst of the courtyard, raised his grotesque hat, and made us a very ceremonious bow, paying his compliments very volubly in execrable French, and German not much better.

Then, disengaging his fiddle, he began to scrape a lively air to which he sang with a merry discord, dancing with ludicrous airs and activity, that made me laugh, in spite of the dog's howling.

Then he advanced to the window with many smiles and salutations, and his hat in his left hand, his fiddle under his arm, and with a fluency that never took breath, he gabbled a long advertisement of all his accomplishments, and the resources of the various arts which he placed at our service, and the curiosities and entertainments which it was in his power, at our bidding, to display. "Will your ladyships be pleased to buy an amulet against the *oupire*, which is going like the wolf, I hear, through these woods," he said dropping his hat on the pavement. "They are dying of it right and left and here is a charm that never fails; only pinned to the pillow, and you may laugh in his face."

These charms consisted of oblong slips of vellum, with cabalistic ciphers and diagrams upon them.

Carmilla instantly purchased one, and so did I.

He was looking up, and we were smiling down upon him, amused; at least, I can answer for myself. His piercing black eye, as he looked up in our faces, seemed to detect something that fixed for a moment his curiosity. In an instant he unrolled a leather case, full of all manner of odd little steel instruments.

"See here, my lady," he said, displaying it, and addressing me, "I profess, among other things less useful, the art of dentistry. Plague take the dog!" he interpolated. "Silence, beast! He howls so that your ladyships can scarcely hear a word. Your noble friend, the young lady at your right, has the sharpest tooth,—long, thin, pointed, like an awl, like a needle; ha, ha! With my sharp and long sight, as I look up, I have seen it distinctly; now if it happens to hurt the young lady, and I think it must, here am I, here

---

are said to grow under gallows, spontaneously generating when the victim's semen drips onto the ground. The mandrake in this story was probably the product of a taxidermist's art blended with a vegetative crown.

are my file, my punch, my nippers; I will make it round and blunt, if her ladyship pleases; no longer the tooth of a fish, but of a beautiful young lady as she is. Hey? Is the young lady displeased? Have I been too bold? Have I offended her?"

The young lady, indeed, looked very angry as she drew back from the window.

"How dares that mountebank insult us so? Where is your father? I shall demand redress from him. My father would have had the wretch tied up to the pump, and flogged with a cart whip, and burnt to the bones with the castle brand!"

She retired from the window a step or two, and sat down, and had hardly lost sight of the offender, when her wrath subsided as suddenly as it had risen, and she gradually recovered her usual tone, and seemed to forget the little hunchback and his follies.

My father was out of spirits that evening. On coming in he told us that there had been another case very similar to the two fatal ones which had lately occurred. The sister of a young peasant on his estate, only a mile away, was very ill, had been, as she described it, attacked very nearly in the same way, and was now slowly but steadily sinking.

"All this," said my father, "is strictly referable to natural causes. These poor people infect one another with their superstitions, and so repeat in imagination the images of terror that have infested their neighbours."

"But that very circumstance frightens one horribly," said Carmilla.

"How so?" inquired my father.

"I am so afraid of fancying I see such things; I think it would be as bad as reality."

"We are in God's hands: nothing can happen without his permission, and all will end well for those who love him. He is our faithful creator; He has made us all, and will take care of us."

"Creator! *Nature!*" said the young lady in answer to my gentle father. "And this disease that invades the country is natural. Nature. All things proceed from Nature—don't they? All things in the heaven, in the earth, and under the earth, act and live as Nature ordains? I think so."

"The doctor said he would come here today," said my father, after a silence. "I want to know what he thinks about it, and what he thinks we had better do."

"Doctors never did me any good," said Carmilla.

"Then you have been ill?" I asked.

"More ill than ever you were," she answered.

"Long ago?"

"Yes, a long time. I suffered from this very illness; but I forget all but my pain and weakness, and they were not so bad as are suffered in other diseases."

"You were very young then?"

"I dare say, let us talk no more of it. You would not wound a friend?"

She looked languidly in my eyes, and passed her arm round my waist lovingly, and led me out of the room. My father was busy over some papers near the window.

"Why does your papa like to frighten us?" said the pretty girl with a sigh and a little shudder.

"He doesn't, dear Carmilla, it is the very furthest thing from his mind."

"Are you afraid, dearest?"

"I should be very much if I fancied there was any real danger of my being attacked as those poor people were."

"You are afraid to die?"

"Yes, every one is."

"But to die as lovers may—to die together, so that they may live together."

"Girls are caterpillars while they live in the world, to be finally butterflies when the summer comes; but in the meantime there are grubs and larvae, don't you see—each with their peculiar propensities, necessities and structure. So says Monsieur Buffon, in his big book[28], in the next room."

Later in the day the doctor came, and was closeted with papa for some time.

He was a skilful man, of sixty and upwards, he wore powder, and shaved his pale face as smooth as a pumpkin. He and papa emerged from the room together, and I heard papa laugh, and say as they came out:

"Well, I do wonder at a wise man like you. What do you say to hippogriffs[29] and dragons?"

The doctor was smiling, and made answer, shaking his head—

"Nevertheless life and death are mysterious states, and we know little of the resources of either."

And so they walked on, and I heard no more. I did not then know what the doctor had been broaching, but I think I guess it now.

---

28   Georges-Louis Leclerc, Compte de Buffon (1707–1788), was an influential French naturalist. His 35-volume *Histoire Naturelle, générale et particulière*, was a big book indeed, particularly if the additional nine posthumous volumes are included.

29   The popularity of Harry Potter may make this unnecessary, but for the benefit of that rare soul who has neither read the books (highly recommended), nor seen the movies, a hippogriff is a winged horse with the head, forelimb, and talons of a hawk or eagle. In legend, hippogriffs result from the mating of a griffin and a mare, an exceedingly rare occurrence, given that a griffin's usual inclination upon seeing a horse is to eat it, not mate with it.

V
A Wonderful Likeness

This evening there arrived from Gratz the grave, dark-faced son of the picture cleaner, with a horse and cart laden with two large packing cases, having many pictures in each. It was a journey of ten leagues, and whenever a messenger arrived at the *schloss* from our little capital of Gratz, we used to crowd about him in the hall, to hear the news.

This arrival created in our secluded quarters quite a sensation. The cases remained in the hall, and the messenger was taken charge of by the servants till he had eaten his supper. Then with assistants, and armed with hammer, ripping chisel, and turnscrew, he met us in the hall, where we had assembled to witness the unpacking of the cases.

Carmilla sat looking listlessly on, while one after the other the old pictures, nearly all portraits, which had undergone the process of renovation, were brought to light. My mother was of an old Hungarian family, and most of these pictures, which were about to be restored to their places, had come to us through her.

My father had a list in his hand, from which he read, as the artist rummaged out the corresponding numbers. I don't know that the pictures were very good, but they were, undoubtedly, very old, and some of them very curious also. They had, for the most part, the merit of being now seen by me, I may say, for the first time; for the smoke and dust of time had all but obliterated them.

"There is a picture that I have not seen yet," said my father. "In one corner, at the top of it, is the name, as well as I could read, "Marcia Karnstein," and the date "1698"; and I am curious to see how it has turned out."

I remembered it; it was a small picture, about a foot and a half high, and nearly square, without a frame; but it was so blackened by age that I could not make it out.

The artist now produced it, with evident pride. It was quite beautiful; it

62

was startling; it seemed to live. It was the effigy of Carmilla!

"Carmilla, dear, here is an absolute miracle. Here you are, living, smiling, ready to speak, in this picture. Isn't it beautiful, Papa? And see, even the little mole on her throat."

My father laughed, and said "Certainly it is a wonderful likeness," but he looked away, and to my surprise seemed but little struck by it, and went on talking to the picture cleaner, who was also something of an artist, and discoursed with intelligence about the portraits or other works, which his art had just brought into light and color, while I was more and more lost in wonder the more I looked at the picture.

"Will you let me hang this picture in my room, papa?"

"Certainly, dear," said he, smiling, "I'm very glad you think it so like. It must be prettier even than I thought it, if it is."

The young lady did not acknowledge this pretty speech, did not seem to hear it. She was leaning back in her seat, her fine eyes under their long lashes gazing on me in contemplation, and she smiled in a kind of rapture.

"And now you can read quite plainly the name that is written in the corner. It is not Marcia; it looks as if it was done in gold. The name is Mircalla, Countess Karnstein, and this is a little coronet over and underneath A.D. 1698. I am descended from the Karnsteins; that is, mamma was."

"Ah!" said the lady, languidly, "so am I, I think, a very long descent, very ancient. Are there any Karnsteins living now?"

"None who bear the name, I believe. The family were ruined, I believe, in some civil wars, long ago, but the ruins of the castle are only about three miles away."

"How interesting!" she said, languidly. "But see what beautiful moonlight!" She glanced through the hall door, which stood a little open. "Suppose you take a little ramble round the court, and look down at the road and river."

"It is so like the night you came to us," I said.

She sighed; smiling.

She rose, and each with her arm about the other's waist, we walked out upon the pavement.

In silence, slowly we walked down to the drawbridge, where the beautiful landscape opened before us.

"And so you were thinking of the night I came here?" she almost whispered.

"Are you glad I came?"

"Delighted, dear Carmilla," I answered.

"And you asked for the picture you think like me, to hang in your room," she murmured with a sigh, as she drew her arm closer about my waist, and let her pretty head sink upon my shoulder.

"How romantic you are, Carmilla," I said. "Whenever you tell me your story, it will be made up chiefly of some one great romance."

She kissed me silently.

"I am sure, Carmilla, you have been in love; that there is, at this moment, an affair of the heart going on."

"I have been in love with no one, and never shall," she whispered, "unless it should be with you."

How beautiful she looked in the moonlight!

Shy and strange was the look with which she quickly hid her face in my neck and hair, with tumultuous sighs, that seemed almost to sob, and pressed in mine a hand that trembled.

Her soft cheek was glowing against mine. "Darling, darling," she murmured, "I live in you; and you would die for me, I love you so."

I started from her.

She was gazing on me with eyes from which all fire, all meaning had flown, and a face colourless and apathetic.

"Is there a chill in the air, dear?" she said drowsily. "I almost shiver; have I been dreaming? Let us come in. Come; come; come in."

"You look ill, Carmilla; a little faint. You certainly must take some wine," I said.

"Yes. I will. I'm better now. I shall be quite well in a few minutes. Yes, do give me a little wine," answered Carmilla, as we approached the door. "Let us look again for a moment; it is the last time, perhaps, I shall see the moonlight with you."

"How do you feel now, dear Carmilla? Are you really better?" I asked.

I was beginning to take alarm, lest she should have been stricken with the strange epidemic that they said had invaded the country about us.

"Papa would be grieved beyond measure." I added, "if he thought you were ever so little ill, without immediately letting us know. We have a very skilful doctor near this, the physician who was with papa today."

"I'm sure he is. I know how kind you all are; but, dear child, I am quite well again. There is nothing ever wrong with me, but a little weakness.

"People say I am languid; I am incapable of exertion; I can scarcely walk as far as a child of three years old: and every now and then the little strength I have falters, and I become as you have just seen me. But after all I am very easily set up again; in a moment I am perfectly myself. See how I have recovered."

So, indeed, she had; and she and I talked a great deal, and very animated she was; and the remainder of that evening passed without any recurrence of what I called her infatuations. I mean her crazy talk and looks, which embarrassed, and even frightened me.

But there occurred that night an event which gave my thoughts quite a new turn, and seemed to startle even Carmilla's languid nature into momentary energy.

VI

A Very Strange Agony

When we got into the drawing room, and had sat down to our coffee and chocolate, although Carmilla did not take any, she seemed quite herself again, and Madame, and Mademoiselle De Lafontaine, joined us, and made a little card party, in the course of which papa came in for what he called his "dish of tea."

When the game was over he sat down beside Carmilla on the sofa, and asked her, a little anxiously, whether she had heard from her mother since her arrival.

She answered, "No."

He then asked whether she knew where a letter would reach her at present.

"I cannot tell," she answered ambiguously, "but I have been thinking of leaving you; you have been already too hospitable and too kind to me. I have given you an infinity of trouble, and I should wish to take a carriage tomorrow, and post in pursuit of her; I know where I shall ultimately find her, although I dare not yet tell you."

"But you must not dream of any such thing," exclaimed my father, to my great relief. "We can't afford to lose you so, and I won't consent to your leaving us, except under the care of your mother, who was so good as to consent to your remaining with us till she should herself return. I should be quite happy if I knew that you heard from her: but this evening the accounts of the progress of the mysterious disease that has invaded our neighbourhood, grow even more alarming; and my beautiful guest, I do feel the responsibility, unaided by advice from your mother, very much. But I shall do my best; and one thing is certain, that you must not think of leaving us without her distinct direction to that effect. We should suffer too much in parting from you to consent to it easily."

"Thank you, sir, a thousand times for your hospitality," she answered, smiling bashfully. "You have all been too kind to me; I have seldom been so happy in all my life before, as in your beautiful chateau, under your care, and in the society of your dear daughter."

So he gallantly, in his old-fashioned way, kissed her hand, smiling and pleased at her little speech.

I accompanied Carmilla as usual to her room, and sat and chatted with her while she was preparing for bed.

"Do you think," I said at length, "that you will ever confide fully in me?"

She turned round smiling, but made no answer, only continued to smile on me.

"You won't answer that?" I said. "You can't answer pleasantly; I ought not to have asked you."

"You were quite right to ask me that, or anything. You do not know how dear you are to me, or you could not think any confidence too great to look for. But I am under vows, no nun half so awfully, and I dare not tell my story yet, even to you. The time is very near when you shall know everything. You will think me cruel, very selfish, but love is always selfish; the more ardent the more selfish. How jealous I am you cannot know. You must come with me, loving me, to death; or else hate me and still come with me, and *hating* me through death and after. There is no such word as indifference in my apathetic nature."

"Now, Carmilla, you are going to talk your wild nonsense again," I said hastily.

"Not I, silly little fool as I am, and full of whims and fancies; for your sake I'll talk like a sage. Were you ever at a ball?"

"No; how you do run on. What is it like? How charming it must be."

"I almost forget, it is years ago."

I laughed.

"You are not so old. Your first ball can hardly be forgotten yet."

"I remember everything about it—with an effort. I see it all, as divers see what is going on above them, through a medium, dense, rippling, but transparent. There occurred that night what has confused the picture, and made its colours faint. I was all but assassinated in my bed, wounded here," she touched her breast, "and never was the same since."

"Were you near dying?"

"Yes, very—a cruel love—strange love, that would have taken my life. Love will have its sacrifices. No sacrifice without blood. Let us go to sleep now; I feel so lazy. How can I get up just now and lock my door?"

She was lying with her tiny hands buried in her rich wavy hair, under her cheek, her little head upon the pillow, and her glittering eyes followed me wherever I moved, with a kind of shy smile that I could not decipher.

I bid her good night, and crept from the room with an uncomfortable sensation.

I often wondered whether our pretty guest ever said her prayers. I certainly had never seen her upon her knees. In the morning she never came down until long after our family prayers were over, and at night she never left the drawing room to attend our brief evening prayers in the hall.

If it had not been that it had casually come out in one of our careless talks that she had been baptised, I should have doubted her being a Christian. Religion was a subject on which I had never heard her speak a word. If I had known the world better, this particular neglect or antipathy would not have so much surprised me.

The precautions of nervous people are infectious, and persons of a like temperament are pretty sure, after a time, to imitate them. I had adopted Carmilla's habit of locking her bedroom door, having taken into my head all her whimsical alarms about midnight invaders and prowling assassins. I had also adopted her precaution of making a brief search through her room, to satisfy herself that no lurking assassin or robber was "ensconced."

These wise measures taken, I got into my bed and fell asleep. A light was burning in my room. This was an old habit, of very early date, and which nothing could have tempted me to dispense with.

Thus fortified I might take my rest in peace. But dreams come through stone walls, light up dark rooms, or darken light ones, and their persons make their exits and their entrances as they please, and laugh at locksmiths.

I had a dream that night that was the beginning of a very strange agony.

I cannot call it a nightmare, for I was quite conscious of being asleep.

But I was equally conscious of being in my room, and lying in bed, precisely as I actually was. I saw, or fancied I saw, the room and its furniture just as I had seen it last, except that it was very dark, and I saw something moving round the foot of the bed, which at first I could not accurately distinguish. But I soon saw that it was a sooty-black animal that resembled a monstrous cat. It appeared to me about four or five feet long for it measured fully the length of the hearth rug as it passed over it; and it continued to-ing and fro-ing with the lithe, sinister restlessness of a beast in a cage. I could not cry out, although as you may suppose, I was terrified. Its pace was growing faster, and the room rapidly darker and darker, and at length so dark that I could no longer see anything of it but its eyes. I felt it spring lightly on the bed. The two broad eyes approached my face, and suddenly I felt a stinging pain as if two large needles darted, an inch or two apart, deep into my breast. I waked with a scream. The room was lighted by the candle that burnt there all through the night, and I saw a female figure standing at the foot of the bed, a little at the right side. It was in a dark loose dress, and its hair was down and covered its shoulders. A block of stone could not have been more still. There was not the slightest stir of respiration. As I stared at it, the figure appeared to have changed its place, and was now nearer the door; then, close to it, the door opened, and it passed out.

I was now relieved, and able to breathe and move. My first thought was that Carmilla had been playing me a trick, and that I had forgotten to secure my door. I hastened to it, and found it locked as usual on the inside. I was afraid to open it—I was horrified. I sprang into my bed and covered my head up in the bedclothes, and lay there more dead than alive till morning.

VII
Descending

It would be vain my attempting to tell you the horror with which, even now, I recall the occurrence of that night. It was no such transitory terror as a dream leaves behind it. It seemed to deepen by time, and communicated itself to the room and the very furniture that had encompassed the apparition.

I could not bear next day to be alone for a moment. I should have told papa, but for two opposite reasons. At one time I thought he would laugh at my story, and I could not bear its being treated as a jest; and at another I thought he might fancy that I had been attacked by the mysterious complaint which had invaded our neighbourhood. I had myself no misgiving of the kind, and as he had been rather an invalid for some time, I was afraid of alarming him.

I was comfortable enough with my good-natured companions, Madame Perrodon, and the vivacious Mademoiselle Lafontaine. They both perceived that I was out of spirits and nervous, and at length I told them what lay so heavy at my heart.

Mademoiselle laughed, but I fancied that Madame Perrodon looked anxious.

"By-the-by," said Mademoiselle, laughing, "the long lime tree walk, behind Carmilla's bedroom window, is haunted!"

"Nonsense!" exclaimed Madame, who probably thought the theme rather inopportune, "and who tells that story, my dear?"

"Martin says that he came up twice, when the old yard gate was being repaired, before sunrise, and twice saw the same female figure walking down the lime tree avenue."

"So he well might, as long as there are cows to milk in the river fields," said Madame.

"I daresay; but Martin chooses to be frightened, and never did I see fool more frightened."

"You must not say a word about it to Carmilla, because she can see down that walk from her room window," I interposed, "and she is, if possible, a greater coward than I."

Carmilla came down rather later than usual that day.

"I was so frightened last night," she said, so soon as were together, "and I am sure I should have seen something dreadful if it had not been for that charm I bought from the poor little hunchback whom I called such hard names. I had a dream of something black coming round my bed, and I awoke in a perfect horror, and I really thought, for some seconds, I saw a dark figure near the chimney-piece, but I felt under my pillow for my charm, and the moment my fingers touched it, the figure disappeared, and I felt quite certain, only that I had it by me, that something frightful would have made its appearance, and, perhaps, throttled me, as it did those poor people we heard of."

"Well, listen to me," I began, and recounted my adventure, at the recital of which she appeared horrified.

"And had you the charm near you?" she asked, earnestly.

"No, I had dropped it into a china vase in the drawing room, but I shall certainly take it with me tonight, as you have so much faith in it."

At this distance of time I cannot tell you, or even understand, how I overcame my horror so effectually as to lie alone in my room that night. I remember distinctly that I pinned the charm to my pillow. I fell asleep almost immediately, and slept even more soundly than usual all night.

Next night I passed as well. My sleep was delightfully deep and dreamless.

But I wakened with a sense of lassitude and melancholy, which, however, did not exceed a degree that was almost luxurious.

"Well, I told you so," said Carmilla, when I described my quiet sleep, "I had such delightful sleep myself last night; I pinned the charm to the breast of my nightdress. It was too far away the night before. I am quite sure it was all fancy, except the dreams. I used to think that evil spirits made dreams, but our doctor told me it is no such thing. Only a fever passing by, or some other malady, as they often do, he said, knocks at the door, and not being able to get in, passes on, with that alarm."

"And what do you think the charm is?" said I.

"It has been fumigated or immersed in some drug, and is an antidote against the malaria," she answered.

"Then it acts only on the body?"

"Certainly; you don't suppose that evil spirits are frightened by bits of ribbon, or the perfumes of a druggist's shop? No, these complaints, wandering in the air, begin by trying the nerves, and so infect the brain, but before they can seize upon you, the antidote repels them. That I am sure is what the charm has done for us. It is nothing magical, it is simply natural."

I should have been happier if I could have quite agreed with Carmilla, but I did my best, and the impression was a little losing its force.

For some nights I slept profoundly; but still every morning I felt the same lassitude, and a languor weighed upon me all day. I felt myself a changed girl. A strange melancholy was stealing over me, a melancholy that I would not have interrupted. Dim thoughts of death began to open, and an idea that I was slowly sinking took gentle, and, somehow, not unwelcome, possession of me. If it was sad, the tone of mind which this induced was also sweet.

Whatever it might be, my soul acquiesced in it.

I would not admit that I was ill, I would not consent to tell my papa, or to have the doctor sent for.

Carmilla became more devoted to me than ever, and her strange paroxysms of languid adoration more frequent. She used to gloat on me with increasing ardour the more my strength and spirits waned. This always shocked me like a momentary glare of insanity.

Without knowing it, I was now in a pretty advanced stage of the strangest illness under which mortal ever suffered. There was an unaccountable fascination in its earlier symptoms that more than reconciled me to the incapacitating effect of that stage of the malady. This fascination increased for a time, until it reached a certain point, when gradually a sense of the horrible mingled itself with it, deepening, as you shall hear, until it discoloured and perverted the whole state of my life.

The first change I experienced was rather agreeable. It was very near the turning point from which began the descent of Avernus.[30]

Certain vague and strange sensations visited me in my sleep. The prevailing one was of that pleasant, peculiar cold thrill which we feel in bathing, when we move against the current of a river. This was soon accompanied by dreams that seemed interminable, and were so vague that I could never recollect their scenery and persons, or any one connected portion of their action. But they left an awful impression, and a sense of exhaustion, as if I had passed through a long period of great mental exertion and danger.

After all these dreams there remained on waking a remembrance of having been in a place very nearly dark, and of having spoken to people whom I could not see; and especially of one clear voice, of a female's, very deep, that spoke as if at a distance, slowly, and producing always the same sensation of indescribable solemnity and fear. Sometime there came a sen-

---

30   A crater in the Campania region, west of Naples, containing Lake Avernus. In ancient times, the crater was believed to be the entrance to the Underworld.

sation as if a hand was drawn softly along my cheek and neck. Sometimes it was as if warm lips kissed me, and longer and longer and more lovingly as they reached my throat, but there the caress fixed itself. My heart beat faster, my breathing rose and fell rapidly and full drawn; a sobbing, that rose into a sense of strangulation, supervened, and turned into a dreadful convulsion, in which my senses left me and I became unconscious.

It was now three weeks since the commencement of this unaccountable state.

My sufferings had, during the last week, told upon my appearance. I had grown pale, my eyes were dilated and darkened underneath, and the languor which I had long felt began to display itself in my countenance.

My father asked me often whether I was ill; but, with an obstinacy which now seems to me unaccountable, I persisted in assuring him that I was quite well.

In a sense this was true. I had no pain, I could complain of no bodily derangement. My complaint seemed to be one of the imagination, or the nerves, and, horrible as my sufferings were, I kept them, with a morbid reserve, very nearly to myself.

It could not be that terrible complaint which the peasants called the *oupire*, for I had now been suffering for three weeks, and they were seldom ill for much more than three days, when death put an end to their miseries.

Carmilla complained of dreams and feverish sensations, but by no means of so alarming a kind as mine. I say that mine were extremely alarming. Had I been capable of comprehending my condition, I would have invoked aid and advice on my knees. The narcotic of an unsuspected influence was acting upon me, and my perceptions were benumbed.

I am going to tell you now of a dream that led immediately to an odd discovery.

One night, instead of the voice I was accustomed to hear in the dark, I heard one, sweet and tender, and at the same time terrible, which said, "Your mother warns you to beware of the assassin." At the same time a light unexpectedly sprang up, and I saw Carmilla, standing, near the foot of my bed, in her white nightdress, bathed, from her chin to her feet, in one great stain of blood.

I wakened with a shriek, possessed with the one idea that Carmilla was being murdered. I remember springing from my bed, and my next recollection is that of standing on the lobby, crying for help.

Madame and Mademoiselle came scurrying out of their rooms in alarm; a lamp burned always on the lobby, and seeing me, they soon learned the cause of my terror.

I insisted on our knocking at Carmilla's door. Our knocking was unanswered.

It soon became a pounding and an uproar. We shrieked her name, but all was vain.

We all grew frightened, for the door was locked. We hurried back, in panic, to my room. There we rang the bell long and furiously. If my father's room had been at that side of the house, we would have called him up at once to our aid. But, alas! he was quite out of hearing, and to reach him involved an excursion for which we none of us had courage.

Servants, however, soon came running up the stairs; I had got on my dressing gown and slippers meanwhile, and my companions were already similarly furnished. Recognizing the voices of the servants on the lobby, we sallied out together; and having renewed, as fruitlessly, our summons at Carmilla's door, I ordered the men to force the lock. They did so, and we stood, holding our lights aloft, in the doorway, and so stared into the room.

We called her by name; but there was still no reply. We looked round the room. Everything was undisturbed. It was exactly in the state in which I had left it on bidding her good night. But Carmilla was gone.

VIII
Search

At sight of the room, perfectly undisturbed except for our violent entrance, we began to cool a little, and soon recovered our senses sufficiently to dismiss the men. It had struck Mademoiselle that possibly Carmilla had been wakened by the uproar at her door, and in her first panic had jumped from her bed, and hid herself in a press, or behind a curtain, from which she could not, of course, emerge until the majordomo and his myrmidons had withdrawn. We now recommenced our search, and began to call her name again.

It was all to no purpose. Our perplexity and agitation increased. We examined the windows, but they were secured. I implored of Carmilla, if she had concealed herself, to play this cruel trick no longer—to come out and to end our anxieties. It was all useless. I was by this time convinced that she was not in the room, nor in the dressing room, the door of which was still locked on this side. She could not have passed it. I was utterly puzzled. Had Carmilla discovered one of those secret passages which the old housekeeper said were known to exist in the *schloss*, although the tradition of their exact situation had been lost? A little time would, no doubt, explain all—utterly perplexed as, for the present, we were.

It was past four o'clock, and I preferred passing the remaining hours of darkness in Madame's room. Daylight brought no solution of the difficulty.

The whole household, with my father at its head, was in a state of agitation next morning. Every part of the chateau was searched. The grounds were explored. No trace of the missing lady could be discovered. The stream was about to be dragged; my father was in distraction; what a tale to have to tell the poor girl's mother on her return. I, too, was almost beside myself, though my grief was quite of a different kind.

The morning was passed in alarm and excitement. It was now one o'clock, and still no tidings. I ran up to Carmilla's room, and found her standing at her dressing table. I was astounded. I could not believe my eyes. She beckoned me to her with her pretty finger, in silence. Her face expressed extreme fear.

I ran to her in an ecstasy of joy; I kissed and embraced her again and again. I ran to the bell and rang it vehemently, to bring others to the spot who might at once relieve my father's anxiety.

"Dear Carmilla, what has become of you all this time? We have been in agonies of anxiety about you," I exclaimed. "Where have you been? How did you come back?"

"Last night has been a night of wonders," she said.

"For mercy's sake, explain all you can."

"It was past two last night," she said, "when I went to sleep as usual in my bed, with my doors locked, that of the dressing room, and that opening upon the gallery. My sleep was uninterrupted, and, so far as I know, dreamless; but I woke just now on the sofa in the dressing room there, and I found the door between the rooms open, and the other door forced. How could all this have happened without my being wakened? It must have been accompanied with a great deal of noise, and I am particularly easily wakened; and how could I have been carried out of my bed without my sleep having been interrupted, I whom the slightest stir startles?"

By this time, Madame, Mademoiselle, my father, and a number of the servants were in the room. Carmilla was, of course, overwhelmed with inquiries, congratulations, and welcomes. She had but one story to tell, and seemed the least able of all the party to suggest any way of accounting for what had happened.

My father took a turn up and down the room, thinking. I saw Carmilla's eye follow him for a moment with a sly, dark glance.

When my father had sent the servants away, Mademoiselle having gone in search of a little bottle of valerian and salvolatile, and there being no one now in the room with Carmilla, except my father, Madame, and myself, he came to her thoughtfully, took her hand very kindly, led her to the sofa, and sat down beside her.

"Will you forgive me, my dear, if I risk a conjecture, and ask a question?"

"Who can have a better right?" she said. "Ask what you please, and I will tell you everything. But my story is simply one of bewilderment and darkness. I know absolutely nothing. Put any question you please, but you know, of course, the limitations mamma has placed me under."

"Perfectly, my dear child. I need not approach the topics on which she desires your silence. Now, the marvel of last night consists in your having been removed from your bed and your room, without being wakened, and this removal having occurred apparently while the windows were still secured, and the two doors locked upon the inside. I will tell you my theory and ask you a question."

Carmilla was leaning on her hand dejectedly; Madame and I were listening breathlessly.

"Now, my question is this. Have you ever been suspected of walking in your sleep?"

"Never, since I was very young indeed."

"But you did walk in your sleep when you were young?"

"Yes; I know I did. I have been told so often by my old nurse."

My father smiled and nodded.

"Well, what has happened is this. You got up in your sleep, unlocked the door, not leaving the key, as usual, in the lock, but taking it out and locking it on the outside; you again took the key out, and carried it away with you to someone of the five-and-twenty rooms on this floor, or perhaps upstairs or downstairs. There are so many rooms and closets, so much heavy furniture, and such accumulations of lumber, that it would require a week to search this old house thoroughly. Do you see, now, what I mean?"

"I do, but not all," she answered.

"And how, papa, do you account for her finding herself on the sofa in the dressing room, which we had searched so carefully?"

"She came there after you had searched it, still in her sleep, and at last awoke spontaneously, and was as much surprised to find herself where she was as any one else. I wish all mysteries were as easily and innocently explained as yours, Carmilla," he said, laughing. "And so we may congratulate ourselves on the certainty that the most natural explanation of the occurrence is one that involves no drugging, no tampering with locks, no burglars, or poisoners, or witches—nothing that need alarm Carmilla, or anyone else, for our safety."

Carmilla was looking charmingly. Nothing could be more beautiful than her tints. Her beauty was, I think, enhanced by that graceful languor that was peculiar to her. I think my father was silently contrasting her looks with mine, for he said:

"I wish my poor Laura was looking more like herself"; and he sighed.

So our alarms were happily ended, and Carmilla restored to her friends.

IX
The Doctor

As Carmilla would not hear of an attendant sleeping in her room, my father arranged that a servant should sleep outside her door, so that she would not attempt to make another such excursion without being arrested at her own door.

That night passed quietly; and next morning early, the doctor, whom my father had sent for without telling me a word about it, arrived to see me.

Madame accompanied me to the library; and there the grave little doctor, with white hair and spectacles, whom I mentioned before, was waiting to receive me.

I told him my story, and as I proceeded he grew graver and graver.

We were standing, he and I, in the recess of one of the windows, facing one another. When my statement was over, he leaned with his shoulders against the wall, and with his eyes fixed on me earnestly, with an interest in which was a dash of horror.

After a minute's reflection, he asked Madame if he could see my father.

He was sent for accordingly, and as he entered, smiling, he said:

"I dare say, doctor, you are going to tell me that I am an old fool for having brought you here; I hope I am."

But his smile faded into shadow as the doctor, with a very grave face, beckoned him to him.

He and the doctor talked for some time in the same recess where I had just conferred with the physician. It seemed an earnest and argumentative conversation. The room is very large, and I and Madame stood together, burning with curiosity, at the farther end. Not a word could we hear, however, for they spoke in a very low tone, and the deep recess of the window quite concealed the doctor from view, and very nearly my father, whose foot, arm, and shoulder only could we see; and the voices were, I suppose, all the less audible for the sort of closet which the thick wall and window formed.

After a time my father's face looked into the room; it was pale, thoughtful, and, I fancied, agitated.

"Laura, dear, come here for a moment. Madame, we shan't trouble you, the doctor says, at present."

Accordingly I approached, for the first time a little alarmed; for, although I felt very weak, I did not feel ill; and strength, one always fancies, is a thing that may be picked up when we please.

My father held out his hand to me, as I drew near, but he was looking at the doctor, and he said:

"It certainly is very odd; I don't understand it quite. Laura, come here, dear; now attend to Doctor Spielsberg, and recollect yourself."

"You mentioned a sensation like that of two needles piercing the skin, somewhere about your neck, on the night when you experienced your first horrible dream. Is there still any soreness?"

"None at all," I answered.

"Can you indicate with your finger about the point at which you think this occurred?"

"Very little below my throat—here," I answered.

I wore a morning dress, which covered the place I pointed to.

"Now you can satisfy yourself," said the doctor. "You won't mind your papa's lowering your dress a very little. It is necessary, to detect a symptom of the complaint under which you have been suffering."

I acquiesced. It was only an inch or two below the edge of my collar.

"God bless me!—so it is," exclaimed my father, growing pale.

"You see it now with your own eyes," said the doctor, with a gloomy triumph.

"What is it?" I exclaimed, beginning to be frightened.

"Nothing, my dear young lady, but a small blue spot, about the size of the tip of your little finger; and now," he continued, turning to papa, "the question is what is best to be done?"

"Is there any danger?" I urged, in great trepidation.

"I trust not, my dear," answered the doctor. "I don't see why you should not recover. I don't see why you should not begin immediately to get better. That is the point at which the sense of strangulation begins?"

"Yes," I answered.

"And—recollect as well as you can—the same point was a kind of center of that thrill which you described just now, like the current of a cold stream running against you?"

"It may have been; I think it was."

"Ay, you see?" he added, turning to my father. "Shall I say a word to Madame?"

"Certainly," said my father.

He called Madame to him, and said:

"I find my young friend here far from well. It won't be of any great consequence, I hope; but it will be necessary that some steps be taken, which I will explain by-and-by; but in the meantime, Madame, you will be so good as not to let Miss Laura be alone for one moment. That is the only direction I need give for the present. It is indispensable."

"We may rely upon your kindness, Madame, I know," added my father.

Madame satisfied him eagerly.

"And you, dear Laura, I know you will observe the doctor's direction."

"I shall have to ask your opinion upon another patient, whose symptoms slightly resemble those of my daughter, that have just been detailed to you—very much milder in degree, but I believe quite of the same sort. She is a young lady—our guest; but as you say you will be passing this way again this evening, you can't do better than take your supper here, and you can then see her. She does not come down till the afternoon."

"I thank you," said the doctor. "I shall be with you, then, at about seven this evening."

And then they repeated their directions to me and to Madame, and with this parting charge my father left us, and walked out with the doctor; and I saw them pacing together up and down between the road and the moat, on the grassy platform in front of the castle, evidently absorbed in earnest conversation.

The doctor did not return. I saw him mount his horse there, take his leave, and ride away eastward through the forest.

Nearly at the same time I saw the man arrive from Dranfield with the letters, and dismount and hand the bag to my father.

In the meantime, Madame and I were both busy, lost in conjecture as to the reasons of the singular and earnest direction which the doctor and my father had concurred in imposing. Madame, as she afterwards told me, was afraid the doctor apprehended a sudden seizure, and that, without prompt assistance, I might either lose my life in a fit, or at least be seriously hurt.

The interpretation did not strike me; and I fancied, perhaps luckily for my nerves, that the arrangement was prescribed simply to secure a companion, who would prevent my taking too much exercise, or eating unripe fruit, or doing any of the fifty foolish things to which young people are supposed to be prone.

About half an hour after my father came in—he had a letter in his hand—and said:

"This letter had been delayed; it is from General Spielsdorf. He might have been here yesterday, he may not come till tomorrow or he may be here today."

He put the open letter into my hand; but he did not look pleased, as he used to when a guest, especially one so much loved as the General, was coming.

On the contrary, he looked as if he wished him at the bottom of the Red Sea. There was plainly something on his mind which he did not choose to divulge.

"Papa, darling, will you tell me this?" said I, suddenly laying my hand on his arm, and looking, I am sure, imploringly in his face.

"Perhaps," he answered, smoothing my hair caressingly over my eyes.

"Does the doctor think me very ill?"

"No, dear; he thinks, if right steps are taken, you will be quite well again, at least, on the high road to a complete recovery, in a day or two," he answered, a little dryly. "I wish our good friend, the General, had chosen any other time; that is, I wish you had been perfectly well to receive him."

"But do tell me, papa," I insisted, "what does he think is the matter with me?"

"Nothing; you must not plague me with questions," he answered, with more irritation than I ever remember him to have displayed before; and seeing that I looked wounded, I suppose, he kissed me, and added, "You shall know all about it in a day or two; that is, all that I know. In the meantime you are not to trouble your head about it."

He turned and left the room, but came back before I had done wondering and puzzling over the oddity of all this; it was merely to say that he was going to Karnstein, and had ordered the carriage to be ready at twelve, and that I and Madame should accompany him; he was going to see the priest who lived near those picturesque grounds, upon business, and as Carmilla had never seen them, she could follow, when she came down, with Mademoiselle, who would bring materials for what you call a picnic, which might be laid for us in the ruined castle.

At twelve o'clock, accordingly, I was ready, and not long after, my father, Madame and I set out upon our projected drive.

Passing the drawbridge we turn to the right, and follow the road over the steep Gothic bridge, westward, to reach the deserted village and ruined castle of Karnstein.

No sylvan drive can be fancied prettier. The ground breaks into gentle hills and hollows, all clothed with beautiful wood, totally destitute of the comparative formality which artificial planting and early culture and pruning impart.

The irregularities of the ground often lead the road out of its course, and cause it to wind beautifully round the sides of broken hollows and the steeper sides of the hills, among varieties of ground almost inexhaustible.

Turning one of these points, we suddenly encountered our old friend, the General, riding towards us, attended by a mounted servant. His portmanteaus were following in a hired wagon, such as we term a cart.

The General dismounted as we pulled up, and, after the usual greetings, was easily persuaded to accept the vacant seat in the carriage and send his horse on with his servant to the *schloss*.

X
Bereaved

It was about ten months since we had last seen him: but that time had sufficed to make an alteration of years in his appearance. He had grown thinner; something of gloom and anxiety had taken the place of that cordial serenity which used to characterize his features. His dark blue eyes, always penetrating, now gleamed with a sterner light from under his shaggy grey eyebrows. It was not such a change as grief alone usually induces, and angrier passions seemed to have had their share in bringing it about.

We had not long resumed our drive, when the General began to talk, with his usual soldierly directness, of the bereavement, as he termed it, which he had sustained in the death of his beloved niece and ward; and he then broke out in a tone of intense bitterness and fury, inveighing against the "hellish arts" to which she had fallen a victim, and expressing, with more exasperation than piety, his wonder that Heaven should tolerate so monstrous an indulgence of the lusts and malignity of hell.

My father, who saw at once that something very extraordinary had befallen, asked him, if not too painful to him, to detail the circumstances which he thought justified the strong terms in which he expressed himself.

"I should tell you all with pleasure," said the General, "but you would not believe me."

"Why should I not?" he asked.

"Because," he answered testily, "you believe in nothing but what consists with your own prejudices and illusions. I remember when I was like you, but I have learned better."

"Try me," said my father; "I am not such a dogmatist as you suppose. Besides which, I very well know that you generally require proof for what you believe, and am, therefore, very strongly predisposed to respect your conclusions."

"You are right in supposing that I have not been led lightly into a belief in the marvelous—for what I have experienced is marvelous—and I have been forced by extraordinary evidence to credit that which ran counter, diametrically, to all my theories. I have been made the dupe of a preternatural conspiracy."

Notwithstanding his professions of confidence in the General's penetration, I saw my father, at this point, glance at the General, with, as I thought, a marked suspicion of his sanity.

The General did not see it, luckily. He was looking gloomily and curiously into the glades and vistas of the woods that were opening before us.

"You are going to the Ruins of Karnstein?" he said. "Yes, it is a lucky coincidence; do you know I was going to ask you to bring me there to inspect them. I have a special object in exploring. There is a ruined chapel, ain't there, with a great many tombs of that extinct family?"

"So there are—highly interesting," said my father. "I hope you are thinking of claiming the title and estates?"

My father said this gaily, but the General did not recollect the laugh, or even the smile, which courtesy exacts for a friend's joke; on the contrary, he looked grave and even fierce, ruminating on a matter that stirred his anger and horror.

"Something very different," he said, gruffly. "I mean to unearth some of those fine people. I hope, by God's blessing, to accomplish a pious sacrilege here, which will relieve our earth of certain monsters, and enable honest people to sleep in their beds without being assailed by murderers. I have strange things to tell you, my dear friend, such as I myself would have scouted as incredible a few months since."

My father looked at him again, but this time not with a glance of suspicion—with an eye, rather, of keen intelligence and alarm.

"The house of Karnstein," he said, "has been long extinct: a hundred years at least. My dear wife was maternally descended from the Karnsteins. But the name and title have long ceased to exist. The castle is a ruin; the very village is deserted; it is fifty years since the smoke of a chimney was seen there; not a roof left."

"Quite true. I have heard a great deal about that since I last saw you; a great deal that will astonish you. But I had better relate everything in the order in which it occurred," said the General. "You saw my dear ward—my child, I may call her. No creature could have been more beautiful, and only three months ago none more blooming."

"Yes, poor thing! when I saw her last she certainly was quite lovely," said my father. "I was grieved and shocked more than I can tell you, my dear friend; I knew what a blow it was to you."

He took the General's hand, and they exchanged a kind pressure.

Tears gathered in the old soldier's eyes. He did not seek to conceal them. He said:

"We have been very old friends; I knew you would feel for me, childless as I am. She had become an object of very near interest to me, and repaid my care by an affection that cheered my home and made my life happy. That is all gone. The years that remain to me on earth may not be very long; but by God's mercy I hope to accomplish a service to mankind before I die, and to subserve the vengeance of Heaven upon the fiends who have murdered my poor child in the spring of her hopes and beauty!"

"You said, just now, that you intended relating everything as it occurred," said my father. "Pray do; I assure you that it is not mere curiosity that prompts me."

By this time we had reached the point at which the Drunstall road, by which the General had come, diverges from the road which we were traveling to Karnstein.

"How far is it to the ruins?" inquired the General, looking anxiously forward.

"About half a league," answered my father. "Pray let us hear the story you were so good as to promise."

XI
The Story

"With all my heart," said the General, with an effort; and after a short pause in which to arrange his subject, he commenced one of the strangest narratives I ever heard.

"My dear child was looking forward with great pleasure to the visit you had been so good as to arrange for her to your charming daughter." Here he made me a gallant but melancholy bow. "In the meantime we had an invitation to my old friend the Count Carlsfeld, whose *schloss* is about six leagues to the other side of Karnstein. It was to attend the series of fêtes which, you remember, were given by him in honour of his illustrious visitor, the Grand Duke Charles."

"Yes; and very splendid, I believe, they were," said my father.

"Princely! But then his hospitalities are quite regal. He has Aladdin's lamp. The night from which my sorrow dates was devoted to a magnificent masquerade. The grounds were thrown open, the trees hung with colored lamps. There was such a display of fireworks as Paris itself had never witnessed. And such music—music, you know, is my weakness—such ravishing music! The finest instrumental band, perhaps, in the world, and the finest singers who could be collected from all the great operas in Europe. As you wandered through these fantastically illuminated grounds, the moon-lighted chateau throwing a rosy light from its long rows of windows, you would suddenly hear these ravishing voices stealing from the silence of some grove, or rising from boats upon the lake. I felt myself, as I looked and listened, carried back into the romance and poetry of my early youth.

"When the fireworks were ended, and the ball beginning, we returned to the noble suite of rooms that were thrown open to the dancers. A masked ball, you know, is a beautiful sight; but so brilliant a spectacle of the kind I never saw before.

"It was a very aristocratic assembly. I was myself almost the only 'nobody' present.

"My dear child was looking quite beautiful. She wore no mask. Her excitement and delight added an unspeakable charm to her features, always lovely. I remarked a young lady, dressed magnificently, but wearing a mask, who appeared to me to be observing my ward with extraordinary interest. I had seen her, earlier in the evening, in the great hall, and again, for a few minutes, walking near us, on the terrace under the castle windows, similarly employed. A lady, also masked, richly and gravely dressed, and with a stately air, like a person of rank, accompanied her as a chaperon.

"Had the young lady not worn a mask, I could, of course, have been much more certain upon the question whether she was really watching my poor darling.

"I am now well assured that she was.

"We were now in one of the salons. My poor dear child had been dancing, and was resting a little in one of the chairs near the door; I was standing near. The two ladies I have mentioned had approached and the younger took the chair next my ward; while her companion stood beside me, and for a little time addressed herself, in a low tone, to her charge.

"Availing herself of the privilege of her mask, she turned to me, and in the tone of an old friend, and calling me by my name, opened a conversation with me, which piqued my curiosity a good deal. She referred to many scenes where she had met me—at Court, and at distinguished houses. She alluded to little incidents which I had long ceased to think of, but which, I found, had only lain in abeyance in my memory, for they instantly started into life at her touch.

"I became more and more curious to ascertain who she was, every moment. She parried my attempts to discover very adroitly and pleasantly. The knowledge she showed of many passages in my life seemed to me all but unaccountable; and she appeared to take a not unnatural pleasure in foiling my curiosity, and in seeing me flounder in my eager perplexity, from one conjecture to another.

"In the meantime the young lady, whom her mother called by the odd name of Millarca, when she once or twice addressed her, had, with the same ease and grace, got into conversation with my ward.

"She introduced herself by saying that her mother was a very old acquaintance of mine. She spoke of the agreeable audacity which a mask rendered practicable; she talked like a friend; she admired her dress, and insinuated very prettily her admiration of her beauty. She amused her with laughing criticisms upon the people who crowded the ballroom, and laughed at my poor child's fun. She was very witty and lively when she pleased, and after a time they had grown very good friends, and the young stranger lowered her mask, displaying a remarkably beautiful face. I had never seen it before, neither had my dear child. But though it was new to us, the features were so engaging, as well as lovely, that it was impossible not to feel the attraction powerfully. My poor girl did so. I never saw anyone more taken with another at first sight, unless, indeed, it was the stranger herself, who seemed quite to have lost her heart to her.

"In the meantime, availing myself of the license of a masquerade, I put not a few questions to the elder lady.

"'You have puzzled me utterly,' I said, laughing. 'Is that not enough? Won't you, now, consent to stand on equal terms, and do me the kindness to remove your mask?'

"'Can any request be more unreasonable?' she replied. 'Ask a lady to yield an advantage! Beside, how do you know you should recognize me? Years make changes.'

"'As you see,' I said, with a bow, and, I suppose, a rather melancholy little laugh.

"'As philosophers tell us,' she said; 'and how do you know that a sight of my face would help you?'

"'I should take chance for that,' I answered. 'It is vain trying to make yourself out an old woman; your figure betrays you.'

"'Years, nevertheless, have passed since I saw you, rather since you saw me, for that is what I am considering. Millarca, there, is my daughter; I cannot then be young, even in the opinion of people whom time has taught to be indulgent, and I may not like to be compared with what you remember me. You have no mask to remove. You can offer me nothing in exchange.'

"'My petition is to your pity, to remove it.'

"'And mine to yours, to let it stay where it is,' she replied.

"'Well, then, at least you will tell me whether you are French or German; you speak both languages so perfectly.'

"'I don't think I shall tell you that, General; you intend a surprise, and are meditating the particular point of attack.'

"'At all events, you won't deny this,' I said, 'that being honored by your permission to converse, I ought to know how to address you. Shall I say Madame la Comtesse?'

"She laughed, and she would, no doubt, have met me with another evasion—if, indeed, I can treat any occurrence in an interview every circumstance of which was prearranged, as I now believe, with the profoundest cunning, as liable to be modified by accident.

"'As to that,' she began; but she was interrupted, almost as she opened her lips, by a gentleman, dressed in black, who looked particularly elegant and distinguished, with this drawback, that his face was the most deadly pale I ever saw, except in death. He was in no masquerade—in the plain evening dress of a gentleman; and he said, without a smile, but with a courtly and unusually low bow:—

"'Will Madame la Comtesse permit me to say a very few words which may interest her?'

"The lady turned quickly to him, and touched her lip in token of silence; she then said to me, 'Keep my place for me, General; I shall return when I have said a few words.'

"And with this injunction, playfully given, she walked a little aside with the gentleman in black, and talked for some minutes, apparently very earnestly. They then walked away slowly together in the crowd, and I lost them for some minutes.

"I spent the interval in cudgeling my brains for a conjecture as to the identity of the lady who seemed to remember me so kindly, and I was thinking of turning about and joining in the conversation between my pretty ward and the Countess's daughter, and trying whether, by the time she returned, I might not have a surprise in store for her, by having her name, title, chateau, and estates at my fingers' ends. But at this moment she returned, accompanied by the pale man in black, who said:

"'I shall return and inform Madame la Comtesse when her carriage is at the door.'

"He withdrew with a bow."

XII
A Petition

Then we are to lose Madame la Comtesse, but I hope only for a few hours,' I said, with a low bow.

"'It may be that only, or it may be a few weeks. It was very unlucky his speaking to me just now as he did. Do you now know me?'

"I assured her I did not.

"'You shall know me,' she said, 'but not at present. We are older and better friends than, perhaps, you suspect. I cannot yet declare myself. I shall in three weeks pass your beautiful *schloss*, about which I have been making enquiries. I shall then look in upon you for an hour or two, and renew a friendship which I never think of without a thousand pleasant recollections. This moment a piece of news has reached me like a thunderbolt. I must set out now, and travel by a devious route, nearly a hundred miles, with all the dispatch I can possibly make. My perplexities multiply. I am only deterred by the compulsory reserve I practice as to my name from making a very singular request of you. My poor child has not quite recovered her strength. Her horse fell with her, at a hunt which she had ridden out to witness, her nerves have not yet recovered the shock, and our physician says that she must on no account exert herself for some time to come. We came here, in consequence, by very easy stages—hardly six leagues a day. I must now travel day and night, on a mission of life and death—a mission the critical and momentous nature of which I shall be able to explain to you when we meet, as I hope we shall, in a few weeks, without the necessity of any concealment.'

"She went on to make her petition, and it was in the tone of a person from whom such a request amounted to conferring, rather than seeking a favour.

"This was only in manner, and, as it seemed, quite unconsciously. Than the terms in which it was expressed, nothing could be more deprecatory.

It was simply that I would consent to take charge of her daughter during her absence.

"This was, all things considered, a strange, not to say, an audacious request. She in some sort disarmed me, by stating and admitting everything that could be urged against it, and throwing herself entirely upon my chivalry. At the same moment, by a fatality that seems to have predetermined all that happened, my poor child came to my side, and, in an undertone, besought me to invite her new friend, Millarca, to pay us a visit. She had just been sounding her, and thought, if her mamma would allow her, she would like it extremely.

"At another time I should have told her to wait a little, until, at least, we knew who they were. But I had not a moment to think in. The two ladies assailed me together, and I must confess the refined and beautiful face of the young lady, about which there was something extremely engaging, as well as the elegance and fire of high birth, determined me; and, quite overpowered, I submitted, and undertook, too easily, the care of the young lady, whom her mother called Millarca.

"The Countess beckoned to her daughter, who listened with grave attention while she told her, in general terms, how suddenly and peremptorily she had been summoned, and also of the arrangement she had made for her under my care, adding that I was one of her earliest and most valued friends.

"I made, of course, such speeches as the case seemed to call for, and found myself, on reflection, in a position which I did not half like.

"The gentleman in black returned, and very ceremoniously conducted the lady from the room.

"The demeanour of this gentleman was such as to impress me with the conviction that the Countess was a lady of very much more importance than her modest title alone might have led me to assume.

"Her last charge to me was that no attempt was to be made to learn more about her than I might have already guessed, until her return. Our distinguished host, whose guest she was, knew her reasons.

"'But here,' she said, 'neither I nor my daughter could safely remain for more than a day. I removed my mask imprudently for a moment, about an hour ago, and, too late, I fancied you saw me. So I resolved to seek an opportunity of talking a little to you. Had I found that you had seen me, I would have thrown myself on your high sense of honour to keep my secret some weeks. As it is, I am satisfied that you did not see me; but if you now suspect, or, on reflection, should suspect, who I am, I commit myself, in like manner, entirely to your honour. My daughter will observe the same secrecy, and I well know that you will, from time to time, remind her, lest she should thoughtlessly disclose it.'

"She whispered a few words to her daughter, kissed her hurriedly twice, and went away, accompanied by the pale gentleman in black, and disappeared in the crowd.

"'In the next room,' said Millarca, 'there is a window that looks upon the hall door. I should like to see the last of mamma, and to kiss my hand to her.'

"We assented, of course, and accompanied her to the window. We looked out, and saw a handsome old-fashioned carriage, with a troop of couriers and footmen. We saw the slim figure of the pale gentleman in black, as he held a thick velvet cloak, and placed it about her shoulders and threw the hood over her head. She nodded to him, and just touched his hand with hers. He bowed low repeatedly as the door closed, and the carriage began to move.

"'She is gone,' said Millarca, with a sigh.

"'She is gone,' I repeated to myself, for the first time—in the hurried moments that had elapsed since my consent—reflecting upon the folly of my act.

"'She did not look up,' said the young lady, plaintively.

"'The Countess had taken off her mask, perhaps, and did not care to show her face,' I said; 'and she could not know that you were in the window.'

"She sighed, and looked in my face. She was so beautiful that I relented. I was sorry I had for a moment repented of my hospitality, and I determined to make her amends for the unavowed churlishness of my reception.

"The young lady, replacing her mask, joined my ward in persuading me to return to the grounds, where the concert was soon to be renewed. We did so, and walked up and down the terrace that lies under the castle windows.

"Millarca became very intimate with us, and amused us with lively descriptions and stories of most of the great people whom we saw upon the terrace. I liked her more and more every minute. Her gossip without being ill-natured, was extremely diverting to me, who had been so long out of the great world. I thought what life she would give to our sometimes lonely evenings at home.

"This ball was not over until the morning sun had almost reached the horizon. It pleased the Grand Duke to dance till then, so loyal people could not go away, or think of bed.

"We had just got through a crowded saloon, when my ward asked me what had become of Millarca. I thought she had been by her side, and she fancied she was by mine. The fact was, we had lost her.

"All my efforts to find her were vain. I feared that she had mistaken, in the confusion of a momentary separation from us, other people for her new friends, and had, possibly, pursued and lost them in the extensive grounds which were thrown open to us.

"Now, in its full force, I recognized a new folly in my having undertaken the charge of a young lady without so much as knowing her name; and fettered as I was by promises, of the reasons for imposing which I knew nothing, I could not even point my inquiries by saying that the missing young lady was the daughter of the Countess who had taken her departure a few hours before.

"Morning broke. It was clear daylight before I gave up my search. It was not till near two o'clock next day that we heard anything of my missing charge.

"At about that time a servant knocked at my niece's door, to say that he had been earnestly requested by a young lady, who appeared to be in great distress, to make out where she could find the General Baron Spielsdorf and the young lady his daughter, in whose charge she had been left by her mother.

"There could be no doubt, notwithstanding the slight inaccuracy, that our young friend had turned up; and so she had. Would to heaven we had lost her!

"She told my poor child a story to account for her having failed to recover us for so long. Very late, she said, she had got to the housekeeper's bedroom in despair of finding us, and had then fallen into a deep sleep which, long as it was, had hardly sufficed to recruit her strength after the fatigues of the ball.

"That day Millarca came home with us. I was only too happy, after all, to have secured so charming a companion for my dear girl."

XIII

The Woodman

There soon, however, appeared some drawbacks. In the first place, Millarca complained of extreme languor—the weakness that remained after her late illness—and she never emerged from her room till the afternoon was pretty far advanced. In the next place, it was accidentally discovered, although she always locked her door on the inside, and never disturbed the key from its place till she admitted the maid to assist at her toilet, that she was undoubtedly sometimes absent from her room in the very early morning, and at various times later in the day, before she wished it to be understood that she was stirring. She was repeatedly seen from the windows of the *schloss*, in the first faint grey of the morning, walking through the trees, in an easterly direction, and looking like a person in a trance. This convinced me that she walked in her sleep. But this hypothesis did not solve the puzzle. How did she pass out from her room, leaving the door locked on the inside? How did she escape from the house without unbarring door or window?

"In the midst of my perplexities, an anxiety of a far more urgent kind presented itself.

"My dear child began to lose her looks and health, and that in a manner so mysterious, and even horrible, that I became thoroughly frightened.

"She was at first visited by appalling dreams; then, as she fancied, by a specter, sometimes resembling Millarca, sometimes in the shape of a beast, indistinctly seen, walking round the foot of her bed, from side to side.

"Lastly came sensations. One, not unpleasant, but very peculiar, she said, resembled the flow of an icy stream against her breast. At a later time, she felt something like a pair of large needles pierce her, a little below the throat, with a very sharp pain. A few nights after, followed a gradual and convulsive sense of strangulation; then came unconsciousness."

I could hear distinctly every word the kind old General was saying, because by this time we were driving upon the short grass that spreads on either side of the road as you approach the roofless village which had not shown the smoke of a chimney for more than half a century.

You may guess how strangely I felt as I heard my own symptoms so exactly described in those which had been experienced by the poor girl who, but for the catastrophe which followed, would have been at that moment a visitor at my father's chateau. You may suppose, also, how I felt as I heard him detail habits and mysterious peculiarities which were, in fact, those of our beautiful guest, Carmilla!

A vista opened in the forest; we were on a sudden under the chimneys and gables of the ruined village, and the towers and battlements of the dismantled castle, round which gigantic trees are grouped, overhung us from a slight eminence.

In a frightened dream I got down from the carriage, and in silence, for we had each abundant matter for thinking; we soon mounted the ascent, and were among the spacious chambers, winding stairs, and dark corridors of the castle.

"And this was once the palatial residence of the Karnsteins!" said the old General at length, as from a great window he looked out across the village, and saw the wide, undulating expanse of forest. "It was a bad family, and here its bloodstained annals were written," he continued. "It is hard that they should, after death, continue to plague the human race with their atrocious lusts. That is the chapel of the Karnsteins, down there."

He pointed down to the grey walls of the Gothic building partly visible through the foliage, a little way down the steep. "And I hear the axe of a woodman," he added, "busy among the trees that surround it; he possibly may give us the information of which I am in search, and point out the grave of Mircalla, Countess of Karnstein. These rustics preserve the local traditions of great families, whose stories die out among the rich and titled so soon as the families themselves become extinct."

"We have a portrait, at home, of Mircalla, the Countess Karnstein; should you like to see it?" asked my father.

"Time enough, dear friend," replied the General. "I believe that I have seen the original; and one motive which has led me to you earlier than I at first intended, was to explore the chapel which we are now approaching."

"What! see the Countess Mircalla," exclaimed my father; "why, she has been dead more than a century!"

"Not so dead as you fancy, I am told," answered the General.

"I confess, General, you puzzle me utterly," replied my father, looking at him, I fancied, for a moment with a return of the suspicion I detected before. But although there was anger and detestation, at times, in the old General's manner, there was nothing flighty.

"There remains to me," he said, as we passed under the heavy arch of the Gothic church—for its dimensions would have justified its being so styled—"but one object which can interest me during the few years that remain to me on earth, and that is to wreak on her the vengeance which, I thank God, may still be accomplished by a mortal arm."

"What vengeance can you mean?" asked my father, in increasing amazement.

"I mean, to decapitate the monster," he answered, with a fierce flush, and a stamp that echoed mournfully through the hollow ruin, and his clenched hand was at the same moment raised, as if it grasped the handle of an axe, while he shook it ferociously in the air.

"What?" exclaimed my father, more than ever bewildered.

"To strike her head off."

"Cut her head off!"

"Aye, with a hatchet, with a spade, or with anything that can cleave through her murderous throat. You shall hear," he answered, trembling with rage. And hurrying forward he said:

"That beam will answer for a seat; your dear child is fatigued; let her be seated, and I will, in a few sentences, close my dreadful story."

The squared block of wood, which lay on the grass-grown pavement of the chapel, formed a bench on which I was very glad to seat myself, and in the meantime the General called to the woodman, who had been removing some boughs which leaned upon the old walls; and, axe in hand, the hardy old fellow stood before us.

He could not tell us anything of these monuments; but there was an old man, he said, a ranger of this forest, at present sojourning in the house of the priest, about two miles away, who could point out every monument of the old Karnstein family; and, for a trifle, he undertook to bring him back with him, if we would lend him one of our horses, in little more than half an hour.

"Have you been long employed about this forest?" asked my father of the old man.

"I have been a woodman here," he answered in his patois, "under the forester, all my days; so has my father before me, and so on, as many generations as I can count up. I could show You the very house in the village here, in which my ancestors lived."

"How came the village to be deserted?" asked the General.

"It was troubled by revenants, sir; several were tracked to their graves, there detected by the usual tests, and extinguished in the usual way, by decapitation, by the stake, and by burning; but not until many of the villagers were killed.

"But after all these proceedings according to law," he continued— "so many graves opened, and so many vampires deprived of their horrible animation—the village was not relieved. But a Moravian nobleman, who happened to be traveling this way, heard how matters were, and being skilled—as many people are in his country—in such affairs, he offered to deliver the village from its tormentor. He did so thus: There being a bright moon that night, he ascended, shortly after sunset, the towers of the chapel here, from whence he could distinctly see the churchyard beneath him; you can see it from that window. From this point he watched until he saw the vampire come out of his grave, and place near it the linen clothes in which he had been folded, and then glide away towards the village to plague its inhabitants.

"The stranger, having seen all this, came down from the steeple, took the linen wrappings of the vampire, and carried them up to the top of the tower, which he again mounted. When the vampire returned from his prowlings and missed his clothes, he cried furiously to the Moravian, whom he saw at the summit of the tower, and who, in reply, beckoned him to ascend and take them. Whereupon the vampire, accepting his invitation, began to climb the steeple, and so soon as he had reached the battlements, the Moravian, with a stroke of his sword, clove his skull in twain, hurling him down to the churchyard, whither, descending by the winding stairs, the stranger followed and cut his head off, and next day delivered it and the body to the villagers, who duly impaled and burnt them.

"This Moravian nobleman had authority from the then head of the family to remove the tomb of Mircalla, Countess Karnstein, which he did effectually, so that in a little while its site was quite forgotten."

"Can you point out where it stood?" asked the General, eagerly.

The forester shook his head, and smiled.

"Not a soul living could tell you that now," he said; "besides, they say her body was removed; but no one is sure of that either."

Having thus spoken, as time pressed, he dropped his axe and departed, leaving us to hear the remainder of the General's strange story.

XIV
The Meeting

M y beloved child," he resumed, "was now growing rapidly worse. The physician who attended her had failed to produce the slightest impression on her disease, for such I then supposed it to be. He saw my alarm, and suggested a consultation. I called in an abler physician, from Gratz.

"Several days elapsed before he arrived. He was a good and pious, as well as a leaned man. Having seen my poor ward together, they withdrew to my library to confer and discuss. I, from the adjoining room, where I awaited their summons, heard these two gentlemen's voices raised in something sharper than a strictly philosophical discussion. I knocked at the door and entered. I found the old physician from Gratz maintaining his theory. His rival was combating it with undisguised ridicule, accompanied with bursts of laughter. This unseemly manifestation subsided and the altercation ended on my entrance.

"'Sir,' said my first physician, 'my learned brother seems to think that you want a conjuror, and not a doctor.'

"'Pardon me,' said the old physician from Gratz, looking displeased, 'I shall state my own view of the case in my own way another time. I grieve, Monsieur le General, that by my skill and science I can be of no use. Before I go I shall do myself the honour to suggest something to you.'

"He seemed thoughtful, and sat down at a table and began to write.

"Profoundly disappointed, I made my bow, and as I turned to go, the other doctor pointed over his shoulder to his companion who was writing, and then, with a shrug, significantly touched his forehead.

"This consultation, then, left me precisely where I was. I walked out into the grounds, all but distracted. The doctor from Gratz, in ten or fifteen minutes, overtook me. He apologized for having followed me, but said that he could not conscientiously take his leave without a few words more. He told me that he could not be mistaken; no natural disease exhibited the same symptoms; and that death was already very near. There remained, however, a day, or possibly two, of life. If the fatal seizure were at once arrested, with great care and skill her strength might possibly return. But all hung now upon the confines of the irrevocable. One more assault might extinguish the last spark of vitality which is, every moment, ready to die.

"'And what is the nature of the seizure you speak of?' I entreated.

"'I have stated all fully in this note, which I place in your hands upon the distinct condition that you send for the nearest clergyman, and open my letter in his presence, and on no account read it till he is with you; you would despise it else, and it is a matter of life and death. Should the priest fail you, then, indeed, you may read it.'

"He asked me, before taking his leave finally, whether I would wish to see a man curiously learned upon the very subject, which, after I had read his letter, would probably interest me above all others, and he urged me earnestly to invite him to visit him there; and so took his leave.

"The ecclesiastic was absent, and I read the letter by myself. At another time, or in another case, it might have excited my ridicule. But into what quackeries will not people rush for a last chance, where all accustomed means have failed, and the life of a beloved object is at stake?

"Nothing, you will say, could be more absurd than the learned man's letter.

"It was monstrous enough to have consigned him to a madhouse. He said that the patient was suffering from the visits of a vampire! The punctures which she described as having occurred near the throat, were, he insisted, the insertion of those two long, thin, and sharp teeth which, it is well known, are peculiar to vampires; and there could be no doubt, he added, as to the well-defined presence of the small livid mark which all concurred in describing as that induced by the demon's lips, and every symptom described by the sufferer was in exact conformity with those recorded in every case of a similar visitation.

"Being myself wholly skeptical as to the existence of any such portent as the vampire, the supernatural theory of the good doctor furnished, in my opinion, but another instance of learning and intelligence oddly associated with someone's hallucination. I was so miserable, however, that, rather than try nothing, I acted upon the instructions of the letter.

"I concealed myself in the dark dressing room, that opened upon the poor patient's room, in which a candle was burning, and watched there till she was fast asleep. I stood at the door, peeping through the small crevice, my sword laid on the table beside me, as my directions prescribed, until, a little after one, I saw a large black object, very ill-defined, crawl, as it seemed to me, over the foot of the bed, and swiftly spread itself up to the poor girl's throat, where it swelled, in a moment, into a great, palpitating mass.

"For a few moments I had stood petrified. I now sprang forward, with my sword in my hand. The black creature suddenly contracted towards the foot of the bed, glided over it, and, standing on the floor about a yard below the foot of the bed, with a glare of skulking ferocity and horror fixed on me, I saw Millarca. Speculating I know not what, I struck at her instantly with my sword; but I saw her standing near the door, unscathed. Horrified, I pursued, and struck again. She was gone; and my sword flew to shivers against the door.

"I can't describe to you all that passed on that horrible night. The whole house was up and stirring. The specter Millarca was gone. But her victim was sinking fast, and before the morning dawned, she died."

The old General was agitated. We did not speak to him. My father walked to some little distance, and began reading the inscriptions on the tombstones; and thus occupied, he strolled into the door of a side chapel to prosecute his researches. The General leaned against the wall, dried his eyes, and sighed heavily. I was relieved on hearing the voices of Carmilla and Madame, who were at that moment approaching. The voices died away.

In this solitude, having just listened to so strange a story, connected, as it was, with the great and titled dead, whose monuments were moldering among the dust and ivy round us, and every incident of which bore so awfully upon my own mysterious case—in this haunted spot, darkened by the towering foliage that rose on every side, dense and high above its noiseless walls—a horror began to steal over me, and my heart sank as I thought that my friends were, after all, not about to enter and disturb this triste and ominous scene.

The old General's eyes were fixed on the ground, as he leaned with his hand upon the basement of a shattered monument.

Under a narrow, arched doorway, surmounted by one of those demoniacal grotesques in which the cynical and ghastly fancy of old Gothic carving delights, I saw very gladly the beautiful face and figure of Carmilla enter the shadowy chapel.

I was just about to rise and speak, and nodded smiling, in answer to her peculiarly engaging smile; when with a cry, the old man by my side caught up the woodman's hatchet, and started forward. On seeing him a brutalized change came over her features. It was an instantaneous and horrible transformation, as she made a crouching step backwards. Before I could utter a scream, he struck at her with all his force, but she dived under his blow, and unscathed, caught him in her tiny grasp by the wrist. He struggled for a moment to release his arm, but his hand opened, the axe fell to the ground, and the girl was gone.

He staggered against the wall. His grey hair stood upon his head, and a moisture shone over his face, as if he were at the point of death.

The frightful scene had passed in a moment. The first thing I recollect after, is Madame standing before me, and impatiently repeating again and again, the question, "Where is Mademoiselle Carmilla?"

I answered at length, "I don't know—I can't tell—she went there," and I pointed to the door through which Madame had just entered; "only a minute or two since."

"But I have been standing there, in the passage, ever since Mademoiselle Carmilla entered; and she did not return."

She then began to call "Carmilla," through every door and passage and from the windows, but no answer came.

"She called herself Carmilla?" asked the General, still agitated.

"Carmilla, yes," I answered.

";Aye," he said; "that is Millarca. That is the same person who long ago was called Mircalla, Countess Karnstein. Depart from this accursed ground, my poor child, as quickly as you can. Drive to the clergyman's house, and stay there till we come. Begone! May you never behold Carmilla more; you will not find her here."

XV
Ordeal and Execution

As he spoke one of the strangest looking men I ever beheld entered the chapel at the door through which Carmilla had made her entrance and her exit. He was tall, narrow-chested, stooping, with high shoulders, and dressed in black. His face was brown and dried with deep furrows; he wore an oddly-shaped hat with a broad leaf. His hair, long and grizzled, hung on his shoulders. He wore a pair of gold spectacles, and walked slowly, with an odd shambling gait, with his face sometimes turned up to the sky, and sometimes bowed down towards the ground, seemed to wear a perpetual smile; his long thin arms were swinging, and his lank hands, in old black gloves ever so much too wide for them, waving and gesticulating in utter abstraction.

"The very man!" exclaimed the General, advancing with manifest delight. "My dear Baron, how happy I am to see you, I had no hope of meeting you so soon." He signed to my father, who had by this time returned, and leading the fantastic old gentleman, whom he called the Baron to meet him. He introduced him formally, and they at once entered into earnest conversation. The stranger took a roll of paper from his pocket, and spread it on the worn surface of a tomb that stood by. He had a pencil case in his fingers, with which he traced imaginary lines from point to point on the paper, which from their often glancing from it, together, at certain points of the building, I concluded to be a plan of the chapel. He accompanied, what I may term, his lecture, with occasional readings from a dirty little book, whose yellow leaves were closely written over.

They sauntered together down the side aisle, opposite to the spot where I was standing, conversing as they went; then they began measuring distances by paces, and finally they all stood together, facing a piece of the sidewall, which they began to examine with great minuteness; pulling off the ivy that clung over it, and rapping the plaster with the ends of their sticks, scraping here, and knocking there. At length they ascertained the existence of a broad marble tablet, with letters carved in relief upon it.

With the assistance of the woodman, who soon returned, a monumental inscription, and carved escutcheon, were disclosed. They proved to be those of the long lost monument of Mircalla, Countess Karnstein.

The old General, though not I fear given to the praying mood, raised his hands and eyes to heaven, in mute thanksgiving for some moments.

"Tomorrow," I heard him say; "the commissioner will be here, and the Inquisition will be held according to law."

Then turning to the old man with the gold spectacles, whom I have described, he shook him warmly by both hands and said:

"Baron, how can I thank you? How can we all thank you? You will have delivered this region from a plague that has scourged its inhabitants for more than a century. The horrible enemy, thank God, is at last tracked."

My father led the stranger aside, and the General followed. I know that he had led them out of hearing, that he might relate my case, and I saw them glance often quickly at me, as the discussion proceeded.

My father came to me, kissed me again and again, and leading me from the chapel, said:

"It is time to return, but before we go home, we must add to our party the good priest, who lives but a little way from this; and persuade him to accompany us to the *schloss.*"

In this quest we were successful: and I was glad, being unspeakably fatigued when we reached home. But my satisfaction was changed to dismay, on discovering that there were no tidings of Carmilla. Of the scene that had occurred in the ruined chapel, no explanation was offered to me, and it was clear that it was a secret which my father for the present determined to keep from me.

The sinister absence of Carmilla made the remembrance of the scene more horrible to me. The arrangements for the night were singular. Two servants, and Madame were to sit up in my room that night; and the ecclesiastic with my father kept watch in the adjoining dressing room.

The priest had performed certain solemn rites that night, the purport of which I did not understand any more than I comprehended the reason of this extraordinary precaution taken for my safety during sleep.

I saw all clearly a few days later.

The disappearance of Carmilla was followed by the discontinuance of my nightly sufferings.

You have heard, no doubt, of the appalling superstition that prevails in Upper and Lower Styria, in Moravia, Silesia, in Turkish Serbia, in Poland, even in Russia; the superstition, so we must call it, of the Vampire.

If human testimony, taken with every care and solemnity, judicially, before commissions innumerable, each consisting of many members, all chosen for integrity and intelligence, and constituting reports more voluminous perhaps than exist upon any one other class of cases, is worth anything, it is difficult to deny, or even to doubt the existence of such a phenomenon as the Vampire.

For my part I have heard no theory by which to explain what I myself have witnessed and experienced, other than that supplied by the ancient and well-attested belief of the country.

The next day the formal proceedings took place in the Chapel of Karnstein.

The grave of the Countess Mircalla was opened; and the General and my father recognized each his perfidious and beautiful guest, in the face now disclosed to view. The features, though a hundred and fifty years had passed since her funeral, were tinted with the warmth of life. Her eyes were open; no cadaverous smell exhaled from the coffin. The two medical men, one officially present, the other on the part of the promoter of the inquiry, attested the marvelous fact that there was a faint but appreciable respiration, and a corresponding action of the heart. The limbs were perfectly flexible, the flesh elastic; and the leaden coffin floated with blood, in which to a depth of seven inches, the body lay immersed.

Here then, were all the admitted signs and proofs of vampirism. The body, therefore, in accordance with the ancient practice, was raised, and a sharp stake driven through the heart of the vampire, who uttered a piercing shriek at the moment, in all respects such as might escape from a living person in the last agony. Then the head was struck off, and a torrent of blood flowed from the severed neck. The body and head was next placed on a pile of wood, and reduced to ashes, which were thrown upon the river and borne away, and that territory has never since been plagued by the visits of a vampire.

My father has a copy of the report of the Imperial Commission, with the signatures of all who were present at these proceedings, attached in verification of the statement. It is from this official paper that I have summarized my account of this last shocking scene.

XVI
Conclusion

I write all this you suppose with composure. But far from it; I cannot think of it without agitation. Nothing but your earnest desire so repeatedly expressed, could have induced me to sit down to a task that has unstrung my nerves for months to come, and reinduced a shadow of the unspeakable horror which years after my deliverance continued to make my days and nights dreadful, and solitude insupportably terrific.

Let me add a word or two about that quaint Baron Vordenburg, to whose curious lore we were indebted for the discovery of the Countess Mircalla's grave.

He had taken up his abode in Gratz, where, living upon a mere pittance, which was all that remained to him of the once princely estates of his family, in Upper Styria, he devoted himself to the minute and laborious investigation of the marvelously authenticated tradition of Vampirism. He had at his fingers' ends all the great and little works upon the subject.

Magia Posthuma, Phlegon de Mirabilibus, Augustinus de cura pro Mortuis, Philosophicæ et Christianæ, Cogitationes de Vampiris, by John Christofer Herenberg; and a thousand others, among which I remember only a few of those which he lent to my father. He had a voluminous digest of all the judicial cases, from which he had extracted a system of principles that appear to govern—some always, and others occasionally only—the condition of the vampire. I may mention, in passing, that the deadly pallour attributed to that sort of revenants, is a mere melodramatic fiction. They present, in the grave, and when they show themselves in human society, the appearance of healthy life. When disclosed to light in their coffins, they exhibit all the symptoms that are enumerated as those which proved the vampire-life of the long-dead Countess Karnstein.

How they escape from their graves and return to them for certain hours every day, without displacing the clay or leaving any trace of disturbance in the state of the coffin or the cerements, has always been admitted to be utterly inexplicable. The amphibious existence of the vampire is sustained by daily renewed slumber in the grave. Its horrible lust for living blood supplies the vigour of its waking existence. The vampire is prone to be fascinated with an engrossing vehemence, resembling the passion of love, by particular persons. In pursuit of these it will exercise inexhaustible patience and stratagem, for access to a particular object may be obstructed in a hundred ways. It will never desist until it has satiated its passion, and drained the very life of its coveted victim. But it will, in these cases, husband and protract its murderous enjoyment with the refinement of an epicure, and heighten it by the gradual approaches of an artful courtship. In these cases it seems to yearn for something like sympathy and consent. In ordinary ones it goes direct to its object, overpowers with violence, and strangles and exhausts often at a single feast.

The vampire is, apparently, subject, in certain situations, to special conditions. In the particular instance of which I have given you a relation, Mircalla seemed to be limited to a name which, if not her real one, should at least reproduce, without the omission or addition of a single letter, those, as we say, anagrammatically, which compose it.

Carmilla did this; so did Millarca.

My father related to the Baron Vordenburg, who remained with us for two or three weeks after the expulsion of Carmilla, the story about the Moravian nobleman and the vampire at Karnstein churchyard, and then he asked the Baron how he had discovered the exact position of the long-concealed tomb of the Countess Mircalla? The Baron's grotesque features puckered up into a mysterious smile; he looked down, still smiling on his worn spectacle case and fumbled with it. Then looking up, he said:

"I have many journals, and other papers, written by that remarkable man; the most curious among them is one treating of the visit of which you speak, to Karnstein. The tradition, of course, discolours and distorts a little. He might have been termed a Moravian nobleman, for he had changed his abode to that territory, and was, beside, a noble. But he was, in truth, a native of Upper Styria. It is enough to say that in very early youth he had been a passionate and favoured lover of the beautiful Mircalla, Countess Karnstein. Her early death plunged him into inconsolable grief. It is the nature of vampires to increase and multiply, but according to an ascertained and ghostly law.

"Assume, at starting, a territory perfectly free from that pest. How does it begin, and how does it multiply itself? I will tell you. A person, more or less wicked, puts an end to himself. A suicide, under certain circumstances, becomes a vampire. That specter visits living people in their slumbers; they die, and almost invariably, in the grave, develop into vampires. This happened in the case of the beautiful Mircalla, who was haunted by one of those demons. My ancestor, Vordenburg, whose title I still bear, soon discovered this, and in the course of the studies to which he devoted himself, learned a great deal more.

"Among other things, he concluded that suspicion of vampirism would probably fall, sooner or later, upon the dead Countess, who in life had been his idol. He conceived a horror, be she what she might, of her remains being profaned by the outrage of a posthumous execution. He has left a curious paper to prove that the vampire, on its expulsion from its amphibious existence, is projected into a far more horrible life; and he resolved to save his once beloved Mircalla from this.

"He adopted the stratagem of a journey here, a pretended removal of her remains, and a real obliteration of her monument. When age had stolen upon him, and from the vale of years, he looked back on the scenes he was leaving, he considered, in a different spirit, what he had done, and a horror took possession of him. He made the tracings and notes which have guided me to the very spot, and drew up a confession of the deception that he had practiced. If he had intended any further action in this matter, death prevented him; and the hand of a remote descendant has, too late for many, directed the pursuit to the lair of the beast."

We talked a little more, and among other things he said was this:

"One sign of the vampire is the power of the hand. The slender hand of Mircalla closed like a vice of steel on the General's wrist when he raised the hatchet to strike. But its power is not confined to its grasp; it leaves a numbness in the limb it seizes, which is slowly, if ever, recovered from."

The following Spring my father took me a tour through Italy. We remained away for more than a year. It was long before the terror of recent events subsided; and to this hour the image of Carmilla returns to memory with ambiguous alternations—sometimes the playful, languid, beautiful girl; sometimes the writhing fiend I saw in the ruined church; and often from a reverie I have started, fancying I heard the light step of Carmilla at the drawing room door.

107

The Predator
Jacob Thomson
2005

He thought of himself as a predator. In nature, predation was an important part of the ecological system. Predators removed the animals who could no longer keep up with the herd. They culled the weak, the sick, the unfit specimens that needed to be removed from the gene pool for the benefit of the others.

Nature wasn't a cartoon, he thought. The cute little animals didn't spend their days frolicking in a bright, sunny meadow. Mostly, he thought, a lot of them spent the day eating grass, or twigs, or other vegetation, while the rest spent the day killing and eating the herbivores. It was all a part of the natural balance, and if you left it alone it usually worked out for the best.

At least, for the best in an overall sense. It was obviously hard on the individual deer or rabbit that found itself as a predator's supper. But it was good for the majority of those who didn't.

That was one of the problems with people, he thought. They had done too much in the way of tampering with the natural balance. If a child was born it had something like a 96% chance of surviving to adulthood, and nearly as good a chance of reproducing.

And this was true both of the superior individuals, whose progeny could be expected to contribute the most to the collective good of humanity, and of the sickly and weak, who could probably contribute best by not reproducing at all.

Curiously, he had never taken this idea to the usual conclusion. He wasn't a racist. It had never once occurred to him that a particular race was superior. Strong, healthy individuals of any race were included in his definition of superior. The same was true when he classified the inferior.

The problem, to his way of thinking, was that too many of the wrong people were growing up and having inferior children. In earlier times, when the human race was steadily progressing, slightly more than half of all children could be expected to die before they were two. It was nature's way of culling the weak and inferior before they were old enough to mate and pass on their bad genes.

But this no longer happened, which left it up to him. He knew, as surely as he was alive, that this was the reason he had been created and placed on the earth.

Now, he didn't hurt children. It wasn't their fault, really, that modern medicine was extending their lives past the point where nature should have removed them from the gene pool. Instead, he culled the inferior adults. Mostly, he hoped, *before* they could reproduce.

He had an inborn gift for finding these people. He could tell just by looking at someone whether they deserved to live or die. He wasn't sure how he knew—he just did. How did the wolf know which caribou needed to be culled from the herd? It was an instinct; something that simply *was*.

He never thought it odd that all of the inferior specimens he culled were women. Again, this was simply something that just *was*. He had nothing against women in general. He merely had a talent for recognizing the ones who needed to be removed from the gene pool. He thought there were probably men who also needed culling, but he hadn't found any of them yet.

He had managed to discover 28 women so far. They were all dead now, of course. After all, what was the value of these insights into the natural order if he didn't follow up on them? Once he recognized that a woman needed to be removed, it became his duty to nature to remove her.

He wasn't sure just how he knew. It wasn't anything obvious. Most of them had looked normal enough—even healthy and attractive. But he knew that an outward appearance of good health could conceal the truth; that her genes were bad, and that she would produce more weak, useless children to further drag down the quality of the human race.

This knowledge came to him from some instinctive source. He could look at any woman and know if she was supposed to live or die. On this single topic, his judgment was never wrong. Every woman he believed should die did die. So he had to be right. Otherwise, they would easily have defended themselves, and would still be alive.

It was a basic law of nature that the fit would always survive. If they didn't, they obviously didn't deserve to.

Just now he was searching. It was never ending, this mission he had set for himself. He had to go out each night, looking at every person he encountered, waiting for that intuitive recognition of the inferior that would set him on the trail of yet another genetic misprint in need of erasure.

Most of the people he encountered this night were just fine. There was nothing about them crying out to his instincts, alerting him that something needed to be done. It was like that most nights. He would prowl the city and no one would draw his interest.

But some nights it was different. On those nights he would notice a particular woman, and something deep in his highly- developed brain would instantly identify her as one of the bad ones. He might not do anything that night, but he would remember her.

Once he knew where she lived, the rest was easy enough. At some point he would get into her home, or catch her in a place where there was no danger of being disturbed. If she was unmarried, and not involved with anyone, he might take longer. If she had a husband, though, he felt compelled to work more quickly. She might get pregnant and, as his purpose was to prevent any more genetically inferior children from being born, it was important to remove her from the gene pool as expeditiously as possible.

The girl walking ahead of him caught his eye. She was tall and slender, dressed in a sheath skirt and a white, fitted blouse. Physically, she was a wonderful specimen, with a perfect figure, good legs, and long, shiny hair in a striking coppery red color.

But she was also one of *them*. His instincts were screaming at him, warning him that, beautiful as this girl might be, she was one of the genetic defectives, and should not be allowed to live long enough to pass on her imperfect genes to the next generation.

Of course, the knowledge that he would have to kill her didn't preclude having a little fun at the same time. That was one of the privileges of his special position in nature's genetic enforcement corps. Should he so choose, he was allowed to have sex with the women before killing them.

His own genes were, obviously, superior, and so should be combined only with the genes of an equally superior woman when it was time to reproduce. Still, as the defective women would die once he'd had them, it didn't matter. They would serve the useful function of giving him pleasure before they died.

Like this one, he thought. She was turning into an alley now, probably taking a short cut over to the next avenue. All the better for him. He wondered if that was what he had recognized in her, that she was one who would take foolish chances. She was making it easy on him. He could simply follow her down the alley, take her in the darkness, and then kill her right there.

He knew the city in every detail. There was a narrow side alley about halfway along the wider alley, between an old theatre on one side and the back of a row of three-story retail buildings on the other. You couldn't see into that side alley from either main street. It was a perfect venue for what he had in mind.

He quickly glanced around, pleased to discover that he was virtually alone on the street. With another quick look back he slipped into the alley. The girl was about 50 feet in front of him, strolling toward the next street as if she hadn't a care in the world.

He always tried to move quietly, but this time it was as if she simply wasn't listening. He caught up with her just as she was passing the side alley and swiftly dragged her into it, his hand clasped tightly over her mouth to prevent her crying out. She hardly seemed to resist, and in a moment he had her pushed up against the back of the old theatre's loading dock. Soon, he thought, there would be one more misfit removed from the gene pool.

But she was fighting back now. He was a big man, three inches over six feet tall, weighing 225 pounds and hardly an ounce of fat on his well-muscled body. Yet the girl was pushing him away, catching hold of his wrists and wrenching them from her lithe body, the effort hardly showing on her lovely face.

"You're not very smart, are you?" she said. Her tone was flat, dismissive. "Why so rough? I hate it when men act like brutes."

He couldn't believe it. Despite his size, the girl was pushing him back, forcing him up against the opposite wall, his arms pinned at his sides as she leaned toward him, her lips inches from his.

"Foolish," she said. "It didn't have to be like this."

She leaned forward, her lips lightly brushing his cheek. His mind was reeling. Was she coming on to him? He felt her kissing him, her soft lips against his throat, the tip of her tongue flicking out against the sensitive skin.

There was hardly any pain at all. He felt a slight pressure on his throat, a sharp twinge as the girl's canine teeth pierced the skin and plunged into the artery beneath. But it didn't really hurt, even as the world began to fade, and the only sound was the frantic pumping of his heart.

Five minutes later the girl walked out of the alley and turned east on the broad sidewalk. It had been easier than she'd expected, and curiously satisfying. She didn't think she was a bad person, after all. It was just her nature. And this time, in this man, she had sensed true evil. A predator, he thought of himself. She had sensed that, taken in his thoughts with his blood.

But he was, after all, only an amateur. One who killed from some psychotic delusion, not out of necessity. A mere child. And he had forgotten the most basic rule of predation. That predators come in all sizes. Foxes ate rabbits, but coyotes ate foxes, and cougars ate coyotes. And there was always a bigger fish. How was he to know that his intended prey was by far the more experienced predator?

You could learn a lot about your craft, she thought, when you'd been at it for more than seven centuries.

Castle Grosshelm
Jacob Thomson
2004

Naught but scattered rubble remains upon the ancient hill, where antique stones here and there thrust up through the bare earth. Black soil, rich and fertile appearing, yet strangely barren. Around the hill lies a vast, virgin forest, with here and there an ancient wagon track, or a peasant's small hut and garden, the blue-gray smoke rising from the chimney. The forest ends perhaps halfway up the slope of the hill, turning to a lovely green meadow, sprinkled in summer with wildflowers.

But the crest is barren. Where once an ancient castle keep rose to challenge the sky, surrounded by a tall, crenelated wall, there is now only rubble and the rich black loam that should support luxuriant greenery, but where nothing at all will grow. Grass seed had been scattered there, and the summer flower seeds, carried on the breeze, fell into the soil and there they died.

The local peasants never venture more than a few yards above the tree line, and never after dark. No one can remember when the castle still dominated the hill. There is only a story, generations old, of how a strange plague slowly wiped out the noble family who dwelt in that place, until the last had been carried down the winding stairs and laid to rest in the venerable crypt buried deep in the bedrock of the hill, and the castle was left to the elements.

More generations passed, and the wind and rain broke through the castle roof, until the floors collapsed into the lowest levels and only the crumbling wall remained. And then, just after the beginning of the 19th Century, a fire had swept through the tumbled beams and boards piled up inside the keep and the heat had finished the work of centuries and the ancient edifice collapsed in upon itself.

The outer curtain wall had long ago succumbed to the need for building stone. It was said that there was hardly a house in the district that did not have at least a few of its stones built into a foundation or wall. With the fire having tumbled the keep, those stones, as well, slowly vanished from the site, to be incorporated into some newer structure. At last, only those half buried stones that remain today were left, marking the burial site of the ancient Von Grosshelm family, whose name was memorialized only in the memories of the oldest peasants, for the great stone lintel of the burial crypt, where it was chiseled deep in the hard granite, was itself buried deep beneath the earth and rubble and out of sight of modern man.

And so it remained until the 1950s, when an avaricious government became aware of the stories of great wealth buried along with the corpses in the Von Grosshelm crypt. There was gold there, it was said, gold in great abundance. Chests of old coins, and rich religious treasure in the tiny chapel at the entrance to the crypt. It seemed strange even to the supposedly benevolent men in Bucharest that no one had plundered the crypt ages ago, but the story was that a fear of the plague breaking out again kept the locals away, and men from farther away had never heard the stories.

So men were brought to the hill to excavate. Ragged men, still dressed in the tattered remains of the field gray uniforms they had been captured in back in 1945. Men brought from prison camps in Siberia, who knew they were never going to return home. They had suffered the misfortune of being captured by the Red Army, and the Soviet Union was not so forgiving as the western powers. Prisoners must be made to pay for the crimes of their government, and for the crimes they had committed themselves, even if those crimes were no more than an administrative excuse to make slaves of a former enemy's troops.

It was doubly hard, this grueling work of excavating the ruined castle, for the prisoners knew they were only a few hundred miles from Germany—closer than they had been since the day they marched off to the east in expectation of a short campaign and an easy victory. Nor did the knowledge of the place they were digging help, for Grosshelm is a German name, meaning "great helmet," and no doubt adopted in honor of some ancient knight's oversized jousting helm. They were digging up the tomb of one of the old Teutonic overlords of this country, perhaps even the grave of a distant relative. Coming of age in the ardently nationalistic Hitlerian years, where the old Teutonic Knights were given the awe and veneration of national demi-gods, such an act seemed little short of sacrilege.

The Russian guards, who had no great love of their socialist comrades in Bucharest, fenced off the perimeter of the hill twenty meters above the tree line. The fence, made of barbed wire, served a dual purpose. It functioned both the keep the prisoners in, and to keep the Romanians out.

If greed in Bucharest had prompted the excavation of Castle Grosshelm, an even greater greed in Moscow was determined to insure that any wealth found made its way back to the Kremlin, and to hell with the Romanians.

It was slow work. Moscow had provided the prisoners and the guards, but they had not provided proper equipment. The workers were given shovels, long pry bars, picks and other hand tools, but there were no cranes or steam shovels or bulldozers. Each of the massive stones had to be dug out, then pried from its place and somehow dragged or carried away by the prisoners. What a properly equipped work force could have done in a week dragged on for nearly a year before the prisoners at last unearthed the top of a rubble filled stairway leading down into the living rock.

Even then, four more weeks passed before the rubble was laboriously hauled up and the full depth of the stairway exposed. At the bottom, a broad landing connected the stair with the chapel entrance, where a massive, iron-bound door, locked tight, barred entry.

The Russian officer in charge of the working party was momentarily stymied. Before the war he had been trained as an art historian, and his first thought was that the chapel door itself was part of the vanished castle's treasure. The wooden panels were heavily carved with religious figures. In the capitalist world, he thought, the door would be worth thousands of dollars. Comrade Stalin, he decided, would not appreciate it if he simply put his men to work breaking it down.

But it was hinged on the inside, so neither could he knock the pins out of the hinges and remove the door from the frame. "I don't suppose," he said, "that any of you men was a locksmith—or a burglar?"

One of the prisoners had been a locksmith in civilian life, but the Russians had never been told that bit of information and he wasn't about to volunteer it now. There were German dead inside the vault beyond the chapel, and he would do nothing extra to help the Russian steal from them.

The prisoners were herded back to the surface. A soldier was sent to the village for a locksmith, but returned an hour later with the news that none was to be found. If the lieutenant needed a locksmith, he would have to send to Bucharest. The village was so poor that, having nothing for anyone to steal, the peasants had no real locks on their doors.

The lieutenant decided he would attempt other methods. A cold chisel and hammer were procured and one of the prisoners was put to work cutting the rivet heads off the thick iron lockplate. The lock was two or three centuries old, at least, he reasoned, so it was probably a fairly simple warded type that could be easily defeated as long as he could get to the guts. Cutting off the rivet heads, he thought, should not cause irreparable damage.

This proved to be the case, and at last the massive door swung into the chapel. The officer entered first, shining his flashlight around the interior.

The room was square, about twenty feet on each side and topped by a barrel-vaulted ceiling. The entry door was on the east side, or so the lieutenant believed—his compass wouldn't work inside the mountain, and the stair changed directions several times on the way down.

There was an elaborate altar against the northern wall, covered by a gold brocade altar cloth. A tall, gold crucifix was at the center of the altar, flanked by a pair of four-branched gold candelabra, the candles still in them. In the center of the chapel, in front of the altar, was a long, stone catafalque, where a coffin would rest during a committal service, before being taken into the burial vault.

The entrance to the vault was in the west wall, a tall, gothic-arched opening, blocked by a wrought iron gate. There was a short marble column placed directly in front of the gate, with another, even larger, gold crucifix resting on its flat top.

"Collect all of this and take it to the top," the lieutenant ordered. "I will record each piece as it is removed," he added, "just in case one of you might be thinking of stealing something."

Despite having had the poor judgment to serve in the army of a tyrant, the prisoners were all honest men. So far as they were concerned, the only thief was the Soviet government that was looting the chapel and tomb.

It was nearly dark by the time the last of the loot was removed from the chapel. The Russian officer decided that enough had been accomplished for one day. He would worry about getting through the gate, and to any treasure in the burial vault, in the morning.

◆   ◆   ◆

Dieter Krause jerked awake to the staccato sound of a guard's Kalashnikov on full automatic. A moment later the shooting stopped, followed instantly by a terrified scream that was itself shut off as if someone had slammed a door on the source.

Around him, Krause could see the other prisoners also sitting upright on their cots, peering about in the dim light that filtered through the canvas walls and roof of their leaky tent. He motioned for them to remain silent and cautiously got to his feet. Before he was captured, Krause had been a captain of infantry, and he was now the highest ranking prisoner in the group. They all wanted to know what was going on, but it was his place to take the risk of peeking through the tent's door. The Prussian sense of duty and leadership was still there.

He wouldn't dare go into the floodlit compound. The Russians had made it quite clear that leaving the tent after lights out would be instantly punished by shooting the transgressor. He could only peek through the canvas flap and hope no one noticed.

Cautiously, he moved the flap to one side, opening a narrow slit sufficient to peer through with one eye. Just inside the main gate a guard opened fire, shooting at something moving along the barbed wire fence. Another figure appeared from the opposite direction, moving swiftly up behind the guard. The figure was clearly not a prisoner, for even from his vantage point Krause could see the slim, white form covered by a flowing gown, and the long, black hair flowing down her back.

The mysterious girl was within inches of the guard before he realized anyone was behind him. Her arm slipped around his chest, lifting him off his feet, and then she slammed him to the ground. The girl knelt over him. Another figure, this time clearly male and dressed in a costume that seemed out of a Renaissance movie, rushed in from the direction where the guard had been firing. Like the girl, he knelt over the fallen guard.

At that moment Krause's view was abruptly blocked by a face. The man standing before the tent was tall and gaunt, his narrow face framed by flowing white hair, worn in a fashion that had gone out of style centuries before. His eyes were deep set, dark as midnight. But it was his mouth that riveted Krause's attention.

The man's lips were thin, his mouth partly open, revealing a line of unusually white teeth. The lower lip with slightly distended, and there was fresh blood dripping down his long chin.

"*Himmel!*"

The man looked closer at the single eye peering out at him him. "*Deutscher?*" he said.

"*Ja,*" Krause could hardly speak. He had gone to sleep a prisoner and somehow awakened in a horror movie.

"Why are you here?" the man asked, his German oddly accented and curiously phrased, sounding like some of the old books Krause had studied in University.

"We are war prisoners," he managed to say.

"Working for these Russians?"

"More like their slaves."

"No longer. Stay where you are, and in the morning you may leave." He smiled suddenly. "We shall also be gone, of course. This castle, what is left of it, will not be safe for us now."

Krause let the tent flap open a bit more. "Who are you?" he asked.

The man bowed slightly. Now Krause could see his body as well as his terrifying face. He was dressed in black, in the fashion of a 16th Century nobleman, complete with sword. "I am Helmut, *Graf* von Grosshelm," he said. "I will not enter your tent, and you would be wise not to invite me in. It has been far too long since last I dined and I would not wish to harm my countrymen."

With that, the man turned on his heel and disappeared from sight.

The noise continued for another hour. Here and there came the sound of firing, mingled with the screams of the dying guards. The Germans remained in their tent, lying on the ground and hoping that no stray shot would find them. Krause had moved away from the door and was huddled with his men.

Eventually it grew silent in the compound, but still none of the Germans moved. Krause had told them what the ominous nobleman had said. No one really believed him. If there was no firing now, it could as easily be presumed to mean that the Russians had triumphed.

Dawn came at last. Now the Germans began to hope. No one came to roust them out of their cots. No sound at all came from outside the tent. Only the soft whisper of the wind as it blew across the bare mountain top.

When they emerged the gates were wide open, and the compound was littered with the bodies of the Russian detachment. One of the braver men descended into the mountain, returning minutes later, his eyes wide with terror.

"They're all gone," he informed them. "The gate to the tomb is open, and all the coffins have been removed."

They would be, he thought. By now he knew what had happened, even if he couldn't quite bring himself to believe it. He was a modern man, not given to superstitious foolishness. Yet here it was before him. The Russian bodies all had their throats torn out, and there was no blood soaking into the ground around them.

It was the golden crucifix set on the short column directly in front of the tomb's gate, he thought. That had been the key, in a very literal sense. Someone had placed it there centuries before, knowing that the members of the ancient family entombed there were not really at rest. So long as the crucifix was in place they could not leave the tomb.

Then the Russian officer had taken it away. Krause didn't know how many vampires had been in the tomb. Enough, certainly. But the old *Graf* had somehow retained his sense of obligation to his own countrymen. The Russians were all dead, and the Germans were all alive.

And the vampires, after slaughtering the Russians, had taken up their coffins and moved to a safer place. If the Russians hadn't known what was in the tomb, it was certain that the locals did. Von Grosshelm and his undead clan would have wasted no time in relocating.

It was time, Krause decided, that his men did the same.

The Succubus
Honoré de Balzac

Prologue

A number of persons of the noble country of Touraine, considerably edified by the warm search which the author is making into the antiquities, adventures, good jokes, and pretty tales of that blessed land, and believing for certain that he should know everything, have asked him (after drinking with him of course understood), if he had discovered the etymological reason, concerning which all the ladies of the town are so curious, and from which a certain street in Tours is called the Rue Chaude. By him it was replied, that he was much astonished to see that the ancient inhabitants had forgotten the great number of convents situated in this street, where the severe continence of the monks and nuns might have caused the walls to be made so hot that some woman of position should increase in size from walking too slowly along them to vespers. A troublesome fellow, wishing to appear learned, declared that formerly all the scandalmongers of the neighbourhood were wont to meet in this place. Another entangled himself in the minute suffrages of science, and poured forth golden words without being understood, qualifying words, harmonising the melodies of the ancient and modern, congregating customs, distilling verbs, alchemising all languages since the Deluge, of the Hebrew, Chaldeans, Egyptians, Greeks, Latins, and of Turnus, the ancient founder of Tours; and the good man finished by declaring that *chaude* or *chaulde* with the exception of the H and the L, came from *Cauda*, and that there was a tail in the affair, but the ladies only understood the end of it. An old man observed that in this same place was formerly a source of thermal water, of which his great great grandfather had drunk. In short, in less time than it takes a fly to embrace its sweetheart, there had been a pocketful of etymologies, in which the truth of the matter had been less easily found than a louse in the filthy beard of

119

a Capuchin friar. But a man well learned and well informed, through having left his footprint in many monasteries, consumed much midnight oil, and manured his brain with many a volume—himself more encumbered with pieces, dyptic fragments, boxes, charters, and registers concerning the history of Touraine than is a gleaner with stalks of straw in the month of August—this man, old, infirm, and gouty, who had been drinking in his corner without saying a word, smiled the smile of a wise man and knitted his brows, the said smile finally resolving itself into a pish! well articulated, which the Author heard and understood it to be big with an adventure historically good, the delights of which he would be able to unfold in this sweet collection.

To be brief, on the morrow this gouty old fellow said to him, "By your poem, which is called 'The Venial Sin,' you have forever gained my esteem, because everything therein is true from head to foot—which I believe to be a precious superabundance in such matters. But doubtless you do not know what became of the Moor placed in religion by the said knight, Bruyn de la Roche-Corbon. I know very well. Now if this etymology of the street harass you, and also the Egyptian nun, I will lend you a curious and antique parchment, found by me in the Olim of the episcopal palace, of which the libraries were a little knocked about at a period when none of us knew if he would have the pleasure of his head's society on the morrow. Now will not this yield you a perfect contentment?"

"Good!" said the author.

Then this worthy collector of truths gave certain rare and dusty parchments to the author, the which he has, not without great labour, translated into French, and which were fragments of a most ancient ecclesiastical process. He has believed that nothing would be more amusing than the actual resurrection of this antique affair, wherein shines forth the illiterate simplicity of the good old times. Now, then, give ear. This is the order in which were the manuscripts, of which the author has made use in his own fashion, because the language was devilishly difficult.

I
What the Succubus Was

In nomine Patris, et Filii, et Spiritus Sancti. Amen.

In the year of our Lord, one thousand two hundred and seventy-one, before me, Hierome Cornille, grand inquisitor and ecclesiastical judge (thereto commissioned by the members of the chapter of Saint Maurice, the cathedral of Tours, having of this deliberated in the presence of our Lord Jean de Montsoreau, archbishop—namely, the grievances and complaints of the inhabitants of the said town, whose request is here subjoined), have appeared certain noblemen, citizens, and inhabitants of the diocese, who have stated the following facts concerning a demon suspected of having taken the features of a woman, who has much afflicted the minds of the diocese, and is at present a prisoner in the jail of the chapter; and in order to arrive at the truth of the said charge we have opened the present court, this Monday, the eleventh day of December, after mass, to communicate the evidence of each witness to the said demon, to interrogate her upon the said crimes to her imputed, and to judge her according to the laws enforced *contra demonios.*

In this inquiry has assisted me to write the evidence therein given, Guillaume Tournebouche, rubrican of the chapter, a learned man.

Firstly has come before us one Jehan, surnamed Tortebras, a citizen of Tours, keeping by licence the hostelry of La Cigoyne, situated on the Place du Pont, and who has sworn by the salvation of his soul, his hand upon the holy Evangelists, to state no other thing than that which by himself hath been seen and heard.

He hath stated as here followeth:—

"I declare that about two years before the feast of St. Jehan, upon which are the grand illuminations, a gentleman, at first unknown to me, but belonging without doubt to our lord the King, and at that time returned to our country from the Holy Land, came to me with the proposition that I should let to him at rental a certain country-house by me built, in the quit rent of the chapter over against the place called of St. Etienne, and the which I let to him for nine years, for the consideration of three besans of fine gold. In the said house was placed by the said knight a fair wench having the appearance of a woman, dressed in the strange fashion of the Saracens Mohammedans, whom he would allow by none to be seen or to be approached within a bow-shot, but whom I have seen with mine own eyes, weird feathers upon her head, and eyes so flaming that I cannot adequately describe them, and from which gleamed forth a fire of hell. The defunct knight having threatened with death whoever should appear to spy about the said house, I have by reason of great fear left the said house, and I have until this day secretly kept to my mind certain presumptions and doubts concerning the bad appearance of the said foreigner, who was more strange than any woman, her equal not having as yet by me been seen.

"Many persons of all conditions having at the time believed the said knight to be dead, but kept upon his feet by virtue of the said charms, philters, spells, and diabolical sorceries of this seeming woman, who wished to settle in our country, I declare that I have always seen the said knight so ghastly pale that I can only compare his face to the wax of a Paschal candle, and to the knowledge of all the people of the hostelry of La Cigoyne, this knight was interred nine days after his first coming. According to the statement of his groom, the defunct had been chalorously[31] coupled with the said Moorish woman during seven whole days shut up in my house, without coming out from her, the which I heard him horribly avow upon his deathbed. Certain persons at the present time have accused this she-devil of holding the said gentleman in her clutches by her long hair, the which was furnished with certain warm properties by means of which are communicated to Christians the flames of hell in the form of love, which work in them until their souls are by this means drawn from their bodies and possessed by Satan. But I declare that I have seen nothing of this excepting the said dead knight, bowelless, emaciated, wishing, in spite of his confessor, still to go to this wench; and then he has been recognised as the Lord de Bueil, who was a crusader, and who was, according to certain persons of the town, under the spell of a demon whom he had met in the Asiatic country of Damascus or elsewhere.

"Afterwards I have let my house to the said unknown lady, according to the clauses of the deed of lease. The said Lord of Bueil, being defunct, I had nevertheless been into my house in order to learn from the said foreign woman if she wished to remain in my dwelling, and after great trouble

---

31   Hotly, from *chaleur*, heat or warmth.

was led before her by a strange, half-naked black man, whose eyes were white.

"Then I have seen the said Moorish woman in a little room, shining with gold and jewels, lighted with strange lights, upon an Asiatic carpet, where she was seated, lightly attired, with another gentleman, who was there imperiling his soul; and I had not the heart bold enough to look upon her, seeing that her eyes would have incited me immediately to yield myself up to her, for already her voice thrilled into my very belly, filled my brain, and debauched my mind. Finding this, from the fear of God, and also of hell, I have departed with swift feet, leaving my house to her as long as she liked to retain it, so dangerous was it to behold that Moorish complexion from which radiated diabolical heats, besides a foot smaller than it was lawful in a real woman to possess; and to hear her voice, which pierced into one's heart! And from that day I have lacked the courage to enter my house from great fear of falling into hell. I have said my say."

To the said Tortebras we have then shown an Abyssinian, Nubian or Ethiopian, who, black from head to foot, had been found wanting in certain virile properties with which all good Christians are usually furnished[32], who, having persevered in his silence, after having been tormented and tortured many times, not without much moaning, has persisted in being unable to speak the language of our country. And the said Tortebras has recognised the said Abyssinian heretic as having been in his house in company with the said demoniacal spirit, and is suspected of having lent his aid to her sorcery.

And the said Tortebras has confessed his great faith in the Catholic religion, and declared no other things to be within his knowledge save certain rumours which were known to every one, of which he had been in no way a witness except in the hearing of them.

In obedience to the citations served upon him, has appeared then, Matthew, surname Cognefestu, a day-labourer of St. Etienne, whom, after having sworn by the holy Evangelists to speak the truth, has confessed to us always to have seen a bright light in the dwelling of the said foreign woman, and heard much wild and diabolical laughter on the days and nights of feasts and fasts, notably during the days of the holy and Christmas weeks, as if a great number of people were in the house. And he has sworn to have seen by the windows of the said dwellings, green buds of all kinds in the winter, growing as if by magic, especially roses in a time of frost, and other things for which there was a need of a great heat; but of this he was in no way astonished, seeing that the said foreigner threw out so much heat that when she walked in the evening by the side of his wall he found on the morrow his salad grown; and on certain occasions she had by the touching

---

32 That is, he was a eunuch.

of her petticoats, caused the trees to put forth leaves and hasten the buds. Finally, the said, Cognefestu has declared to us to know no more, because he worked from early morning, and went to bed at the same hour as the fowls.

Afterwards the wife of the aforesaid Cognefestu has by us been required to state also upon oath the things come to her cognisance in this process, and has avowed naught save praises of the said foreigner, because since her coming her man had treated her better in consequence of the neighbourhood of this good lady, who filled the air with love, as the sun did light, and other incongruous nonsense, which we have not committed to writing.

To the said Cognefestu and to his wife we have shown the said unknown African, who has been seen by them in the gardens of the house, and is stated by them for certain to belong to the said demon. In the third place, has advanced Harduin V., lord of Maille, who being by us reverentially begged to enlighten the religion of the church, has expressed his willingness so to do, and has, moreover, engaged his word, as a gallant knight, to say no other thing than that which he has seen. Then he has testified to have known in the army of the Crusades the demon in question, and in the town of Damascus to have seen the knight of Bueil, since defunct, fight at close quarters to be her sole possessor. The above-mentioned wench, or demon, belonged at that time to the knight Geoffroy IV, Lord of Roche-Pozay, by whom she was said to have been brought from Touraine, although she was a Saracen; concerning which the knights of France marvelled much, as well as at her beauty, which made a great noise and a thousand scandalous ravages in the camp. During the voyage this wench was the cause of many deaths, seeing that Roche-Pozay had already discomfited certain Crusaders, who wished to keep her to themselves, because she shed, according to certain knights petted by her in secret, joys around her comparable to none others. But in the end the knight of Bueil, having killed Geoffroy de la Roche-Pozay, became lord and master of this young murderess, and placed her in a convent, or harem, according to the Saracen custom. About this time one used to see her and hear her chattering as entertainment many foreign dialects, such as the Greek or the Latin empire, Moorish, and, above all, French better than any of those who knew the language of France best in the Christian host, from which sprang the belief that she was demoniacal.

The said knight Harduin has confessed to us not to have tilted for her in the Holy Land, not from fear, coldness or other cause, so much as that he believed the time had arrived for him to bear away a portion of the true cross, and also he had belonging to him a noble lady of the Greek country, who saved him from this danger in denuding him of love, morning and night, seeing that she took all of it substantially from him, leaving him none in his heart or elsewhere for others.

And the said knight has assured us that the woman living in the country house of Tortebras, was really the said Saracen woman, come into the country from Syria, because he had been invited to a midnight feast at her house by the young Lord of Croixmare, who expired the seventh day afterwards, according to the statement of the Dame de Croixmare, his mother, ruined all points by the said wench, whose commerce with him had consumed his vital spirit, and whose strange phantasies had squandered his fortune.

Afterwards questioned in his quality of a man full of prudence, wisdom and authority in this country, upon the ideas entertained concerning the said woman, and summoned by us to open his conscience, seeing that it was a question of a most abominable case of Christian faith and divine justice, answer has been made by the said knight:—

That by certain of the host of Crusaders it has been stated to him that always this she-devil was a maid to him who embraced her, and that Mammon was for certain occupied in her, making for her a new virtue for each of her lovers, and a thousand other foolish sayings of drunken men, which were not of a nature to form a fifth gospel. But for a fact, he, an old knight on that turn of life, and knowing nothing more of the aforesaid, felt himself again a young man in that last supper with which he had been regaled by the lord of Croixmare; then the voice of this demon went straight to his heart before flowing into his ears, and had awakened so great a love in his body that his life was ebbing from the place whence it should flow, and that eventually, but for the assistance of Cyprus wine, which he had drunk to blind his sight, and his getting under the table in order no longer to gaze upon the fiery eyes of his diabolical hostess, and not to rend his heart from her, without doubt he would have fought the young Croixmare, in order to enjoy for a single moment this supernatural woman. Since then he had had absolution from his confessor for the wicked thought. Then, by advice from on high, he had carried back to his house his portion of the true Cross[33], and had remained in his own manor, where, in spite of his Christian precautions, the said voice still at certain times tickled his brain, and in the morning often had he in remembrance this demon, warm as brimstone; and because the look of this wench was so warm that it made him burn like a young man, be half dead, and because it cost him then many transshipments of the vital spirit, the said knight has requested us not to confront him with the empress of love to whom, if it were not the

---

33   It has sometimes been suggested that, based upon the quantity of fragments of the "true cross" brought back by Crusaders, pilgrims, and other travelers to the Holy Land, Jesus must have been crucified on a tree the size of a giant Sequoia. One rather suspects that this was not the case, and that when they weren't occupied in fighting the Crusaders, the local population was busy swindling them.

devil, God the Father had granted strange liberties with the minds of men. Afterwards, he retired, after reading over his statement, not without having first recognised the above-mentioned African to be the servant and page of the lady.

In the fourth place, upon the faith pledged in us in the name of the Chapter and of our Lord Archbishop, that he should not be tormented, tortured, nor harassed in any manner, nor further cited after his statement, in consequence of his commercial journeys, and upon the assurance that he should retire in perfect freedom, has come before us a Jew, Solomon al Rastchid, who, in spite of the infamy of his person and his Judaism, has been heard by us to this one end, to know everything concerning the conduct of the aforesaid demon. Thus he has not been required to take any oath this Solomon, seeing that he is beyond the pale of the Church, separated from us by the blood of our saviour (*trucidatus Salvatore inter nos*). Interrogated by us as to why he appeared without the green cap upon his head, and the yellow wheel in the apparent locality of the heart in his garment, according to the ecclesiastical and royal ordinances, the said de Rastchid has exhibited to us letters patent of the seneschal of Touraine and Poitou. Then the said Jew has declared to us to have done a large business for the lady dwelling in the house of the innkeeper Tortebras, to have sold to her golden chandeliers, with many branches, minutely engraved, plates of red silver, cups enriched with stones, emeralds and rubies; to have brought for her from the Levant a number of rare stuffs, Persian carpets, silks, and fine linen; in fact, things so magnificent that no queen in Christendom could say she was so well furnished with jewels and household goods; and that he had for his part received from her three hundred thousand pounds for the rarity of the purchases in which he had been employed, such as Indian flowers, poppingjays[34], birds' feathers, spices, Greek wines, and diamonds. Requested by us, the judge, to say if he had furnished certain ingredients of magical conjuration, the blood of new-born children, conjuring books, and things generally and whatsoever made use of by sorcerers, giving him licence to state his case without that thereupon he should be the subject to any further inquest or inquiry, the said al Rastchid has sworn by his Hebrew faith never to have had any such commerce; and has stated that he was involved in too high interests to give himself to such miseries, seeing that he was the agent of certain most powerful lords, such as the Marquis de Montferrat, the King of England, the King of Cyprus and Jerusalem, the Court of Provence, lords of Venice, and many German gentleman; to have belonging to him merchant galleys of all kinds, going into Egypt with the permission of the Sultan, and he trafficking in precious articles of silver and of gold, which took him often into the exchange of Tours. Moreover,

---

34   In this context, a parrot.

he has declared that he considered the said lady, the subject of inquiry, to be a right royal and natural woman, with the sweetest limbs, and the smallest he has ever seen. That in consequence of her renown for a diabolical spirit, pushed by a wild imagination, and also because that he was smitten with her, he had heard once that she was husbandless, proposed to her to be her gallant, to which proposition she willingly acceded. Now, although from that night he felt his bones disjointed and his bowels crushed, he had not yet experienced, as certain persons say, that who once yielded was free no more; he went to his fate as lead into the crucible of the alchemist. Then the said Solomon, to whom we have granted his liberty according to the safe conduct, in spite of the statement, which proves abundantly his commerce with the devil, because he had been saved there where all Christians have succumbed, has admitted to us an agreement concerning the said demon. To make known that he had made an offer to the chapter of the cathedral to give for the said semblance of a woman such a ransom, if she were condemned to be burned alive, that the highest of the towers of the Church of St. Maurice, at present in course of construction, could therewith be finished.

The which we have noted to be deliberated upon at an opportune time by the assembled chapter. And the said Solomon has taken his departure without being willing to indicate his residence, and has told us that he can be informed of the deliberation of the chapter by a Jew of the synagogue of Tours, by name Tobias Nathaneus. The said Jew has before his departure been shown the African, and has recognised him as the page of the demon, and has stated the Saracens to have the custom of mutilating their slaves thus, to commit to them the task of guarding their women by an ancient usage, as it appears in the profane histories of Narsez, general of Constantinople, and others.

On the morrow after mass has appeared before us the most noble and illustrious lady of Croixmare. The same has worn her faith in the holy Evangelists, and has related to us with tears how she had placed her eldest son beneath the earth, dead by reason of his extravagant amours with this female demon. The which noble gentleman was three-and-twenty years of age; of good complexion, very manly and well bearded like his defunct sire. Notwithstanding his great vigour, in ninety days he had little by little withered, ruined by his commerce with the succubus of the Rue Chaude, according to the statement of the common people; and her maternal authority over the son had been powerless. Finally in his latter days he appeared like a poor dried up worm, such as housekeepers meet with in a corner when they clean out the dwelling-rooms. And always, so long as he had the strength to go, he went to shorten his life with this cursed woman; where, also, he emptied his cash-box. When he was in his bed, and knew his last hour had come, he swore at, cursed, and threatened and heaped upon all—his sister, his brother, and upon her his mother—a thousand insults, rebelled in the face of the chaplain; denied God, and wished to die in damnation; at which were much afflicted the retainers of the family, who, to save his soul and pluck it from hell, have founded two annual masses in the cathedral. And in order to have him buried in consecrated ground, the house of Croixmare has undertaken to give to the chapter, during one hundred years, the wax candles for the chapels and the church, upon the day of the Paschal feast. And, in conclusion, saving the wicked words heard by the reverend person, Dom Loys Pot, a nun of Marmoustiers, who came to assist in his last hours the said Baron de Croixmaire affirms never to have heard any words offered by the defunct, touching the demon who had undone him.

And therewith has retired the noble and illustrious lady in deep mourning.

In the sixth place has appeared before us, after adjournment, Jacquette, called Vieux-Oing, a kitchen scullion, going to houses to wash dishes, residing at present in the Fishmarket, who, after having placed her word to say nothing she did not hold to be true, has declared as here follows:— Namely, that one day she, being come into the kitchen of the said demon, of whom she had no fear, because she was wont to regale herself only upon males, she had the opportunity of seeing in the garden this female demon, superbly attired, walking in company with a knight, with whom she was laughing, like a natural woman. Then she had recognised in this demon that true likeness of the Moorish woman placed as a nun in the convent of Notre Dame de l'Egrignolles by the defunct seneschal of Touraine and Poitou, Messire Bruyn, Count of Roche-Corbon, the which Moorish woman had been left in the situation and place of the image of our Lady the Virgin, the mother of our Blessed Saviour, stolen by the Egyptians about eighteen years since. Of this time, in consequence of the troubles come about in Touraine, no record has been kept. This girl, aged about twelve years, was saved from the stake at which she would have been burned by being baptised; and the said defunct and his wife had then been godfather and godmother to this child of hell. Being at that time laundress at the convent, she who bears witness has remembrance of the flight which the said Egyptian took twenty months after her entry into the convent, so subtlety that it has never been known how or by what means she escaped. At that time it was thought by all, that with the devil's aid she had flown away in the air, seeing that not withstanding much search, no trace of her flight was found in the convent, where everything remained in its accustomed order.

The African having been shown to the said scullion, she has declared not to have seen him before, although she was curious to do so, as he was commissioned to guard the place in which the Moorish woman combated with those whom she drained through the spigot.

In the seventh place has been brought before us Hugues de Fou, son of the Sieur de Bridore, who, aged twenty years, has been placed in the hands of his father, under caution of his estates, and by him is represented in this process, whom it concerns if should be duly attained and convicted of having, assisted by several unknown and bad young men, laid siege to the jail of the archbishop and of the chapter, and of having lent himself to disturb the force of ecclesiastical justice, by causing the escape of the demon now under consideration. In spite of the evil disposition we have commanded the said Hugues de Fou to testify truly, touching the things he should know concerning the said demon, with whom he is vehemently reputed to have had commerce, pointing out to him that it was a question of his salvation and of the life of the said demon. He, after having taken the oath, he said:—

"I swear by my eternal salvation, and by the holy Evangelists here present under my hand, to hold the woman suspected of being a demon to be an angel, a perfect woman, and even more so in mind than in body, living in all honesty, full of the *mignard*[35] charms and delights of love, in no way wicked, but most generous, assisting greatly the poor and suffering. I declare that I have seen her weeping veritable tears for the death of my friend, the knight of Croixmare. And because on that day she had made a vow to our Lady the Virgin no more to receive the love of young noblemen too weak in her service; she has to me constantly and with great courage denied the enjoyment of her body, and has only granted to me love, and the possession of her heart, of which she has made sovereign. Since this gracious gift, in spite of my increasing flame I have remained alone in her dwelling, where I have spent the greater part of my days, happy in seeing and in hearing her. Oh! I would eat near her, partake of the air which entered into her lungs, of the light which shone in her sweet eyes, and found in this occupation more joy than have the lords of paradise. Elected by me to be forever my lady, chosen to be one day my dove, my wife, and only sweetheart, I, poor fool, have received from her no advances on the joys of the future, but, on the contrary, a thousand virtuous admonitions; such as that I should acquire renown as a good knight, become a strong man and a fine one, fear nothing except God; honour the ladies, serve but one and love them in memory of that one; that when I should be strengthened by the work of war, if her heart still pleased mine, at that time only would she be mine, because she would be able to wait for me, loving me so much."

So saying the young Sire Hugues wept, and weeping, added:—

---

35   Graceful or delicate.

"That thinking of this graceful and feeble woman, whose arms seemed scarcely large enough to sustain the light weight of her golden chains, he did not know how to contain himself while fancying the irons which would wound her, and the miseries with which she would traitorously be loaded, and from this cause came his rebellion. And that he had licence to express his sorrow before justice, because his life was so bound up with that of his delicious mistress and sweetheart that on the day when evil came to her he would surely die."

And the same young man has vociferated a thousand other praises of the said demon, which bear witness to the vehement sorcery practised upon him, and prove, moreover, the abominable, unalterable, and incurable life and the fraudulent witcheries to which he is at present subject, concerning which our lord the archbishop will judge, in order to save by exorcisms and penitences this young soul from the snares of hell, if the devil has not gained too strong a hold of it.

Then we have handed back the said young nobleman into the custody of the noble lord his father, after that by the said Hugues, the African has been recognised as the servant of the accused.

In the eighth place, before us, have the footguards of our lord the archbishop led in great state the *Most High and Reverend Lady Jaqueline de Champchevrier, Abbess of the Convent of Notre-Dame,* under the invocation of Mount Carmel, to whose control has been submitted by the late seneschal of Touraine, father of Monseigneur the Count of Roche-Corbon, present advocate of the said convent, the Egyptian, named at the baptismal font Blanche Bruyn.

To the said abbess we have shortly stated the present cause, in which is involved the holy church, the glory of God, and the eternal future of the people of the diocese afflicted with a demon, and also the life of a creature who it was possible might be quite innocent. Then the cause elaborated, we have requested the said noble abbess to testify that which was within her knowledge concerning the magical disappearance of her daughter in God, Blanche Bruyn, espoused by our Saviour under the name of Sister Clare.

Then has stated the very high, very noble, and very illustrious lady abbess as follows:—

"The Sister Clare, of origin to her unknown, but suspected to be of an heretic father and mother, people inimical to God, has truly been placed in religion in the convent of which the government had canonically come to her in spite of her unworthiness; that the said sister had properly concluded her novitiate, and made her vows according to the holy rule of the order. That the vows taken, she had fallen into great sadness, and had much drooped. Interrogated by her, the abbess, concerning her melancholy malady, the said sister had replied with tears that she herself did not know the cause. That one thousand and one tears engendered themselves in her at feeling no more her splendid hair upon her head; that besides this she thirsted for air, and could not resist her desire to jump up into the trees, to climb and tumble about according to her wont during her open air life; that she passed her nights in tears, dreaming of the forests under the leaves of which in other days she slept; and in remembrance of this she abhorred the quality of the air of the cloisters, which troubled her respiration; that in her inside she was troubled with evil vapours; that at times she was inwardly diverted in church by thoughts which made her lose countenance. Then I have repeated over and over again to the poor creature the holy directions of the church, have reminded her of the eternal happiness which women without seeing enjoy in paradise, and how transitory was life here below, and certain the goodness of God, who for first certain bitter pleasures lost, kept for us a love without end. Is spite of this wise maternal advice the evil spirit has persisted in the said sister; and always would she gaze upon the leaves of the trees and grass of the meadows through the windows of the church during the offices and times of prayer; and persisted in becoming as white as linen in order that she might stay in her bed, and at certain times she would run about the cloisters like a goat broken loose from its fastening. Finally, she had grown thin, lost much of the great beauty, and shrunk away to nothing. While in this condition by us, the abbess her mother, was she placed in the sick-room, we daily expecting her to die. One winter's morning the said sister had fled, without leaving any trace of her steps, without breaking the door, forcing of locks, or opening of windows, nor any sign whatever of the manner of her passage; a frightful adventure which was believed to have taken place by the aid of the demon which has annoyed and tormented her. For the rest it was settled by the authorities of the metropolitan church that the mission of this daughter of hell was to divert the nuns from their holy ways, and blinded by their perfect lives, she had returned through the air on the wings of the sorcerer, who had left her for mockery of our holy religion in the place of our Virgin Mary."

The which having said, the lady abbess was, with great honour and according to the command of our lord the archbishop, accompanied as far as the convent of Carmel.

In the ninth place, before us has come, agreeably to the citation served upon him, Joseph, called Leschalopier, a money-changer, living on the bridge at the sign of the Besant d'Or, who, after having pledged his Catholic faith to say no other thing than the truth, and that known to him, touching the process before the ecclesiastical tribunal, has testified as follows:— "I am a poor father, much afflicted by the sacred will of God. Before the coming of the Succubus of the Rue Chaude, I had, for all good, a son as handsome as a noble, learned as a clerk, and having made more than a dozen voyages into foreign lands; for the rest a good Catholic; keeping himself on guard against the needles of love, because he avoided marriage, knowing himself to be the support of my old days, the love for my eyes, and the constant delight of my heart. He was a son of whom the King of France might have been proud—a good and courageous man, the light on my commerce, the joy of my roof, and, above all, an inestimable blessing, seeing that I am alone in the world, having had the misfortune to lose my wife, and being too old to take another. Now, monseigneur, this treasure without equal has been taken from me, and cast into hell by the demon. Yes, my lord judge, directly he beheld this mischievous jade, this she-devil, in whom it is a whole workshop of perdition, a conjunction of pleasure and delectation, and whom nothing can satiate, my poor child stuck himself fast into the gluepot of love, and afterwards lived only between the columns of Venus, and there did not live long, because in that place like so great a heat that nothing can satisfy the thirst of this gulf, not even should you plunge therein the germs of the entire world. Alas! then, my poor boy—his fortune, his generative hopes, his eternal future, his entire self, more than himself, have been engulfed in this sewer, like a grain of corn in the jaws of a bull. By this means become an old orphan I, who speak, shall have no greater joy than to see burning, this demon, nourished with blood and gold. This Arachne[36] who has drawn out and sucked more marriages, more families in the seed, more hearts, more Christians then there are lepers in all the lazar houses of Christendom. Burn, torment this fiend—this vampire who feeds on souls, this tigerish nature that drinks blood, this amorous lamp in which burns the venom of all the vipers. Close this abyss, the bottom of which no man can find... I offer my deniers to the chapter for the stake, and my arm to light the fire. Watch well, my lord judge, to surely guard this devil, seeing that she has a fire more flaming than all other terrestrial fires; she has all the fire of hell in her, the strength of Samson in her hair, and the sound of celestial music in her voice. She charms to kill the body and the soul at one stroke; she smiles to bite, she kisses to devour; in short, she would wheedle an angel, and make him deny his God. My son! my son! where is he at this hour? The flower of my life—a flower cut by this feminine needlecase as with scissors. Ha, lord! why have I been called? Who will give me back my son, whose soul has been absorbed by a womb which gives death to all, and life to none? The devil alone copulates, and engenders not. This is my evidence, which I pray Master Tournebouche to write without omitting one iota, and to grant me a schedule, that I may tell it to God every evening in

---

36 In mythology, a mortal woman, skilled in the art of weaving, whose vanity caused her to be transformed into a spider by the goddess Minerva. Arachne (αραχνη) translates in Greek as "spider," and is no doubt being used in a dual sense in this passage, as one who weaves a web and destroys the captive.

my prayer, to this end to make the blood of the innocent cry aloud into His ears, and to obtain from His infinite mercy the pardon for my son."

Here followed twenty and seven other statements, of which the transcription in their true objectivity, in all their quality of space would be overfastidious, would draw to a great length, and divert the thread of this curious process—a narrative which, according to ancient precepts, should go straight to the fact, like a bull to his principal office. Therefore, here is, in a few words, the substance of these testimonies.

A great number of good Christians, townsmen and townswomen, inhabitants of the noble town of Tours, testified the demon to have held every day wedding feasts and royal festivities, never to have been seen in any church, to have cursed God, to have mocked the priests, never to have crossed herself in any place; to have spoken all the languages of the earth—a gift which has only been granted by God to the blessed Apostles; to have been many times met in the fields, mounted upon an unknown animal who went before the clouds; not to grow old, and to have always a youthful face; to have received the father and the son on the same day, saying that her door sinned not; to have visible malign influences which flowed from her, for that a pastrycook, seated on a bench at her door, having perceived her one evening, received such a gust of warm love that, going in and getting to bed, he had with great passion embraced his wife, and was found dead on the morrow, that the old men of the town went to spend the remainder of their days and of their money with her, to taste the joys of the sins of their youth, and that they died like fleas on their bellies, and that certain of them, while dying, became as black as Moors; that this demon never allowed herself to be seen neither at dinner, nor at breakfast, nor at supper, but ate alone, because she lived upon human brains; that several had seen her during the night go to the cemeteries, and there embrace the young dead men, because she was not able to assuage otherwise the devil who worked in her entrails, and there raged like a tempest, and from that came the astringent biting, nitrous shooting, precipitant, and diabolical movements, squeezings, and writhings of love and voluptuousness, from which several men had emerged bruised, torn, bitten, pinched and crushed; and that since the coming of our Saviour, who had imprisoned the master devil in the bellies of the swine, no malignant beast had ever been seen in any portion of the earth so mischievous, venomous and so clutching; so much so that if one threw the town of Tours into this field of Venus, she would there transmute it into the grain of cities, and this demon would swallow it like a strawberry.

And a thousand other statements, sayings, and depositions, from which was evident in perfect clearness the infernal generation of this woman, daughter, sister, niece, spouse, or brother of the devil, beside abundant proofs of her evil doing, and of the calamity spread by her in all families. And if it were possible to put them here conformably with the catalogue preserved by the good man to whom he accused the discovery, it would seem like a sample of the horrible cries which the Egyptians gave forth on the day of the seventh plague.[37] Also this examination has covered with great honour Messire Guillaume Tournebouche, by whom are quoted all the memoranda. In the tenth vacation was thus closed this inquest, arriving at a maturity of proof, furnished with authentic testimony and sufficiently engrossed with the particulars, plaints, interdicts, contradictions, charges, assignments, withdrawals, confessions public and private, oaths, adjournments, appearances and controversies, to which the said demon must reply. And the townspeople say everywhere if there were really a she-devil, and furnished with internal horns planted in her nature, with which she drank the men, and broke them, this woman might swim a long time in this sea of writing before being landed safe and sound in hell.

---

37   For the benefit of those who weren't paying attention in Sunday School, the seventh plague was hail mixed with fire.

II
The Proceedings Taken Relative to this Female Vampire

In nomine Patris, et Filii, et Spiritus Sancti. Amen.

In the year of our Lord one thousand two hundred and seventy-one, before us, Hierome Cornille, grand penitentiary and ecclesiastical judge to this, canonically appointed, have appeared—

The Sire Philippe d'Idre, bailiff of the town and city of Tours and province of Touraine, living in his hotel in the Rue de la Rotisserie, in Chateauneuf; Master Jehan Ribou, provost of the brotherhood and company of drapers, residing on the Quay de Bretaingne, at the image of St. Pierre-es-liens; Messire Antoine Jehan, alderman and chief of the Brotherhood of Changers, residing in the Place du Pont, at the image of St. Mark-counting-tournoise-pounds; Master Martin Beaupertuys, captain of the archers of the town residing at the castle; Jehan Rabelais, a ships'; painter and boat maker residing at the port at the isle of St. Jacques, treasurer of the brotherhood of the mariners of the Loire; Mark Hierome, called Maschefer, hosier, at the sign of Saint-Sebastian, president of the trades council; and Jacques, called de Villedomer, master tavern-keeper and vine dresser, residing in the High Street, at the Pomme de Pin; to the said Sire d'Idre, and to the said citizens, we have read the following petition by them, written, signed, and deliberated upon, to be brought under the notice of the ecclesiastical tribunal:—

PETITION

We, the undersigned, all citizens of Tours, are come into the hotel of his worship the Sire d'Idre, bailiff of Touraine, in the absence of our mayor, and have requested him to hear our plaints and statements concerning the

135

following facts, which we intend to bring before the tribunal of the archbishop, the judge of ecclesiastical crimes, to whom should be deferred the conduct of the cause which we here expose:—

A long time ago there came into this town a wicked demon in the form of a woman, who lives in the parish of Saint-Etienne, in the house of the innkeeper Tortebras, situated in the quit-rent of the chapter, and under the temporal jurisdiction of the archiepiscopal domain. The which foreigner carries on the business of a gay woman in a prodigal and abusive manner, and with such increase of infamy that she threatens to ruin the Catholic faith in this town, because those who go to her come back again with their souls lost in every way, and refuse the assistance of the Church with a thousand scandalous discourses.

Now considering that a great number of those who yielded to her are dead, and that arrived in our town with no other wealth than her beauty, she has, according to public clamour, infinite riches and right royal treasure, the acquisition of which is vehemently attributed to sorcery, or at least to robberies committed by the aid of magical attractions and her supernaturally amorous person.

Considering that it is a question of the honour and security of our families, and that never before has been seen in this country a woman wild of body or a daughter of pleasure, carrying on with such mischief of vocation of light of love, and menacing so openly and bitterly the life, the savings, the morals, chastity, religion, and the everything of the inhabitants of this town;

Considering that there is need of a inquiry into her person, her wealth and her deportment, in order to verify if these effects of love are legitimate, and to not proceed, as would seem indicated by her manners, from a bewitchment of Satan, who often visits Christianity under the form of a female, as appears in the holy books, in which it is stated that our blessed Saviour was carried away into a mountain, from which Lucifer or Astaroth showed him the fertile plains of Judea and that in many places have been seen succubi or demons, having the faces of women, who, not wishing to return to hell, and having with them an insatiable fire, attempt to refresh and sustain themselves by sucking in souls;

Considering that in the case of the said woman a thousand proofs of diablerie are met with, of which certain inhabitants speak openly, and that it is necessary for the repose of the said woman that the matter be sifted, in order that she shall not be attacked by certain people, ruined by the result of her wickedness;

For these causes we pray that it will please you to submit to our spiritual lord, father of this diocese, the most noble and blessed archbishop Jehan de Monsoreau, the troubles of his afflicted flock, to the end that he may advise upon them.

By doing so you will fulfil the duties of your office, as we do those of preservers of the security of this town, each one according to the things of which he has charge in his locality.

And we have signed the present, in the year of our Lord one thousand two hundred and seventy-one, of All Saints' Day, after mass.

Master Tournebouche having finished the reading of this petition, by us, Hierome Cornille, has it been said to the petitioners—

"Gentlemen, do you, at the present time, persist in these statements? have you proofs other than those come within your own knowledge, and do you undertake to maintain the truth of this before God, before man, and before the accused?"

All, with the exception of Master Jehan Rabelais, have persisted in their belief, and the aforesaid Rabelais has withdrawn from the process, saying that he considered the said Moorish woman to be a natural woman and a good wench who had no other fault than that of keeping up a very high temperature of love.

Then we, the judge appointed, have, after mature deliberation, found matter upon which to proceed in the petition of the aforesaid citizens, and have commanded that the woman at present in the jail of the chapter shall be proceeded against by all legal methods, as written in the canons and ordinances, *contra demonios.* The said ordinance, embodied in a writ, shall be published by the town-crier in all parts, and with the sound of the trumpet, in order to make it known to all, and that each witness may, according to his knowledge, be confronted with the said demon, and finally the said accused to be provided with a defender, according to custom, and the interrogations, and the process to be congruously conducted.

{Signed} HIEROME CORNILLE.

And, lower-down.

TOURNEBOUCHE

In nomine Patris, et Filii, et Spiritus Sancti. Amen.

In the year of our Lord one thousand two hundred and seventy-one, the 10th day of February, after mass, by command of us, Hierome Cornille, ecclesiastical judge, has been brought from the jail of the chapter and led before us the woman taken in the house of the innkeeper Tortebras, situated in the domains of the chapter and the cathedral of St. Maurice, and are subject to the temporal and seigneurial justice of the Archbishop of Tours; besides which, in consequence of the nature of the crimes imputed to her, she is liable to the tribunal and council of ecclesiastical justice, the which we have made known to her, to the end that she should not ignore it.

And after a serious reading, entirely at will understood by her, in the first place of the petition of the town, then of the statements, plaints, accusations, and proceedings which written in twenty-four quires by Master Tournebouche, and are above related, we have, with the invocation and assistance of God and the Church, resolved to ascertain the truth, first by interrogatories made to the said accused.

In the first interrogation we have requested the aforesaid to inform us in what land or town she had been born. By her who speaks was it answered: "In Mauritania."

We have then inquired: "If she had a father or mother, or any relations?" By her who speaks has it been replied: "That she had never known them." By us requested to declare her name. By her who speaks has been replied: "Zulma," in Arabian tongue.

By us has it been demanded: "Why she spoke our language?" By her who speaks has it been said: "Because she had come into this country." By us has it been asked: "At what time?" By her who speaks has it been replied: "About twelve years."

By us has it been asked: "What age she then was?" By her who speaks has it been answered: "Fifteen years or thereabout."

By us has it been said: "Then you acknowledge yourself to be twenty-seven years of age?" By her who speaks has it been replied: "Yes."

By us has it been said to her: "That she was then the Moorish child found in the niche of Madame the Virgin, baptised by the Archbishop, held at the font by the late Lord of Roche-Corbon and the Lady of Azay, his wife, afterwards by them placed in religion at the convent of Mount Carmel, where by her had been made vows of chastity, poverty, silence, and the love of God, under the divine assistance of St. Clare?" By her who speaks has been said: "That is true."

By us has it been asked her: "If, then, she allowed to be true the declarations of the very noble and illustrious lady the abbess of Mount Carmel, also the statements of Jacquette, called Vieux-Oing, being kitchen scullion?" By the accused has been answered: "These words are true in great measure."

Then by us has it been said to her: "Then you are a Christian?" And by her who speaks has been answered: "Yes, my father."

Then by us has she been requested to make the sign of the cross, and to take holy water from the brush placed by Master Tournebouche in her hand; the which having been done, and by us having been witnessed, it has been admitted as an indisputable fact, that Zulma, the Moorish woman, called in our country Blanche Bruyn, a nun of the convent under the invocation of Mount Carmel, there named Sister Clare, and suspected to be the false appearance of a woman under which is concealed a demon, has in our presence made act of religion and thus recognised the justice of the ecclesiastical tribunal.[38]

Then by us have these words been said to her: "My daughter, you are vehemently suspected to have had recourse to the devil from the manner in which you left the convent, which was supernatural in every way." By her who speaks has it been stated, that she at that time gained naturally the fields by the street door after vespers, enveloped in the robes of Jehan de Marsilis, visitor of the convent, who had hidden her, the person speaking, in a little hovel belonging to him, situated in the Cupidon Lane, near a tower in the town. That there this said priest had to her then speaking, at great length, and most thoroughly taught the depths of love, of which she then speaking was before in all points ignorant, for which delights she had a

---

38   This is an important plot point. The jurisdiction of ecclesiatic courts was limited to those subject to canon law, and this was obviously limited to members of the Church. Anyone who could not be classified as a communicant could only be tried by civil court, which in all likelihood would impose the same sentence. Punishment, however, was not the most important factor in such cases as that under discussion in this story. The most important factor was the victim's property. If the victim was sentenced by the Church, his property was forfeited to the Church. If he was sentenced by the civil court his property was forfeited to the Crown. This "Christians only" jurisdiction applied even to the most notorious of ecclesiastic courts, the Spanish Inquisition, which was powerless to prosecute any Jew who had not accepted baptism. This is, however, a minor point, as unconverted Jews would be prosecuted by the King's courts for the capital crime of being Jewish in Spain after 1492 (the expulsion decree was not officially repealed until 1968, though it wasn't enforced on an individual basis after 1868, and the Inquisition itself lost the power to prosecute and punish heretics in 1834).

great taste, finding them of great use. That the Sire d'Amboise having perceived her then speaking at the window of this retreat, had been smitten with a great love for her. That she loved him more heartily than the monk, and fled from the hovel where she was detained for profit of his pleasure by Don Marsilis. And then she had gone in great haste to Amboise, the castle of the said lord, where she had had a thousand pastimes, hunting, and dancing, and beautiful dresses fit for a queen. One day the Sire de la Roche-Pozay having been invited by the Sire d'Amboise to come and feast and enjoy himself, the Baron d'Amboise had allowed him to see her then speaking, as she came out naked from her bath. That at this sight the said Sire de la Roche-Pozay having fallen violently in love with her, had on the morrow discomfited in single combat the Sire d'Amboise, and by great violence, had, is spite of her tears, taken her to the Holy Land, where she who was speaking had lived the life of a woman well beloved, and had been held in great respect on account of her great beauty. That after numerous adventures, she who was speaking had returned into this country in spite of the apprehensions of misfortune, because such was the will of her lord and master, the Baron de Bueil, who was dying of grief in Asiatic lands, and desired to return to his patrimonial manor. Now he had promised her who was speaking to preserve her from peril. Now she who was speaking had faith and belief in him, the more so as she loved him very much; but on his arrival in this country, the Sire de Bueil was seized with an illness, and died deplorably, without taking any remedies, this spite of the fervent requests which she who was speaking had addressed to him, but without success, because he hated physicians, master surgeons, and apothecaries; and that this was the whole truth.

Then by us has it been said to the accused that she then held to be true the statements of the good Sire Harduin and of the innkeeper Tortebras. By her who speaks has it been replied, that she recognised as evidence the greater part, and also as malicious, calumnious, and imbecile certain portions.

Then by us has the accused been required to declare if she had had pleasure and carnal commerce with all the men, nobles, citizens, and others as set forth in the plaints and declarations of the inhabitants. To which her who speaks has it been answered with great effrontery: "Pleasure, yes! Commerce, I do not know."

By us has it been said to her, that all had died by her acts. By her who speaks has it been said that their deaths could not be the result of her acts, because she had always refused herself to them, and the more she fled from them the more they came and embraced her with infinite passion, and that when she who was speaking was taken by them she gave herself up to them with all her strength, by the grace of God, because she had in that more joy than in anything, and has stated, she who speaks, that she avows her secret sentiments solely because she had been requested by us to state the whole truth, and that she the speaker stood in great fear of the torments of the torturers.

Then by us has she been requested to answer, under pain of torture, in what state of mind she was when a young nobleman died in consequence of his commerce with her. Then by her speaking has it been replied, that she remained quite melancholy and wished to destroy herself; and prayed God, the Virgin, and the saints to receive her into Paradise, because never had she met with any but lovely and good hearts in which was no guile, and beholding them die she fell into a great sadness, fancying herself to be an evil creature or subject to an evil fate, which she communicated like the plague.

Then by us has she been requested to state where she paid her orisons.

By her speaking has it been said that she prayed in her oratory on her knees before God, who according to the Evangelists, sees and hears all things and resides in all places.

Then by us has it been demanded why she never frequented the churches, the offices, nor the feasts. To this by her speaking has it been answered, that those who came to love her had elected the feast days for that purpose, and that she speaking did all things to their liking.

By us has it been remonstrated that, by so doing, she was submissive to man rather than to the commandments of God.

Then by her speaking has it been stated, that for those who loved her well she speaking would have thrown herself into a flaming pile, never having followed in her love any course but that of nature, and that for the weight of the world in gold she would not have lent her body or her love to a king who did not love her with his heart, feet, hair, forehead, and all over. In short and moreover the speaker had never made an act of harlotry in selling one single grain of love to a man whom she had not chosen to be hers, and that he who held her in his arms one hour or kissed her on the mouth a little, possessed her for the remainder of her days.

Then by us has she been requested to state whence preceded the jewels, gold plate, silver, precious stones, regal furniture, carpets, *et cetera*, worth 200,000 doubloons, according to the inventory found in her residence and placed in the custody of the treasurer of the chapter. By the speaker answer has been made, that in us she placed all her hopes, even as much as in God, but that she dare not reply to this, because it involved the sweetest things of love upon which she had always lived. And interpolated anew, the speaker has said that if the judge knew with what fervour she held him she loved, with what obedience she followed him in good or evil ways, with what study she submitted to him, with what happiness she listened to his desires, and inhaled the sacred words with which his mouth gratified her, in what adoration she held his person, even we, an old judge, would believe with her well-beloved, that no sum could pay for this great affection which all the men ran after. After the speaker has declared never from any man loved by her, to have solicited any present or gift, and that she rested perfectly contented to live in their hearts, that she would there curl herself up with indestructible and ineffable pleasure, finding herself richer with this heart than with anything, and thinking of no other thing than to give them more pleasure and happiness than she received from them. But in spite of the iterated refusals of the speaker her lovers persisted in graciously rewarding her. At times one came to her with a necklace of pearls, saying, "This is to show my darling that the satin of her skin did not falsely appear to me whiter than pearls" and would put it on the speaker's neck, kissing her lovingly. The speaker would be angry at these follies, but could not refuse to keep a jewel that gave them pleasure to see it there where they placed it. Each one had a different fancy. At times another liked to tear the precious garments which the speaker wore to gratify him; another to deck out the speaker with sapphires on her arms, on her legs, on her neck, and in her hair; another to seat her on the carpet, clad in silk or black velvet, and to remain for days together in ecstasy at the perfections of the speaker the whom the things desired by her lovers gave infinite pleasure, because these things rendered them quite happy. And the speaker has said, that as we love nothing so much as our pleasure, and wish that everything should shine in beauty and harmonise, outside as well as inside the heart, so they all wished to see the place inhabited by the speaker adorned with handsome objects, and from this idea all her lovers were pleased as much as she was in spreading thereabout gold, silks and flowers. Now seeing that these lovely things spoil nothing, the speaker had no force or commandment by which to prevent a knight, or even a rich citizen beloved by her, having his will, and thus found herself constrained to receive rare perfumes and other satisfaction with which the speaker was loaded, and that such was the source of the gold, plate, carpets, and jewels seized at her house by the officers of justice. This terminates the first interrogation made to the said Sister Clare, suspected to be a demon, because we the judge and Guillaume Tournebouche, are greatly fatigued with having the voice of the aforesaid, in our ears, and finding our understanding in every way muddled.

By us the judge has the second interrogatory been appointed, three days from to-day, in order that the proofs of the possession and presence of the demon in the body of the aforesaid may be sought, and the accused, according to the order of the judge, has been taken back to the jail under the conduct of Master Guillaume Tournebouche.

◆　　　◆　　　◆

In nomine Patris, et Filii, et Spiritus Sancti. Amen.

On the thirteenth day following of the said month of the February before us, Hierome Cornille, *et cetera*, has been produced the Sister Clare above-mentioned, in order to be interrogated upon the facts and deeds to her imputed, and of them to be convicted.[39]

By us, the judge, has it been said to the accused that, looking at the divers responses by her given to the proceeding interrogatories, it was certain that it never had been in the power of a simple woman, even if she were authorised, if such licence were allowed to lead the life of a loose woman, to give pleasure to all, to cause so many deaths, and to accomplish sorceries so perfect, without the assistance of a special demon lodged in her body, and to whom her soul had been sold by an especial compact. That it had been clearly demonstrated that under her outward appearance lies and moves a demon, the author of these evils, and that she was now called upon to declare at what age she had received the demon, to vow the agreement existing between herself and him, and to tell the truth concerning their common evil doings. By the speaker was it replied that she would answer us, man, as to God, who would be judge of all of us. Then has the speaker pretended never to have seen the demon, neither to have spoken with him, nor in any way to desire to see him; never to have led the life of a courtesan, because she, the speaker, had never practised the various delights that love invents, other than those furnished by the pleasure which the Sovereign Creator has put in the thing, and to have always been incited more from the desire of being sweet and good to the dear lord loved by her, than by an incessantly raging desire. But if such had been her inclination, the speaker begged us to bear in mind that she was a poor African girl, in whom God had placed very hot blood, and in her brain so easy an understanding of the delights of love, that if a man only looked at her she felt greatly moved in her heart. That if from desire of acquaintance an amorous gentleman touched the speaker her on any portion of the body, there passing his hand, she was, in spite of everything, under his power, because her heart failed

---

39   One might here note that the presumption is that interrogation will serve only to prove the case, and that conviction will surely follow. It was the nature of ecclesiastical courts to presume guilt—everyone is a sinner from birth, after all, and has no doubt done *something* to deserve punishment—and when the primary purpose of a trial is to set a seal of official sanction on something that was generally a fixed outcome (and confiscate the defendant's property in the process), that presumption is even stronger. This is part and parcel with the principle that God *has* never, and *would* never, allow an innocent man to be executed, which principle also suggests that sometimes the crime for which the human court executes the man isn't the same crime that caused God to *permit* the execution.

her instantly. By this touch, the apprehension and remembrance of all the sweet joys of love woke again in her breast, and there caused an intense heat, which mounted up, flamed in her veins, and made her love and joy from head to foot. And since the day when Don Marsilis had first awakened the understanding of the speaker concerning these things, she had never had any other thought, and thenceforth recognised love to be a thing so perfectly concordant with her nature, that it had since been proved to the speaker that in default of love and natural relief she would have died, withered at the said convent. As evidence of which, the speaker affirms as a certainty, that after her flight from the said convent she had not passed a single day or one particle of time in melancholy and sadness, but always was she joyous, and thus followed the sacred will of God, which she believed to have been diverted during the time lost by her in the convent.

To this was it objected by us, Hierome Cornille, to the said demon, that in this response she had openly blasphemed against God, because we had all been made to his greater glory, and placed in the world to honour and to serve Him, to have before our eyes His blessed commandments, and to live in sanctity, in order to gain eternal life, and not to be always in bed, doing that which even the beasts only do at a certain time. Then by the said sister, has answer been made, that she honoured God greatly, that in all countries she had taken care of the poor and suffering, giving them both money and raiment, and that at the last judgement-day she hoped to have around her a goodly company of holy works pleasant to God, which would intercede for her. That but for her humility, a fear of being reproached and of displeasing the gentlemen of the chapter, she would with joy have spent her wealth in finishing the cathedral of St. Maurice, and there have established foundations for the welfare of her soul—would have spared therein neither her pleasure nor her person, and that with this idea she would have taken double pleasure in her nights, because each one of her amours would have added a stone to the building of this basilica. Also the more this purpose, and for the eternal welfare of the speaker, would they have right heartily given their wealth.

Then by us has it been said to this demon that she could not justify the fact of her sterility, because in spite of so much commerce, no child had been born of her, the which proved the presence of a demon in her. Moreover, Astaroth alone, or an apostle, could speak all languages, and she spoke after the manner of all countries, the which proved the presence of the devil in her. Thereupon the speaker has asked: "In what consisted the said diversity of language?"—that of Greek she knew nothing but a *Kyrie eleison*, of which she made great use; of Latin, nothing, save Amen[40], which she said to God, wishing therewith to obtain her liberty. That for the rest

---

40   "Amen" is not actually Latin, but a Hebrew loan word adopted into the liturgy.

the speaker had felt great sorrow, being without children, and if the good wives had them, she believed it was because they took so little pleasure in the business, and she, the speaker, a little too much. But that such was doubtless the will of God, who thought that from too great happiness, the world would be in danger of perishing. Taking this into consideration, and a thousand other reasons, which sufficiently establish the presence of the devil in the body of the sister, because the peculiar property of Lucifer is to always find arguments having the semblance of truth, we have ordered that in our presence the torture be applied to the said accused, and that she be well tormented in order to reduce the said demon by suffering to submit to the authority of the Church, and have requested to render us assistance one Francois de Hangest, master surgeon and doctor to the chapter, charging him by a codicil hereunder written to investigate the qualities of the feminine nature (*virtutes vulvæ*) of the above-mentioned woman, to enlighten our religion on the methods employed by this demon to lay hold of souls in that way, and see if any article was there apparent.

Then the said Moorish woman had wept bitterly, tortured in advance, and in spite of her irons, has knelt down imploring with cries and clamour the revocation of this order, objecting that her limbs were in such a feeble state, and her bones so tender, that they would break like glass; and finally, has offered to purchase her freedom from this by the gift all her goods to the chapter, and to quit incontinently the country.

Upon this, by us has she been required to voluntarily declare herself to be, and to have always been, demon of the nature of the Succubus, which is a female devil whose business it is to corrupt Christians by the blandishments and flagitious delights of love. To this the speaker has replied that the affirmation would be an abominable falsehood, seeing that she had always felt herself to be a most natural woman.

Then her irons being struck off by the torturer, the aforesaid has removed her dress, and has maliciously and with evil design bewildered and attacked our understandings with the sight of her body, the which, for a fact, exercises upon a man supernatural coercion.

Master Guillaume Tournebouche has, by reason of nature, quitted the pen at this period, and retired, objecting that he was unable, without incredible temptations, which worked in his brain, to be a witness of this torture, because he felt the devil violently gaining his person.

This finishes the second interrogatory; and as the apparitor and janitor of the chapter have stated Master Francois de Hangest to be in the country, the torture and interrogations are appointed for to-morrow at the hour of noon after mass.

This has been written verbally by me, Hierome, in the absence of Master Guillaume Tournebouche, on whose behalf it is signed.

HIEROME CORNILLE

Grand Penitentiary.

PETITION

Today, the fourteenth day of the month of February, in the presence of me, Hierome Cornille, have appeared the said Masters Jehan Ribou, Antoine Jehan, Martin Beaupertuys, Hierome Maschefer, Jacques de Ville d'Omer, and the Sire d'Idre, in place of the mayor of the city of Tours, for the time absent. All plaintiffs designated in the act of process made at the Town Hall, to whom we have, at the request of Blanche Bruyn (now confessing herself a nun of the convent of Mount Carmel, under the name of Sister Clare), declared the appeal made to the Judgment of God by the said person accused of demonical possession, and her offer to pass through the ordeal of fire and water, in presence of the Chapter and of the town of Tours, in order to prove her reality as a woman and her innocence.

To this request have agreed for their parts, the said accusers, who, on condition that the town is security for it, have engaged to prepare a suitable place and a pile, to be approved by the godparents of the accused.

Then by us, the judge, has the first day of the new year been appointed for the day of the ordeal—which will be next Paschal Day—and we have indicated the hour of noon, after mass, each of the parties having acknowledged this delay to be sufficient.

And the present proclamation shall be cited, at the suit of each of them, in all the towns, boroughs, and castles of Touraine and the land of France, at their request and at their cost and suit.

HIEROME CORNILLE

III

What the Succubus did to Suck Out the Soul of the Old Judge, and What Came of the Diabolical Delectation

This the act of extreme confession made the first day of the month of March, in the year one thousand two hundred and seventy-one, after the coming of our blessed Saviour, by Hierome Cornille, priest, canon of the chapter of the cathedral of St. Maurice, grand penitentiary, of all acknowledging himself unworthy, who, finding his last hour to be come, and contrite of his sins, evil doings, forfeits, bad deeds, and wickednesses, has desired his avowal to be published to serve the preconisation of the truth, the glory of God, the justice of the tribunal, and to be an alleviation to him of his punishment, in the other world. The said Hierome Cornille being on his deathbed, there had been convoked to hear his declarations, Jehan de la Haye (de Hago), vicar of the church of St. Maurice; Pietro Guyard, treasurer of the chapter, appointed by our Lord Jean de Monsoreau, Archbishop, to write his words; and Dom Louis Pot, a monk of *maius Monasterium* (Marmoustier), chosen by him for a spiritual father and confessor; all three assisted by the great and illustrious Dr. Guillaume de Censoris, Roman Archdeacon, at present sent into the diocese (*Legatus*), by our Holy Father the Pope; and, finally, in the presence of a great number of Christians come to be witnesses of the death of the said Hierome Cornille, upon his known wish to make act of public repentance, seeing that he was fast sinking, and that his words might open the eyes of Christians about to fall into hell.

And before him, Hierome, who, by reason of his great weakness could not speak, has Dom Louis Pot read the following confession to the great agitation of the said company:—

"My brethren, until the seventy-first year of my age, which is the one in which I now am, with the exception of the little sins through which, all holy though he be, a Christian renders himself culpable before God, but which it is allowed to us to repurchase by penitence, I believe I led a Christian life, and merited the praise and renown bestowed upon me in this diocese, where I was raised to the high office of grand penitentiary, of which I am unworthy. Now, struck with the knowledge of the infinite glory of God, horrified at the agonies which await the wicked and prevaricators in hell, I have thought to lessen the enormity of my sins by the greatest penitence I can show in the extreme hour at which I am. Thus I have prayed of the Church, whom I have deceived and betrayed, whose rights and judicial renown I have sold, to grant me the opportunity of accusing myself publicly in the manner of ancient Christians. I hoped, in order to show my great repentance, to have still enough life in me to be reviled at the door of the cathedral by all my brethren, to remain there an entire day on my knees, holding a candle, a cord around my neck, and my feet naked, seeing that I had followed the way of hell with regard to the sacred instincts of the Church. But in this great shipwreck of my fragile virtue, which will be to you as a warning to fly from vice and the snares of the demon, and to take refuge in the Church, where all help is, I have been so bewitched by Lucifer that our Saviour Jesus Christ will take, by the intercession of all you whose help and prayers I request, pity on me, a poor abused Christian, whose eyes now stream with tears. So would I have another life to spend in works of penitence. Now then listen and tremble with great fear! Elected by the assembled Chapter to carry it out, instruct, and complete the process commenced against a demon, who had appeared in a feminine shape, in the person of a relapsed nun—an abominable person, denying God, and bearing the name of Zulma in the infidel country whence she comes; the which devil is known in the diocese under that of Clare, of the convent of Mount Carmel, and has much afflicted the town by putting herself under an infinite number of men to gain their souls to Mammon, Astaroth, and Satan—princes of hell, by making them leave this world in a state of mortal sin, and causing their death where life has its source, I have, I the judge, fallen in my latter days into this snare, and have lost my senses, while acquitting myself traitorously of the functions committed with great confidence by the Chapter to my cold senility. Hear how subtle the demon is, and stand firm against her artifices. While listening to the first response of the aforesaid Succubus, I saw with horror that the irons placed upon her feet and hands left no mark there, and was astonished at her hidden strength and at her apparent weakness. Then my mind was troubled suddenly at the sight of the natural perfections with which the devil was endowed. I listened to the music of her voice, which warmed me from head to foot, and made me desire to be young, to give myself up to this demon, thinking that for an hour passed in her company my eternal salvation was but poor payment for the pleasure of love tasted in those slender arms. Then I lost that firmness with which all judges should be furnished. This demon by me questioned, reasoned with me in such a manner that at the second interrogatory I was firmly persuaded I should be committing a crime in fining and torturing a poor little creature who cried like an innocent child. Then warned by a voice from on high to do my duty, and that these golden words, the music of celestial appearance, were diabolical mummeries, that this body, so pretty, so infatuating, would transmute itself into a bristly beast with sharp claws, those eyes so soft into flames of hell, her behind into a scaly tail, the pretty rosebud mouth and gentle lips into the jaws of a crocodile, I came back to my intention of having the said Succubus tortured until she avowed her permission, as this practice had already been followed in Christianity. Now when this demon showed herself stripped to me, to be put to the torture, I was suddenly placed in her power by magical conjurations. I felt my old bones crack, my brain received a warm light, my heart transhipped young and boiling blood. I was light in myself, and by virtue of the magic philter thrown into my eyes the snows on my forehead melted away. I lost all conscience of my Christian life and found myself a schoolboy, running about the country, escaped from class and stealing apples. I had not the power to make the sign of the cross, neither did I remember the Church, God the Father, nor the sweet Saviour of men. A prey to this design, I went about the streets thinking over the delights of that voice, the abominable, pretty body of this demon, and saying a thousand wicked things to myself. Then pierced and drawn by a blow of the devil's fork, who had planted himself already in my head as a serpent in an oak, I was conducted by this sharp prong towards the jail, in spite of my guardian angel, who from time to time pulled me by the arm and defended me against these temptations, but in spite of his holy advice and his assistance I was dragged by a million claws stuck into my heart, and soon found myself in the jail. As soon as the door was opened to me I saw no longer any appearance of a prison, because the Succubus had there, with the assistance of evil genii or fays, constructed a pavilion of purple and silk, full of perfumes and flowers, where she was seated, superbly attired with neither irons on her neck nor chains on her feet. I allowed myself to be stripped of my ecclesiastical vestments, and was put into a scent bath. Then the demon covered me with a Saracen robe, entertained me with a repast of rare viands contained in precious vases, gold cups, Asiatic wines, songs and marvellous music, and a thousand sweet sounds that tickled my soul by means of my ears. At my side kept always the said Succubus, and her sweet, delectable embrace distilled new ardour into my members. My guardian angel quitted me. Then I lived only by the terrible light of the Moorish woman's eyes, coveted the warm embraces of the delicate body, wished always to feel her red lips, that I believed natural, and had no fear of the bite of those teeth which drew me to the bottom of hell, I delighted to feel the unequalled softness of her hands without thinking that they were unnatural claws. In short, I acted like husband desiring to go to his affianced without thinking that that spouse was everlasting death. I had no thought for the things of this world nor the interests of God, dreaming only of love, of the sweet breasts of this woman, who made me burn, and of the gate of hell in which I wished to cast myself. Alas! my brethren, during three days and three nights was I thus constrained to toil without being able to stop the stream which flowed from my reins, in which were plunged, like two pikes, the hands of the Succubus, which communicated to my poor old age and to my dried up bones, I know not what sweat of love. At first this demon, to draw me to her, caused to flow in my inside the softness of milk, then came poignant joys which pricked like a hundred needles my bones, my marrow, my brain, and my nerves. Then all this gone, all things became inflamed, my head, my blood, my nerves, my flesh, my bones, and then I burned with the real fire of hell, which caused me torments in my joints, and an incredible, intolerable, tearing voluptuousness which loosened the bonds of my life. The tresses of this demon, which enveloped my poor body, poured upon me a stream of flame, and I felt each lock like a bar of red iron. During this mortal delectation I saw the ardent face of the said Succubus, who laughed and addressed to me a thousand exciting words; such as that I was her knight, her lord, her lance, her day, her joy, her hero, her life, her good, her rider, and that she would like to clasp me even closer, wishing to be in my skin or have me in hers. Hearing which, under the prick of this tongue which sucked out my soul, I plunged and precipitated myself finally into hell without finding the bottom. And then when I had no more a drop of blood in my veins, when my heart no longer beat in my body, and I was ruined at all points, the demon, still fresh, white, rubicund, glowing, and laughing, said to me—

"'Poor fool, to think me a demon! Had I asked thee to sell thy soul for a kiss, wouldst thou not give it to me with all thy heart?'

"'Yes,' said I.

"'And if always to act thus it were necessary for thee to nourish thyself with the blood of new-born children in order always to have new life to spend in my arms, would you not imbibe it willingly?'

"'Yes,' said I.

"'And to be always my gallant horseman, gay as a man in his prime, feeling life, drinking pleasure, plunging to the depths of joy as a swimmer into the Loire, wouldst thou not deny God, wouldst thou not spit in the face of Jesus?'

"'Yes,' said I.

"Then I felt a hundred sharp claws which tore my diaphragm as if the beaks of a thousand birds there took their bellyfuls, shrieking. Then I was lifted suddenly above the earth upon the said Succubus, who had spread her wings, and cried to me—

"'Ride, ride, my gallant rider! Hold yourself firmly on the back of thy mule, by her mane, by her neck; and ride, ride, my gallant rider—everything rides!' And then I saw, as a thick fog, the cities of the earth, where by a special gift I perceived each one coupled with a female demon, and tossing about, and engendering in great concupiscence, all shrieking a thousand words of love and exclamations of all kinds, and all toiling away with ecstasy. Then my horse with the Moorish head pointed out to me, still flying and galloping beyond the clouds, the earth coupled with the sun in a conjunction, from which proceeded a germ of stars, and there each female world was embracing a male world; but in place of the words used by creatures, the worlds were giving forth the howls of tempests, throwing up lightnings and crying thunders. Then still rising, I saw overhead the female nature of all things in love with the Prince of Movement. Now, by way of mockery, the Succubus placed me in the centre of this horrible and perpetual conflict, where I was lost as a grain of sand in the sea. Then still cried my white mare to me, 'Ride, ride my gallant rider—all things ride!' Now, thinking how little was a priest in this torment of the seed of worlds, nature always clasped together, and metals, stones, waters, airs, thunders, fish, plants, animals, men, spirits, worlds and planets, all embracing with rage, I denied the Catholic faith. Then the Succubus, pointing out to me the great patch of stars seen in heavens, said to me, 'That way is a drop of celestial seed escaped from great flow of the worlds in conjunction.' Thereupon I instantly clasped the Succubus with passion by the light of a thousand million of stars, and I wished in clasping her to feel the nature of those thousand million creatures. Then by this great effort of love I fell impotent in every way, and heard a great infernal laugh. Then I found myself in my bed, surrounded by my servitors, who had had the courage to struggle with the demon, throwing into the bed where I was stretched a basin full of holy water, and saying fervent prayers to God. Then had I to sustain, in spite of this assistance, a horrible combat with the said Succubus, whose claws still clutched my heart, causing me infinite pains; still, while reanimated by the voice of my servitors, relations, and friends, I tried to make the sacred sign of the cross; the Succubus perched on my bed, on the bolster, at the foot, everywhere, occupying herself in distracting my nerves, laughing, grimacing, putting before my eyes a thousand obscene images, and causing me a thousand wicked desires. Nevertheless, taking pity on me, my lord the Archbishop caused the relics of St. Gatien to be brought, and the moment the shrine had touched my bed the said

Succubus was obliged to depart, leaving an odour of sulphur and of hell, which made the throats of my servants, friends, and others sore for a whole day. Then the celestial light of God having enlightened my soul, I knew I was, through my sins and my combat with the evil spirit, in great danger of dying. Then did I implore the especial mercy, to live just a little time to render glory to God and his Church, objecting the infinite merits of Jesus dead upon the cross for the salvation of the Christians. By this prayer I obtained the favour of recovering sufficient strength to accuse myself of my sins, and to beg of the members of the Church of St. Maurice their aid and assistance to deliver me from purgatory, where I am about to atone for my faults by infinite agonies. Finally, I declare that my proclamation, wherein the said demon appeals the judgment of God by the ordeals of holy water and a fire, is a subterfuge due to an evil design suggested by the said demon, who would thus have had the power to escape the justice of the tribunal of the Archbishop and of the Chapter, seeing that she secretly confessed to me, to be able to make another demon accustomed to the ordeal appear in her place. And, in conclusion, I give and bequeath to the Chapter of the Church of St. Maurice my property of all kinds, to found a chapter in the said church, to build it and adorn it and put it under the invocation of St. Hierome and St. Gatien, of whom one is my patron and the other the saviour of my soul."

This, heard by all the company, has been brought to the notice of the ecclesiastical tribunal by Jehan de la Haye (Johannes de Haga).

We, Jehan de la Haye (Johannes de Haga), elected grand penitentiary of St. Maurice by the general assembly of the Chapter, according to the usage and custom of that church, and appointed to pursue afresh the trial of the demon Succubus, at present in the jail of the Chapter, have ordered a new inquest, at which will be heard all those of this diocese having cognisance of the facts relative thereto. We declared void the other proceedings, interrogations, and decrees, and annul them in the name of the members of the Church in general, and sovereign Chapter assembled, and declare that the appeal to God, traitorously made by the demon, shall not take place, in consequence of the notorious treachery of the devil in this affair. And the said judgment shall be cried by sound of trumpet in all parts of the diocese in which have been published the false edicts of the preceding month, all notoriously due to the instigation of the demon, according to the confession of the late Hierome Cornille.

Let all good Christians be of assistance to our Holy Church, and to her commandments.

JEHAN DE LA HAYE.

IV
How the Moorish Woman of the Rue Chaude Twisted About so Briskly that with Great Difficulty was she Burned and Cooked Alive, to the Great Loss of the Infernal Regions

This was written in the month of May, of the year 1360, after the manner of a testament.

"My very dear and well-beloved son, when it shall be lawful for thee to read this I shall be, I thy father, reposing in the tomb, imploring thy prayers, and supplicating thee to conduct thyself in life as it will be commanded thee in this rescript, bequeathed for the good government of thy family, thy future, and safety; for I have done this at a period when I had my senses and understanding, still recently affected by the sovereign injustice of men. In my virile age I had a great ambition to raise myself in the Church, and therein to obtain the highest dignities, because no life appeared to me more splendid. Now with this earnest idea, I learned to read and write, and with great trouble became in a fit condition to enter the clergy. But because I had no protection, or good advice to superintend my training I had an idea of becoming the writer, tabellion, and rubrican of the Chapter of St. Maurice, in which were the highest and richest personages of Christendom, since the King of France is only therein a simple canon. Now there I should be able better than anywhere else to find services to render to certain lords, and thus to find a master or gain patronage, and by this assistance enter into religion, and be mitred and ensconced in an archiepiscopal chair, somewhere or other. But this first vision was over credulous, and a little too ambitious, the which God caused me clearly to perceive by the sequel. In fact, Messire Jepan de Villedomer, who afterwards became cardinal, was given this appointment, and I was rejected, discomfited. Now in this unhappy hour I received an alleviation of my troubles, by the advice of the good old Hierome Cornille, of whom

I have often spoken to you. This dear man induced me, by his kindness, to become penman to the Chapter of St. Maurice and the Archbishop of Tours, the which offer I accepted with joy, since I was reputed a scrivener. At the time I was about to enter into the presbytery commenced the famous process against the devil of the Rue Chaude, of which the old folk still talk, and which in its time, has been recounted in every home in France. Now, believing that it would be of great advantage to my ambition, and that for this assistance the Chapter would raise me to some dignity, my good master had me appointed for the purpose of writing all of that should be in this grave cause, subject to writing. At the very outset Monseigneur Hierome Cornille, a man approaching eighty years, of great sense, justice, and sound understanding, suspected some spitefulness in this cause, although he was not partial to immodest girls, and had never been involved with a woman in his life, and was holy and venerable, with a sanctity which had caused him to be selected as a judge, all this not withstanding. As soon as the depositions were completed, and the poor wench heard, it remained clear that although this merry doxy had broken her religious vows, she was innocent of all devilry, and that her great wealth was coveted by her enemies, and other persons, whom I must not name to thee for reasons of prudence. At this time every one believed her to be so well furnished with silver and gold that she could have bought the whole county of Touraine, if so it had pleased her. A thousand falsehoods and calumnious words concerning the girl, envied by all the honest women, were circulated and believed in as gospel. At this period Master Hierome Cornille, having ascertained that no demon other than that of love was in the girl, made her consent to remain in a convent for the remainder of her days. And having ascertained certain noble knights brave in war and rich in domains, that they would do everything to save her, he invited her secretly to demand of her accusers the judgment of God, at the same time giving her goods to the chapter, in order to silence mischievous tongues. By this means would be saved from the stake the most delicate flower that ever heaven has allowed to fall upon our earth; the which flower yielded only from excessive tenderness and amiability to the malady of love, cast by her eyes into the hearts of all her pursuers. But the real devil, under the form of a monk, mixed himself up in this affair; in this wise: great enemy of the virtue, wisdom, and sanctity of Monsignor Hierome Cornille, named Jehan de la Haye, having learned that in the jail, the poor girl was treated like a queen, wickedly accused the grand penitentiary of connivance with her and of being her servitor, because, said this wicked priest, she makes him young, amorous, and happy, from which the poor old man died of grief in one day, knowing by this that Jehan de la Haye had worn his ruin and coveted his dignities. In fact, our lord the archbishop visited the jail, and found the Moorish woman in a pleasant place, reposing comfortably, and without irons, because, having placed a diamond in a place when none could have believed she could have held it, she had purchased the clemency of her jailer. At the time certain persons said that this jailer was smitten with her, and that from love, or perhaps in great fear of the young barons, lovers of this woman, he had planned her escape. The good man Cornille being at the point of death, through the treachery of Jehan de la Haye, the Chapter thinking it necessary to make null and void the proceedings taken by the penitentiary, and also his decrees, the said Jehan de la Haye, at that time a simple vicar of the cathedral, pointed out that to do this it would be sufficient to obtain a public confession from the good man on his death-bed. Then was the moribund tortured and tormented by the gentleman of the Chapter, those of Saint Martin, those of Marmoustiers, by the archbishop and also by the Pope's legate, in order that he might recant to the advantage of the Church, to which the good man would not consent. But after a thousand ills, the public confession was prepared, at which the most noteworthy people of the town assisted, and the which spread more horror and consternation than I can describe. The churches of the diocese held public prayers for this calamity, and every one expected to see the devil tumble into his house by the chimney. But the truth of it is that the good Master Hierome had a fever, and saw cows in his room, and then was this recantation obtained of him. The access passed, the poor saint wept copiously on learning this trick from me. In fact, he died in my arms, assisted by his physicians, heartbroken at this mummery, telling us that he was going to the feet of God to pray to prevent the consummation of this deplorable iniquity. The poor Moorish woman had touched him much by her tears and repentance, seeing that before making her demand for the judgment of God he had minutely confessed her, and by that means had disentangled the soul divine which was in the body, and of which he spoke as of a diamond worthy of adorning the holy crown of God, when she should have departed this life, after repenting her sins. Then, my dear son, knowing by the statements made in the town, and by the naïve responses of this unhappy wretch, all the trickery of this affair, I determined by the advice of Master Francois de Hangest, physician of the chapter, to feign an illness and quit the service of the Church of St. Maurice and of the archbishopric, in order not to dip my hands in the innocent blood, which still cries and will continue to cry aloud unto God until the day of the last judgment. Then was the jailer dismissed, and in his place was put the second son of the torturer, who threw the Moorish woman into a dungeon, and inhumanly put upon her hands and feet chains weighing fifty pounds, besides a wooden waistband; and the jail were watched by the crossbowmen of the town and the people of the archbishop. The wench was tormented and tortured, and her bones were broken; conquered by sorrow, she made an avowal according to the wishes of Jehan de la Haye, and was instantly condemned to be burned in the enclosure of St. Etienne, having been previously placed in the portals of the church, attired in a chemise of sulphur, and her goods given over to the Chapter, *et cetera.* This order was the cause of great disturbances and fighting in the town, because three young knights of Touraine swore to die in the service of the poor girl, and to deliver her in all possible ways. Then they came into the town, accompanied by thousands of sufferers, labouring people, old soldiers, warriors, courtesans, and others, whom the said girls had succoured, saved from misfortune, from hunger and misery, and searched all the poor dwellings of the town where lay those to whom she had done good. Thus all were stirred up and called together to the plain of Mount-Louis under the protection of the soldiers of the said lords; they had for companions all the scape-graces of the said twenty leagues around, and came one morning to lay siege to the prison of the archbishop, demanding that the Moorish woman should be given up to them as though they would put her to death, but in fact to set her free, and to place her secretly upon a swift horse, that she might gain the open country, seeing that she rode like a groom. Then in this frightful tempest of men have we seen between the battlements of the archiepiscopal palace and the bridges, more than ten thousand men swarming, besides those who were perched upon the roofs of the houses and climbing on all the balconies to see the sedition; in short it was easy to hear the horrible cries of the Christians, who were terribly in earnest, and of those who surrounded the jail with the intention of setting the poor girl free, across the Loire, the other side of Saint Symphorien. The suffocation and squeezing of bodies was so great in this immense crowd, bloodthirsty for the poor creature at whose knees they would have fallen had they had the opportunity of seeing her, that seven children, eleven women, and eight citizens were crushed and smashed beyond all recognition, since they were like splodges of mud; in short, so wide open was the great mouth of this popular leviathan, this horrible monster, that the clamour was heard at Montils-les-Tours. All cried 'Death to the Succubus! Throw out the demon! Ha! I'd like a quarter! I'll have her skin! The foot for me, the mane for thee! The head for me! The something for me! Is it red? Shall we see? Will it be grilled? Death to her! death!' Each one had his say. But the cry, 'Largesse to God! Death to the Succubus!' was yelled at the same time by the crowd so hoarsely and so cruelly that one's ears and heart bled therefrom; and the other cries were scarcely heard in the houses. The archbishop decided, in order to calm this storm which threatened to overthrow everything, to come out with great pomp from the church, bearing the host, which would deliver the Chapter from ruin, since the wicked young men and the lords had sworn to destroy and burn the cloisters and all the canons. Now by this stratagem the crowd was obliged to break up, and from lack of provisions return to their houses. Then the monks of Touraine, the lords, and the citizens, in great apprehension of pillage on the morrow, held a nocturnal council, and accepted the advice of the Chapter. By their efforts the men-at-arms, archers, knights, and citizens, in a large number, kept watch, and killed a party of shepherds, road menders, and vagrants, who, knowing the disturbed state of Tours, came to swell the ranks of the malcontents. The Sire Harduin de Maille, an old nobleman, reasoned with the young knights, who were the champions of the Moorish woman, and argued sagely with them, asking them if for so small a woman they wished to put Touraine to fire and sword; that even if they were victorious they would be masters of the bad characters brought together by them; that these said freebooters, after having sacked the castles of their enemies, would turn to those of their chiefs. That the rebellion commenced had had no success in the first attack, because up to that time the place was untouched, could they have any over the church, which would invoke the aid of the king? And a thousand other arguments. To these reasons the young knights replied, that it was easy for the Chapter to aid the girl's escape in the night, and that thus the cause of the sedition would be removed. To this humane and wise requests replied Monseigneur de Censoris, the Pope's legate, that it was necessary that strength should remain with the religion of the Church. And thereupon the poor wench paid for all, since it was agreed that no inquiry should be made concerning this sedition.

"Then the Chapter had full licence to proceed to the penance of the girl, to which act and ecclesiastical ceremony the people came from twelve leagues around. So that on the day when, after divine satisfaction, the Succubus was to be delivered up to secular justice, in order to be publicly burnt at a stake, not for a gold pound would a lord or even an abbot have been found lodging in the town of Tours. The night before many camped outside the town in tents, or slept upon straw. Provisions were lacking, and many who came with their bellies full, returned with their bellies empty, having seen nothing but the reflection of the fire in the distance. And the bad characters did good strokes of business by the way.

"The poor courtesan was half dead; her hair had whitened. She was, to tell the truth, nothing but a skeleton, scarcely covered with flesh, and her chains weighed more than she did. If she had had joy in her life, she paid dearly for it at this moment. Those who saw her pass say that she wept and shrieked in a way that should have earned the pity of her hardest pursuers; and in the church there were compelled to put a piece of wood in her mouth, which she bit as a lizard bites a stick. Then the executioner tied her to a stake to sustain her, since she let herself roll at times and fell for want of strength. Then she suddenly recovered a vigorous handful, because, this notwithstanding, she was able, it is said to break her cords and escape into the church, where in remembrance of her old vocation, she climbed quickly into galleries above, flying like a bird along the little columns and small friezes. She was about to escape on to the roof when a soldier perceived her, and thrust his spear in the sole of her foot. In spite of her foot half cut through, the poor girl still ran along the church without noticing it, going along with her bones broken and her blood gushing out, so great fear had she of the flames of the stake. At last she was taken and bound, thrown into a tumbrel and led to the stake, without being afterwards heard to utter a cry. The account of her flight in the church assisted in making the common people believe that she was the devil, and some of them said that she had flown in the air. As soon as the executioner of the town threw her into the flames, she made two or three horrible leaps and fell down into the bottom of the pile, which burned day and night. On the following evening I went to see if anything remained of this gentle girl, so sweet, so loving, but I found nothing but a fragment of the 'os stomachal,' in which, is spite of this, there still remained some moisture, and which some say still trembled like a woman does in the same place. It is impossible to tell, my dear son, the sadnesses, without number and without equal, which for about ten years weighed upon me; always was I thinking of this angel burnt by wicked men, and always I beheld her with her eyes full of love. In short the supernatural gifts of this artless child were shining day and night before me, and I prayed for her in the church, where she had been martyred. At length I had neither the strength nor the courage to look without trembling upon the grand penitentiary Jehan de la Haye, who died eaten up by lice. Leprosy was his punishment. Fire burned his house and his wife; and all those who had a hand in the burning had their own hands singed.

"This, my well-beloved son, was the cause of a thousand ideas, which I have here put into writing to be forever the rule of conduct in our family.

"I quitted the service of the church, and espoused your mother, from whom I received infinite blessings, and with whom I shared my life, my goods, my soul, and all. And she agreed with me in following precepts—

Firstly, that to live happily, it is necessary to keep far away from church people, to honour them much without giving them leave to enter your house, any more than to those who by right, just or unjust, are supposed to be superior to us. Secondly, to take a modest condition, and to keep oneself in it without wishing to appear in any way rich. To have a care to excite no envy, nor strike any onesoever in any manner, because it is needful to be as strong as an oak, which kills the plants at its feet, to crush envious heads, and even then would one succumb, since human oaks are especially rare and that no Tournebouche should flatter himself that he is one, granting that he be a Tournebouche. Thirdly, never to spend more than one quarter of one's income, conceal one's wealth, hide one's goods and chattels, to undertake no office, to go to church like other people, and always keep one's thoughts to oneself, seeing that they belong to you and not to others, who twist them about, turn them after their own fashion, and make calumnies therefrom. Fourthly, always to remain in the condition of the Tournebouches, who are now and forever drapers. To marry your daughters to good drapers, send your sons to be drapers in other towns of France furnished with these wise precepts, and to bring them up to the honour of drapery, and without leaving any dream of ambition in their minds. A draper like a Tournebouche should be their glory, their arms, their name, their motto, their life. Thus by being always drapers, they will be always Tournebouches, and rub on like the good little insects, who, once lodged in the beam, made their dens, and go on with security to the end of their ball of thread. Fifthly never to speak any other language than that of drapery, and never to dispute concerning religion or government. And even though the government of the state, the province, religion, and God turn about, or have a fancy to go to the right or to the left, always in your quality of Tournebouche, stick to your cloth. Thus unnoticed by the others of the town, the Tournebouches will live in peace with their little Tournebouches—paying the tithes and taxes, and all that they are required by force to give, be it to God, or to the king, to the town of to the parish, with all of whom it is unwise to struggle. Also it is necessary to keep the patrimonial treasure, to have peace and to buy peace, never to owe anything, to have corn in the house, and enjoy yourselves with the doors and windows shut.

"By this means none will take from the Tournebouches, neither the state, nor the Church, nor the Lords, to whom should the case be that force is employed, you will lend a few crowns without cherishing the idea of ever seeing him again—I mean the crowns.

"Thus, in all seasons people will love the Tournebouches, will mock the Tournebouches as poor people—as the slow Tournebouches, as Tournebouches of no understanding. Let the know-nothings say on. The Tournebouches will neither be burned nor hanged, to the advantage of King or Church, or other people; and the wise Tournebouches will have secretly money in their pockets, and joy in their houses, hidden from all.

"Now, my dear son, follow this the counsel of a modest and middle-class life. Maintain this in thy family as a county charter; and when you die, let your successor maintain it as the sacred gospel of the Tournebouches, until God wills it that there be no longer Tournebouches in this world."

This letter has been found at the time of the inventory made in the house of François Tournebouche, lord of Veretz, chancellor to Monseigneur the Dauphin, and condemned at the time of the rebellion of the said lord against the King to lose his head, and have all his goods confiscated by order of the Parliament of Paris. The said letter has been handed to the Governor of Touraine as an historical curiosity, and joined to the pieces of the process in the archbishopric of Tours, by me, Pierre Gaultier, Sheriff, President of the Trades Council.

The author having finished the transcription and deciphering of these parchments, translating them from their strange language into French, the donor of them declared that the Rue Chaude at Tours was so called, according to certain people, because the sun remained there longer than in all other parts. But in spite of this version, people of lofty understanding will find, in the warm way of the said Succubus, the real origin of the said name. In which acquiesces the author. This teaches us not to abuse our body, but use it wisely in view of our salvation.

Excerpt from *The Alukam*
Jacob Thomson

This excerpt consists of Chapters 25 and 26 of *The Alukam*, Jacob Thomson's curious vampire/police procedural/ kabalistic novel (Riverdale edition published 2004, ISBN: 978-1-932606-02-7). The novel covers a wide time span, from the "death" of the vampire, Itzak ben Nossan Sh'muel (later Isaac Nathanson), in a Jewish ghetto in 1684 Poland, to the main action in 1993 Florida. The portion in this excerpt is a flashback to 1891 Baltimore and concludes in 1993. One might note that it contains a lot less sex than several other chapters.

Friday, November 6, 1891
Baltimore, Maryland

Karl Lager, as Itzak was now calling himself, was getting desperate. A chain of circumstances had frustrated him for nearly two weeks, preventing even a light feeding.

Now he had his chance. He'd found the girl walking along a main street less than ten minutes earlier. The location was fortuitous. His house was no more than five minutes away, and it was now 4:00 in the afternoon, which meant that the sun would be setting in exactly one hour. On a Friday afternoon, that meant he had only an hour until he would have to return to his coffin, hidden beneath the coal cellar of his house, for his Sabbath rest. It didn't give him a lot of time, but it gave him enough.

The girl was a prostitute. She'd made that more than obvious from the moment he first saw her. Lager had no moral qualms about her profession; to him, she was just a source of nourishment. If she presented a public health threat, it was only to her "living" customers. The diseases of the living didn't pass with the blood—or, if they did, they didn't affect him.

She was a plain-looking girl, probably no more than 20, garbed in a

161

plum velvet dress that, on someone of better quality, would have been striking. On her it merely looked cheap. He had long ago come to recognize
that it wasn't so much what someone wore, as it was the *way* they wore it.
This girl carried herself like a prostitute, and her expression was that of a
wanton. At least, it contrived to be. Lager had no doubt that her actual feeling for her profession was one of disgust.

The doctors and clergymen all said that prostitutes were driven to their
trade by their personalities. That they were all nymphomaniacs. Lager, who
had much more experience of prostitutes than even the most profligate
physician or vicar—and who also had the advantage of being able to read
their thoughts as he drained their blood—recognized that the main im-
petus toward that profession was nothing more than simple poverty. They
didn't seek constant sexual release because of some pathological inability
to take any real pleasure in the sex act. It was simply a way to make money.

In the society of 1891 America—and most other places—there was
little honest work available to an illiterate girl, and if she didn't quickly find
a husband, about all that was left for her was to sell her body on the street,
or in one of the many houses the city fathers were so careful to pretend
didn't exist, even as they pocketed the bribes of the madams and pimps.

But just now, Lager thought, there was no time to take the girl back
to his house. With the sun going down in an hour, he wouldn't have time
to drain her and dispose of her body before the Sabbath arrived and he
lapsed into his weekly stasis. If he killed her at home, it was possible that her
body would begin to smell before he could wake up and get rid of it. And
that sort of thing invited official attention.

He noticed a narrow alley and guided her into it. She was smiling. Why
not? He had offered her five dollars to go with him—a fortune to a girl
like this, who could live for a week or more on that sum. And she had no
reason to suspect that he wanted anything different from her usual clients.
He was dressed like a gentleman, and the girl presumed that gentlemen
were simply more willing to pay a proper fee for their pleasure than the
working-class clientele who usually made up her trade.

They went back into the alley about 30 feet. "This will do fine," Lager
said.

"What?" the girl asked, with a slight laugh. "You'll be havin' me up
against the side o' the buildin', will you?"

"It's convenient."

"Well, sure, it is that."

"What do you call yourself, by the way?" he asked.

"Eileen Murphy."

Irish, he thought. Hardly a surprise in Baltimore, which had started as
a Catholic colony in the first place, and continued to attract Catholic im-

migrants at a greater rate than any city south of New York.

"Well, Eileen," he said, "if you don't mind, I think we should get on with it, eh?"

"Sure." She leaned back against the brick wall of the building, letting him unbutton the front of her dress and pull it open, so that her breasts were exposed to his view. With a calculatingly wanton smile, she pulled up her skirt and petticoats. Except for her cotton stockings, she wore nothing underneath.

She had done the same sort of thing a hundred times before. Usually for other unfortunates, who didn't have the money to pay for her *and* a room. This would be the first time with an obvious gentleman, though.

At the moment he was just looking at her. Smiling. Then he laughed softly, and she was astonished to notice the length of the sharp, canine teeth. How had she failed to see those, she wondered. He'd smiled before and his teeth had seemed entirely normal.

Then she looked up at his eyes, and found herself unable to move. His head lowered, tilting to one side, and there was a momentary pain in her neck. Her hands opened, letting her skirt drop back into place. Her body, being rapidly drained of its blood, was moving involuntarily in the familiar sexual rhythms. There was no pain. Only the trembling warmth of the climax she had often simulated, but had never actually felt until now.

His hands were on her breasts, massaging them, the nipples tingling with released passions. Her mind was flashing on a scene from the book her friend Mary had been reading to her. The image of the Transylvanian Count, which she had found curiously erotic at the same time it horrified her.

But that was fiction, and this was reality. Intellectually, she knew that she was dying, yet her body was trembling with weird spasms of pleasure.

And was she now being doomed to roam the night as an undead creature, preying on the blood of the innocent, as the author of that book had suggested?

Creature of the *night?* It was still daylight. And she had been standing in the full afternoon sunlight when this man approached her. Could that book have been wrong about that, she wondered?

There was a final spasm of supreme pleasure, and then she went limp in his arms.

Lager sucked out the final ounces of blood and let her body fall to the brick pavement. And as he turned to leave the alley he heard a shout, followed immediately by a gunshot and a stinging slap against his left arm.

And it was then that he realized he'd taken too long with the girl. In the Jewish section of Baltimore, housewives were beginning to light their Sabbath candles.

In another twenty minutes it would be sunset. Time enough to get home, he thought—if two cops weren't in the way.

He rushed at them, and the bigger one rapped him on the side of the head with his nightstick. Both of them fell on top of him, and in a moment there were handcuffs on his wrists. With the Sabbath about to begin, Lager lacked the strength to fight back.

At any other time, he could have simply brushed them aside like insects. The gunshot in his arm was meaningless. With a vampire's exaggerated healing capacities, the wound would close up completely in only a few hours. But now his strength was draining away as the sun neared the horizon. The alley was already in deep shadow.

♦   ♦   ♦

"What have you got?" the desk sergeant asked.

"A lunatic, I think," the cop said. "Killed a girl in the alley around the corner. Ripped her throat out with his teeth, from the look of her."

"In there." The sergeant pointed to an iron cage in the corner of the room, which served as a holding cell until a prisoner could be interrogated, or until they could think of what to do with him. This one, the sergeant thought, would probably go to the asylum. From what the arresting officers were telling him, the man was clearly insane.

Lager, already weak with the approaching sunset, was thrust into the holding cell and staggered to the bunk, flopping onto the horsehair-stuffed mattress.

And that was where the Sabbath found him, on the metal-framed bunk in the holding cell. At precisely 5:00 PM, as the sun vanished to the west of the city, the link between body and spirit was severed. His spirit would rise to its Sabbath rest and its longed-for—yet curiously terrifying —taste of the world to come. His body would seem, to any who encountered it, to be exactly what it had been since 1684.

Dead.

Vaguely, he had looked on, watching what was happening in a detached way. His spirit, which on the Sabbath was vividly conscious of the horror Itzak had become, actually felt a stirring of hope as the desk sergeant summoned a doctor. Perhaps they would find a way to destroy his body and thus release his spirit to return to its maker?

"He's dead," the doctor said. "No heartbeat and no respiration." Had he encountered Lager when he was up and walking about, there would *also* have been no heartbeat or respiration, unless Lager consciously willed it, but the doctor had no way of knowing that. Even if he'd been told, he wouldn't have believed it. You simply expected that anyone who was moving about was breathing, which meant that when they weren't you would put it down to an illusion of some sort—perhaps created by loose fitting clothing.

Dracula had been published only three years earlier, and the doctor had read it. But the doctor was a modern, up-to-date scientist. The fact that he knew less about medicine that a First Class Boy Scout would know a hundred years later didn't bother him at all; his medical knowledge was state-of-the-art for his own time.

And he was certainly knowledgeable enough to know that people who didn't breath, and whose hearts were no longer beating, were obviously dead. Vampires were a Central European myth. So even the description of this man's crime wasn't sufficient to alert him to the truth.

Besides, he suffered from the same prejudices as Eileen Murphy. His knowledge of vampires was limited to fiction, and fictional vampires didn't walk around in the daylight, or drop dead in jail cells.

"He's been shot," the doctor added.

"Ryan did that," the sergeant said. "Couldn't have killed him, though. Look at the wound—it didn't even bleed."

The doctor nodded. "So I see. Something killed him, though. Send him around to the morgue. And see if you can find out who he was—he may have a family."

♦   ♦   ♦

Autopsy procedures in 1891 were essentially the same as those in 1993. Lager's body was laid out on a steel table—this one coated with white porcelain—and the doctor took his measurements. These were different from those that would be taken a few years later, since the Baltimore police were still using the Bertillion system, which employed precise measurements to identify individuals. They were also taken in inches, pounds, and ounces, instead of millimeters, kilos, and grams.

Bertillion, a Frenchman, had decided that, if you took enough measurements, in a sufficiently precise manner, no two people would have exactly the same set of measurements. He was proven wrong within a few years, but by then Scotland Yard's fingerprint identification system had come into general use, and the old system passed with little notice, except by writers, who continued to use Bertillion's system of "types"—criminals had more prominent brow ridges than honest people, and smaller eyes, according to the good professor—in their character descriptions.

Once the body had been measured, it was washed down, and the doctor took a large scalpel and made the standard "Y" incision. The whole process took less than an hour, and when he was finished the doctor still had no idea what had killed the prisoner.

Having arrived at that non-conclusion, the doctor replaced the internal organs in the body cavity, paying absolutely no attention to their original location, and sewed up the long incisions with coarse, running stitches.

About the only conclusion he had drawn was that the man had probably been Jewish, and he'd figured that out before he ever picked up his scalpel. Clinical circumcision was still extremely rare at that time, so if you found someone who had been circumcised, he was probably a Jew.

Wednesday, September 15, 1993
Port Morrow Beach

The healing process, Nathanson remembered, had taken five weeks. All of those jumbled-up organs to be sorted out and put back in their proper place; the gross tissue damage inflicted during the course of the autopsy to heal. It all complicated and slowed the healing.

One of his neighbors had identified his body, and he had been buried in a small Jewish cemetery. When he finally rose from his coffin at the end of the fifth week, he made a fast kill to build up his strength and then put in an appearance at the police station, where he informed the desk sergeant that he was Emil Lager, Karl's twin brother, who had just learned what had happened and come down from New York to claim his brother's effects.

The sergeant took one look at him and turned him over to the captain. Since it never occurred to either of them that the "twins" were actually the same man, the formalities were observed and the property released.

"Will you be staying in Baltimore, Mr. Lager?" the captain asked, after the papers were duly signed and witnessed.

"I don't believe so. My brother was killed here, after all."

"Your brother, I'm afraid, wasn't quite a model citizen. He was captured in the act of murdering a young woman, and we have reason to believe he may have killed five others in the same way."

"Worse than I thought," Lager said, smiling inwardly. They were still unaware of the other two, it seemed. "We always did have problems with Karl," he went on. "He would do things to animals—no one ever understood why. But no one in the family ever expected it to end *this* way."

The captain nodded. He'd heard the same sort of thing said by parents, siblings, spouses, and even friends of countless other criminals. No one *ever* expected them to turn out that way—but they did. "So, you'll be going back to New York, then?"

"That's right," Lager said. "New York."

A day later, after making the arrangements to have his property packed up and shipped to a warehouse in New York, Lager boarded the train and left Baltimore.

He would return, but not before the 1930s.

But he wasn't about to let that sort of thing happen to him today. It wasn't that he really feared 'dropping dead' in a jail cell when the Sabbath arrived. Or even the mutilation of another autopsy. They could chop him into little pieces, and as long as they all wound up in the same box his body would reassemble itself. Probably, he thought, it would even regenerate a few missing pieces.

But today, he feared, whatever was left after the autopsy would probably be cremated. And he wasn't sure that even *he* could recover from that. Even worse, he was just a little afraid that he *would*. If God could restore the bodies of those who had been buried for centuries to their normal condition—and Nathanson, better than most, knew that this was not only possible, but would eventually happen—what was to stop Him from reconstituting Nathanson's cremated body for further earthly punishment?

Memoir
J.T. McDaniel

I had a different name when I was young. My parents named me Septimus Morenus Altimanus. Septimus, which means seventh, suggests to me that, like many Romans, they simply got tired of thinking up names for their children and started numbering them instead. We were Marcus, Horatius, Drusilla, Brutus, Quintus, Sextus, Septimus, and Octavius, so the first four, including my sister, had real names and the rest of us were numbered.

I was born on the fifth day of October, in what would now be considered 72 BCE, in Herculaneum. On today's calendar that would be August fifth, as this was before Julius and Augustus Cæsar inserted themselves into the calendar, shifting the last four months further back. Given that the last four were numbered, confusion has reigned ever since. This is how it happens that the twelfth month in the year, December, means "tenth month." You probably found this sort of thing annoying in Latin class, presuming you took it.

I did, of course, but when I was born that's what we spoke, so it was a lot easier. There was no translating to worry about, for one thing. I *did* have to study Greek, but we also commonly spoke that. We Romans were something like the Russians of the early 19th Century. Just as they found it somehow more fashionable to speak French in society rather than their own language, so educated Romans made a point of speaking Greek.

Because I was seventh born, and the sixth son of a remarkably healthy family, there was little chance that I would ever inherit more than the few personal items my father might wish me to have. The bulk of the estate would go to my brother Marcus. It was therefore decided that I would go into the army.

My father was a senator, which gave him a certain amount of interest. By the time I was 20 I had been commissioned as centurion, and placed in command of a century in the 14th Legion. The name suggests that I commanded 100 troops, but it was actually 80 combat troops, and another 20 administrative types. Even then the number of non-combatants needed to support the actual fighters was growing.

In the Spring of 47 BCE our legion was sent into Thrace to put down a rebellion. That was when things changed, in the midst of a small battle involving only my own century against a little band of Thracian infantry. During the fight I was wounded by a spear thrust to my right thigh.

It was not, in itself, a serious wound. The iron point didn't so much penetrate as slice, laying open the skin for a length of perhaps two inches, and only slightly damaging the muscle beneath. But there was always a danger of infection in those days, long before anyone had ever heard of antibiotics. Within a few days the wound began to fester.

That was when Meskhenet appeared. She was one of the women who followed in the wake of our army. No one was entirely sure of where she came from, though her name was clearly Egyptian. There was even a question of why she was there. She wasn't a prostitute, nor was she a cook, or a laundress. Sometimes she would sit with the injured, and sometimes they would get well and sometimes they wouldn't. Perhaps two of ten whom she watched over would be healed, and if that does not sound particularly impressive, remember that most physicians did little better and many did less well.

The first time she came into my tent she ejected everyone else, sat by my cot, took my hand in hers, and told me that she could certainly heal me, and even save my infected leg—which our physician wanted to cut off—but that there would be a price.

"What price?" I asked. My father was rich, and would certainly pay well to keep any of his children in health.

"Not money," she explained. "My price is more personal."

"In what way?"

"If I heal you, you will be healthy in the future, but you also be different. You will gain not only the few years you might normally expect, but many more as well."

"How many?"

"Perhaps only a few, perhaps hundreds, perhaps thousands."

"What are you, a goddess offering immortality?"

"No. Many would go so far as to call me accursed, even a demon. I am not. In most ways I am quite ordinary, a woman with all the virtues and faults of any other woman, except that I have lived much longer than anyone you have ever known."

She looked to be but little past twenty.

"But you must know that if you are healed, the day will almost surely come when your friends denounce you. When they are old and you are still young. When their children are old and you are still young." She smiled. "And, you must know, you will take no pleasure in the foods you now love, nor will they nourish you. You will live only on blood."

It was a curious idea. Live on blood?

"Human blood?"

"Any blood will nourish—but human *tastes* best."

"You're a vampire?"

She nodded her head. "As I said, I like you, Septimus. It is only because of this that I offer you this chance. It will hurt far less than you think. I will merely take a little of your blood, hardly more than a thimble-full each time. Each day for a fortnight I will do this, and at the end of that time you will be healed, but you will also be as I am, a drinker of blood, a vampire."

The worst part was that I had to make the choice at once. I did not have the option to think about it for a few days, because in a few days the infection would kill me.

"How old are you, exactly?" I asked.

"I was born in Egypt, in the same year that the Israelites departed our country amidst horrendous plagues. I never knew my father, for he was a first born, and so he died shortly before I was born, along with all the others."

I knew enough of this Jewish story to know that it had supposedly happened centuries ago. Was it possible that this girl was truly immortal?

Still, there was not much of a choice. The worst that could happen was that I would die, something the physicians had determined was almost certainly inevitable. It was a choice between possible immortality and death. Not much of a choice, I thought.

I said, "Yes."

There was almost no pain. Meskhenet's canine teeth sank into my shoulder. She made no attempt to puncture an artery; the blood that welled up from the ruptured capillaries in the skin and muscle was sufficient to her purpose. And, as she had said, she returned to my tent each day for the next two weeks, each day taking a little more blood.

And each day the infection in my leg relented, and my health improved. As she had predicted, my hunger for normal foods diminished as my strength returned. I began to crave blood, and this Meskhenet supplied, bringing it to me in a wine bottle. She said that it came from a cow.

In recent years I have concluded that the transmission of vampirism is the result of a virus injected by the bite. It is not a particularly virulent virus, and requires repeated exposure over many days. Once the infection takes hold, aging ceases, and healing ability is accelerated to such a degree that a wound that would normally heal in a month will fully close up and heal, without a scar, in a matter of minutes. I'm still not sure if we are truly immortal, but if we are not our normal life span extends to thousands of years.

Oh, we can be killed, surely, but not easily. Most injuries will heal. Cut off our heads, or burn our bodies to ashes—that will do the job. Shooting us will not, nor will the traditional stake. Only an injury that makes healing impossible will kill us.

Now it developed that my becoming a vampire was not the only price Meskhenet had in mind. Somehow, perhaps from seeing me around the camp, she had fallen in love with me. It seemed that her usual healing practice did not involve conversion of the patient. This she had reserved for me.

And do not let anyone suggest that a vampire cannot make love in the same manner as any other man. We are not dead, and we are not un-dead—whatever that means—we are as alive as any other, perhaps more so. We can see our reflection in a mirror, and the sun does *less* harm to us than to ordinary people, for with our exaggerated healing abilities even the worst sunburn is no more than a momentary discomfort.

By the time my leg wound had fully healed, and I had been fully con-verted into a vampire, Meskhenet was no longer visiting my tent once a day. She had moved into my tent and was sharing my bed.

Well, she was beautiful, very smart, a good companion, and a wonder-ful lover. I think I got the best of the bargain.

But I have not seen her for many years. I feel that she is still alive, though I could not prove it. There was a strong connection born of my conversion, and perhaps a stronger one developed of a marriage—this seems the most appropriate term, even if the union was not blessed by a priest—lasting some 273 years. That's a very long time, and you get to know each other very well. Unfortunately, even perfection eventually pales, and we have long since gone our separate ways, finding others with whom to share a few years. Never again so long, at least for me, for all but one of my partners since Meskhenet have been mortal.

During nearly all of the last two millennia I have followed the profes-sion of arms. Meskhenet was quite right in saying that any blood will nour-ish, but human blood simply tastes best. Battlefields are a reliable source of fresh blood. The donors no longer have any use for it, and the dangers of "dead" blood are nothing more than a literary device. It matters not at all whether the donor is living or dead.

During nearly all of those centuries life has been relatively easy. Be-cause I do not actually have to spend the daylight hours hiding in a cof-fin—I sleep in a bed, like anyone else, and usually at night—I was in little danger from vampire hunters. On occasion, I even joined in the hunt.

♦   ♦   ♦

It was in 1784, in the Austrian province of Styria, where I was then doing service as a captain of infantry. The little village where I was stationed was experiencing an epidemic of vampirism, or so everyone believed. It was *not* me. I was dining regularly, to be sure, but no one was dying of it. As for the epidemic, I believe it was tuberculosis.

But a vampire was suspected, so find it we must. The Bürgermeister, a fat little man dressed in rust-colored broadcloth and sagging woolen stockings, organized a group of men with the intention of doing just that. I was present, with two of my men, ostensibly to provide additional protection for the vampire hunters. From my own point of view, I simply joined them for the entertainment value. I never thought that desecrating a corpse was a good thing, but I recognized that it didn't actually hurt the corpse and, in these cases, while "killing" the so-called "vampire" would do nothing to stop the tubercular infection in the village, it seemed to make the townspeople feel better.

"Do you suspect anyone in this?" I asked the Bürgermeister.

"There have been six who died in the past year," he replied. "It is almost certainly one of them. So we will begin by examining the graves."

Our little party entered the cemetery, going from one new grave to the next, starting with the oldest. The priest, who was supposed to be an expert on vampires, would get down on his hands and knees and closely examine the ground. He had known me for months, so I had to wonder just how perceptive he really was. Today's movies and television shows are quite wrong, we don't have retractable fangs, and we don't change appearance when we're hungry. My canine teeth are significantly longer and sharper than normal, something the priest had apparently never noticed, I suppose because he mostly saw me in his church and it was well known that no vampire could tolerate the presence of the holy, much less take the Eucharist.

"What are you looking for, Father?" I asked.

"Over a vampire's grave," the priest replied, "you will often find several small, deep holes in the ground, about the size of a thumb. He has to get in and out of his grave, you see, and it seems that he can somehow flow up through these holes." He frowned. "But you do not always find them, and if that is the case we shall have to resort to other means."

The priest went back to examining the graves for holes, while my men and I watched. I found it mildly amusing that this priest—in that age a learned man—thought that vampires could somehow turn into liquid or mist and flow up from their graves through holes in the ground. I suppose this was no stranger than the later notion that a 200 pound vampire could somehow transform himself into a two pound bat and then back again. Physics, I suppose, did not constitute a major portion of a theologian's education in those days, and would later simply be ignored by writers of fantastic fiction.

It took perhaps an hour for the priest to concede that none of the suspect graves had the tell-tale holes, so now it was decided that other measures would have to be taken. A thirteen-year-old village boy was brought to the cemetery. Under questioning, the boy attested that he was still a virgin, and had never so much as contemplated indulging in self-abuse, knowing full well the horrible consequences that would certainly ensue. People really believed that back in those days, and were convinced—despite a total lack of any evidence—that such things would lead to physical weakness, insanity, and blindness. Despite which, naturally, everyone did it anyway and simply presumed that *they* were somehow immune from the consequences, but that it was still dangerous for anyone else.

The boy, having no doubt lied about his solitary habits, but probably having been truthful about his virginity, was then mounted on a white stallion. The horse had not yet been put to stud, so here we had a virgin mounted upon another virgin.

Taking the horse by the reins, a man then led it through the cemetery, being careful to lead it across each of the suspect graves in turn. The horse plodded along placidly, to the thorough frustration of the vampire hunters, who expected it to balk at the vampire's grave, the double virginity of the horse and boy—purity mounted upon purity, as it were—was supposed to naturally shy from the evil contained in the grave.

This new device having failed, the Bürgermeister announced that they would have to resort to the hard way and dig up each suspect. Shovels were procured and the men set to work, my troops included. Being their leader, I naturally employed my time in sitting on a bench under a tree chatting with the Bürgermeister, who, also being a leader, was no more inclined to indulge in physical labor than I.

The oldest graves yielded nothing more than a horrible stench and rotting corpses. They found the vampire in the newest, buried little more than two months. The occupant, in life a rather attractive young lady, was now bloated, with blood seeping from her nose and mouth. More blood stained her white garment. There was, really, nothing at all unusual about her corpse, which was simply decomposing, but the priest assured us that these signs clearly pointed to the girl being a vampire.

Under the priest's direction, a wooden stake was driven through the girl's heart, in response to which she emitted a pitiable groan. I am sure this was no more than some remaining air or gases being driven up through her throat by the pressure, but it certainly convinced the vampire hunters that they had found the right body. One of the men then cut off her head with a sexton's shovel and placed it in the bottom of the coffin, between her feet. After that they cut off enough of the stake to allow the coffin to be closed and refilled the grave.

"Now we shall be safe," the priest informed us. "We have released that poor girl from her curse, and perhaps her soul will now return to God, if she has not already been irredeemably damned for her depredations. We can hope, at least."

I doubted that the girl had ever done anything deserving of eternal punishment. Certainly she wasn't a vampire. Quite possibly, she had been in heaven ever since she died, or, equally, when you're dead you're dead and that's all there is. I really have no particular knowledge of what follows life, nor do I expect to gain any such knowledge until my own is over.

In any event, the putative vampire having been vanquished, life returned to normal in the little village. The epidemic ended, not, I am sure, because of the townspeople having mutilated the poor girl's corpse, but because epidemics generally *do* end after a time.

♦   ♦   ♦

The biggest problem in my life is that I do not age. I have now been physically in my early 20s for over 2,000 years. The result was that I could never put down permanent roots in any one place. Eventually the neighbors notice that sort of thing. I had to move about every ten years or so. If I liked a place, I might stretch it to 15 years, but never more than that. And after perhaps 30 years had passed I could return, for then, even if those same neighbors *did* recognize me, the fact that they were now closing in on 60 and I appeared to be about 23 would make my declaration that I was their old neighbor's son seem perfectly logical.

This is becoming more difficult now. Today there is DNA. Today fingerprints are not only a positive identifier, but reside in a computerized database that may yet unintentionally discover that I am not only walking around today, but was also an Armor officer in World War II. Today there are entire government agencies devoted to making sure that everyone is who he claims to be. They are looking for terrorists, which I certainly am not, but I know I would make them more than a little curious if they once noticed me. People are supposed to be born, live for seventy or eighty years, and then drop dead. They're not supposed to just keep on living. That sort of thing makes people nervous. There have been too many stories, movies, television shows, and mostly about predatory vampires. The idea that there might be utterly innocuous vampires doesn't fit the belief system.

I know where I came from, but I can hardly put Herculaneum on an American government form. And it is no longer possible to lay claim to the identity of some poor child who died within days of birth. Today the government matches birth and death certificates to prevent exactly that sort of thing. Today you need to find a way to create an identity from scratch, which is much harder, but can be done if you know enough about computers.

For now, I am known as Sidney Height, and should I put in a request, Pennsylvania's electronic records would spit out a certified birth certificate indicating that I was born in Pittsburgh in 1984. You always pick a large city for this sort of thing. People know each other in small towns. In a large city you can be anonymous. People don't find it at all odd even if several people they know to be from the same city don't know each other. As often as not today, even people who were in the same high school graduating class may never have met.

I rather count on that sort of thing.

One advantage of being a couple thousand years old is that you have plenty of time to accumulate wealth. If you don't have to work you can remain more anonymous. I have a number of bank accounts, scattered across the country, as well as in the usual havens, Switzerland, the Cayman Islands, and so forth. But most of my wealth is in tangible assets, real estate, gold, and particularly diamonds. I also hold a lot of stock, much of it purchased in 1929 when the shares were as cheap as they would ever be, and periodically "inherited" from a previous self.

I try to keep a low profile. It is better not to be noticed, though this doesn't always work.

My current home is isolated, a large brick mansard Victorian set in the middle of a wooded 35 acre plot. It looks a bit like something from Charles Addams, though much better maintained. You reach it by driving back almost half a mile into the woods on a brick-paved driveway, shaded in the summer by big oak trees planted along the drive. In the winter, with the leaves gone, the drive looks a bit more ominous.

I have lived here for twelve years now. The forested setting provides most of my needs. The woods are full of animals, giving me a handy blood supply. I am, and always have been, a fairly skilled hunter.

But it appears I may soon need to move again.

It happened on Saturday. I was in the garage, washing one of my cars, when I heard a vehicle coming up the drive. I wasn't expecting anyone.

The vehicle was soon in view, a beat-up Chevy van, once royal blue, but now faded to some indeterminate color in the bluish family. It stopped in front of the house and five people got out, three girls and two boys, all of them appearing to be about eighteen or nineteen except for one of the girls, who appeared to be in her late twenties.

As they were all carrying pistols, the older girl in her right hand, the others stuck into their belts, I quickly decided that this was not a friendly visit.

They walked quite boldly up to the front door. By this time I had slipped around behind the bushes to where I could observe them. The older girl rang the bell several times. As I had moved around to the front of the house and was watching them from behind a hedge, no one answered. I would not have done so in any case. While not readily visible unless you're looking very carefully, there are cameras covering the doors. The presence of armed people on my porch would have suggested that answering the bell wasn't very prudent.

"No one home," the older girl, who appeared to be the leader, informed her companions, slipping her gun into the waistband of her jeans.

She nodded to one of the boys, flipping her right thumb in the direction of the van. The boy trotted to the vehicle and returned with a crowbar, which he applied to the locked door. I have good locks, but my house isn't exactly a bank vault. He had the door open in a few seconds and the five of them went inside.

It was time, I thought, to interrupt their party. Staying behind the hedge and plantings, I moved around to the side of the house and entered by way of the bulkhead door to the basement. I could hear people walking around upstairs.

The house was built in 1887, by a true eccentric. It was right up to date for the time, and subsequent owners, myself included, have spent a lot of money keeping it that way, at least as far as heat, air conditioning, electricity, and so forth are concerned. The story was that the original builder had been a fan of Gothic fiction and had built the house accordingly—complete with a number of hidden passages inside the walls. These passages were not documented anywhere, so far as I could tell, but I had managed to find all of them in the time I'd lived in the house.

Slipping through a concealed door at the back of what had once been a coal cellar, I passed along a short hall built into the base of a fireplace and climbed a wooden ladder to the main floor. I found myself in a small, windowless room. Another ladder led up to the second floor, and a narrow passage continued toward the rear of the house. A low, square door would allow access into the formal parlor at the front of the house. From the other side the door was invisible, the edges concealed in the vertical beading of the mahogany wainscotting.

I could hear the intruders in the parlor. Near the concealed door, a hot-air register looked into the room. Behind the ornamental brass grillwork a small periscope allowed me to see into the parlor. The leader was seated on the window seat, dispatching the others to the rest of the house to discover what looked good. They had already piled some of my property on the coffee table. I saw none of the true treasures. They had taken some nice watches from my bedroom, and had accumulated a fair stock of jewelry. Yet no one had bothered to take down the small painting that hung on the wall within a few feet of their booty. I have owned that painting for many years, having purchased it from the artist, so it was "unknown" to the art world in general, but I suspect it would bring more than the house and the entire 35-acre estate should I ever decide to sell it. There are no doubt very, very few undiscovered Da Vincis in the world, but this was one of them.

I decided it would be best to start with the boys, who were physically bigger and stronger than the girls. When the leader sent one of them to check out the attic I decided that was a good place to start.

Knowing the hidden passages and stairs far better than the intruders knew the ordinary ones, I was in the attic before the young man arrived. There was plenty for him to look through up there. Not only did it contain things that I had stored, but there were chests, cabinets, and trunks long abandoned by former owners. He was bending over an open steamer trunk, rummaging through the contents, when I slipped up behind him and hit him over the head with an old Indian club.

There was a very satisfying crunch as the heavy club fractured his skull, and he went down instantly, without making a sound beyond the thump of his body across the trunk. I briefly pondered taking the opportunity of a snack, but decided there were more pressing matters to consider. There were still four people in my house who didn't belong there and I wanted them out.

I slipped back into the hidden staircase and went to find the next intruder. I really wanted to take out the two men first. Call it chivalry or something, killing the men first. But none of these people were going to leave the house alive.

I found the other boy in the library. Unfortunately, he caught sight of me in a mirror as I was slipping up on him. Before I could get to him he had his gun out and put a bullet into my side. It didn't hit anything vital—it couldn't, really, and the wound would heal completely in a few minutes—but it made noise, which was something I had been trying to avoid.

He didn't get a chance to take a second shot. One thing the fiction writers got right was the astonishing speed and strength we can muster when needed. Before he could pull the trigger again I was across the room, had torn the gun from his hand, and lifted him right off the floor.

"You picked the wrong house," I said, opening my mouth as wide as I could manage and hissing in my best Christopher Lee imitation.

The effect seemed to work. The kid shrieked and wet his pants as I pulled him down and ripped out his throat with my teeth. I really don't do that sort of thing very often—it's messy, if you must know—but it just seemed appropriate now.

I didn't take the time to do more than sip quickly. Between the noise of the gun and the kid's screaming I figured his friends would be in there before long. I opened the bookcase door and disappeared back into the wall.

A minute later all three girls were in the library, guns in their hands, standing over their dead accomplice.

"What the hell is this?" the blond one demanded.

The older one, already established as the leader, got down on one knee and examined the dead burglar. The look on her face was one of bewilderment, mixed with curiosity. Obviously she had been expecting to pull off a burglary, not to suddenly find herself in the middle of a horror movie. Still, it seemed somehow to affect her less than it did the other two. As if there was something natural about it.

"Something tore his throat out," she said.

That would be me, I thought.

"What would do that?"

"Damned if I know." Her voice sounded odd, as if she thought that perhaps she *did* know, but wasn't quite ready to admit it to herself. She looked around. "Where's Billy?"

Billy, I presumed, was the corpse in the attic. He would not be joining them.

Having decided to keep the mess confined to one room, I slipped out into the hall through another door hidden in the wainscotting and quickly closed and locked the library door. Now I had them trapped, and it was just a matter of figuring out how to dispatch them.

The problem was simply that there were three of them, each armed, and I didn't want to be shot again. Even if they couldn't kill me, being shot was still painful and I preferred to avoid it.

I could kill the electricity in that room. Darkness would be to my advantage, except it was only a little after one in the afternoon and the windows would let in plenty of light. There were shutters, but they were merely ornamental, bolted to the outside walls alongside the windows.

I wondered if it was time to resort to costuming. Even with a vampire's fangs, I suspected I didn't present a particularly terrifying image. At the moment I was dressed as I had been while washing the car, old blue jeans, sneakers, and a white tee-shirt. The tee-shirt was rather gory, both from the kid's blood, and from a little of my own, where I had bled until the bullet wound healed up. I supposed that might help, though the full outfit of black suit and opera cape might be more effective.

Except, again, it was the middle of the day. People these days are conditioned by movies and television to think that vampires can only be out at night. By popular image, I should have been safely tucked away in a coffin in some hidden crypt in the sub-basement. If I turned up in the library dressed like Dracula the first reaction was more likely to be amusement than terror, even with their dead companion to remind them of what they were facing.

Nevertheless, I ran down to the basement and pulled the fuses for the library. Even if there was still light from the windows, it would be darker than before and that had to help.

Leaving the three girls to ponder this new development, I quickly ran up to my room and changed shirts, getting rid of the bloody tee-shirt and slipping into a black turtleneck.

Before returning to my vantage point inside the library wall I went outside and disabled their van by pulling the wires off the spark plugs. It could be repaired in less than a minute, but you would have to know what was wrong first, and I am still male enough to think that it might take a woman a while to figure out that the neatly replaced plug hole covers concealed a disconnected terminal. Perhaps this is overly technical, stereotypical thinking, but I'm 2,081 years old, so indulge me if I sometimes seem old fashioned. I've spent a lot more of my life in the "old days" than in the modern ones.

The precaution was well advised. I had barely finished and closed the hood when the three girls came around the corner of the house. I presumed from this that they had opened one of the library windows and lowered themselves to the ground outside the house. It was a drop of about ten feet; not too far, really, presuming you were careful.

I ducked behind a hedge and waited to see what they would do.

All three had their guns out as they piled into the van. As the starter ground away I could see determination turning to dismay. It took a few seconds, but as they realized what was happening—or, more precisely, what was *not* happening—the fear was obvious on their faces.

I heard the clunk of the hood release and one of them got out of the van, coming around to the front of the vehicle and raising the hood. She was peering at the engine as the leader turned it over. I didn't think she'd see anything, and the sound of the engine turning over should have been enough to drown out the sharp pop of the sparks jumping to the sides of the metal wells. Unless she pulled on one of the wires she was unlikely to notice anything.

My vantage point was only about eight feet from the front of the van, on the passenger side. With the windowless side door closed—the girl checking the engine had been in the front seat—I would be mostly shielded from the view of anyone in the van.

I took the chance. I move extremely fast, so almost before the leader sitting in the driver's seat could realize that her comrade had suddenly vanished I had dragged the girl back behind the hedge and snapped her neck. I almost felt sorry for her, as she didn't die immediately. The look in her eye was one of curiosity more than pain; consciousness was rapidly fading, for her spinal cord was severed and she couldn't breath.

Fascinating as this might from an academic viewpoint, there was no time to waste. I picked up her gun, a pre-war Belgian Browning Hi-Power, with the rudimentary fixed sights and flat wooden grips, and looked around the hedge. The other two girls were out of the van now. It seemed to me that it was time for direct action.

"Perhaps," I said, stepping from behind the hedge, my gun pointed between them, "you should consider surrendering."

It was a rather ingenuous suggestion, really. I was going to kill both of them whether they gave up or not. I just thought that it would be easier all around if no one else shot me today. The fact that this cannot really harm me is secondary to the fact that it still hurts like hell.

"Maybe *you* should give up," the leader said. "There are two of us and only one of you."

I smiled. "Half an hour ago there were *five* of you and only one of me. I still like the odds."

The younger girl swung her gun toward me and pulled the trigger. Her bullet zipped past my waist, clipping a belt loop but not touching anything else. *So be it,* I thought.

I fired back, automatically squeezing the trigger twice. Both 9 MM slugs slammed into the girl's chest. She would have been dead before she started to fall.

The leader took advantage of the situation and fired a carefully aimed shot into my lower abdomen. Normally, such a shot would have been instantly disabling, even if it didn't kill. Normally. Of course, I'm not normal.

"Damn!" I grunted. "That hurt!"

Then I shot the remaining girl right through the heart.

Instead of falling down, she shot me again. Twice. Then I shot *her* again, with equally inconsequential results.

"Well, hell," I said. "Do you really want to keep doing this? It seems so pointless."

The girl had lowered her gun and was leaning against the front of the van. "I suppose not," she said.

"Why were you robbing my house? With them?"

"It seemed like a good idea at the time." She was poking at the hole in her shirt where the bullet had gone in. "This is nearly healed," she said, sounding surprised.

"Naturally. Did you expect otherwise?"

She glanced at her dead companion. "I'm a little new at this," she said.

I looked down at the dead girl, thinking about the three other bodies in and around my house. There obviously would not be a fifth, which made it important to get to know this girl a little better. Would I be moving immediately, or did I have some time?

"You should have been taught," I said. "You didn't get this way accidentally. The one who converts you has an obligation to teach you."

"He's dead. We were in a car wreck—it took his head off. He never got the chance."

"Then perhaps you need a new teacher? Does anyone know you're here?"

She shook her head. "Only the rest of my crew, and they're all dead now, I suppose."

"Close friends, were they?"

"No. I put this crew together for this job. I hardly knew them, except that they were supposed to be good and didn't seem to worry about whether they hurt anyone."

"Then I suggest we remove the bodies to someplace a bit more discreet. You might also wish to have something to eat, as it seems to have been rather conveniently supplied. Repairing bullet wounds takes a bit out of you."

◆   ◆   ◆

Her name, it developed, was Laura, and she was a burglar by profession. At least, she had been until about a year ago, when she started to get sick. Over the course of several months she had started to waste away, and when the diagnosis of pancreatic cancer was received she was weak enough already to accept the inevitability of death. There was a less than five percent survival rate, her doctor informed her, mostly because that particular form of cancer was generally painless until it was too late to do anything about it.

She had gone into the hospital, presumably for the last time, when an orderly began to visit her. He made the same offer that Meskhenet had made me. Desperate, she accepted, and two weeks later walked out of the hospital, still thin enough to look a bit unhealthy, but now essentially immortal.

She went to live with the orderly, but he had barely begun to teach her when he was decapitated in a car wreck. Most things a vampire can recover from, but not beheading. Not knowing what else to do, Laura returned to her former profession, recruiting the four younger burglars specifically for the attack on my house. She had no real idea of who I was, but I was known to live alone, on a large estate, and presumably had more than a few things worth stealing.

"If I was going to live forever," she told me, "I figured I should start accumulating stuff. I can't be a burglar forever, after all."

"Nor shall you be in the future," I said. "Stay here a while. You have a great deal to learn, and there aren't that many who can teach you."

Did I mention that she was quite beautiful? She was of about average height, slender, with short, dark-brown hair that was still growing back from the chemotherapy. We heal very rapidly, but some things, such as hair and nails, grow at a normal rate. She would be pleasant to be around for a few years. And I liked the fact that she *was* of only average height, for while I was considered quite a tall man in Roman times, at 5'9" I am rather on the short side today.

She nodded, looking around the room. We were sitting in the dining room, side by side at the long table, with tall wine glasses in front of us. They did not contain wine. Her accomplices were providing a final service to us.

What will come next? Laura's career as a thief is over, I think. I can show her far less dangerous ways to gain wealth. A vampire would not do well in prison. Too much surveillance tends to interfere with our diet.

Time would tell. And time was one thing we would have in plenty.

www.ingramcontent.com/pod-product-compliance
Lightning Source LLC
Chambersburg PA
CBHW020611250626
47154CB00004B/1461